More Raves *[proposed]* for Strom's *History*:

"I think this book is stunning. I knew Strom and I didn't know he had this in him."
—PRESIDENT ABE LINCOLN

"In all my days, there has been nothing like it, which is good."
—PRESIDENT WILLIAM HOWARD TAFT

"Finally, a voice that speaks the true black experience!"
—SUPREME COURT JUSTICE CLARENCE THOMAS

"The melody of true virtue, unrelenting rectitude, howls from every line."
—WILLIAM BENNETT

". . . [S]peaks to areas of our minds and bodies seldom spoken to."
—ATTORNEY GENERAL JOHN ASHCROFT

A HISTORY OF THE AFRICAN-AMERICAN PEOPLE

[PROPOSED]

BY STROM THURMOND

AS TOLD TO
PERCIVAL EVERETT
& JAMES KINCAID

[A NOVEL]

Akashic Books
New York

The authors wish to make clear to the reader that this is a work of fiction (i.e., none of it is true). Though there are many references to actual people, all of our interactions with those people (and the fictitious ones as well) are, in fact, fictitious. This includes all of the characters and events in the novel involving the Simon & Schuster publishing company. If any of the matter of this novel should be found offensive by anyone, we understand (if not completely) and suggest you find another book to read. We wish we could say that we mean no disrespect.

Published by Akashic Books
©2004 Percival Everett & James Kincaid
Excerpts from this book appeared in an earlier form in *Transition* magazine.

Cover photo ©AP/World Wide Photos Photo/Ken Lambert, Strom Thurmond greeted by two staff assistants for Mississippi Senator Trent Lott in the Capitol, September 24, 2002.

ISBN: 1-888451-57-2
Library of Congress Control Number: 2003116549
First printing
Printed in Canada

Akashic Books
PO Box 1456
New York, NY 10009
Akashic7@aol.com
www.akashicbooks.com

TO CHESSIE AND NITA

MEMO

March 1, 2002

From: Barton Wilkes
To: The Senator

You will doubtless remember me but maybe not. You commented last Tuesday on my tie (bow, new) and red hair (not so much red as auburn, like the school).

But to get to the point, you know that you hold a peculiar place in history. You must know that, for all your modesty, and know too that I mean nothing special by peculiar. That place in history is perhaps nowhere so remarkable as vis a vis the colored people (aka Afro-Americans, negroes, people of color, and blacks). Now that your career has fully matured (you know I mean nothing special by matured), perhaps it is time to explore the true and unmistakable understanding (ripe right to the core) that you have attained vis a vis the subject(s) aforementioned to a nation failing to appreciate not only its most glittering jewels but the true depth and thickness of its historical roots.

While to many in our nation, the new diversity, as we may call it unhappily, may appear as cute as a speckled pup, I feel (and the nation will echo my feeling) it is your place to point out the route we have traveled to arrive at this place. Map it, I say! Like a 21st-century Vasco da Gama.

To this end, I trust I am not overstepping my bounds as I suggest to you that we initiate a discussion leading to the potential production of a possible mode of transport to allow us to travel that route aforementioned. And by this I mean a good old-fashioned Southern Greyhound Bus.

I await your pleasure, having taken such initial steps, baby though they may be, (Did you ever play Mother, May I?) that will pour starter fluid on the briquets.

Devotedly,
Barton Wilkes
Barton Wilkes, Assistant to Aide

March 3, 2002

To: Barton Wilkes
From: Strom

Come to think of it, I did play Mother May I. That's been a while.

Who are you?

What?

OFFICE OF SENATOR STROM THURMOND
217 RUSSELL SENATE BUILDING
WASHINGTON, D.C. 20515

March 13, 2002

Simon & Schuster, Publishers
1230 Avenue of the Americas
New York, NY 10020

Dear Sir/Madam:

I will be brief.

The project is this: <u>A History of the African-American People by Strom Thurmond.</u> As Advisor to Senator Thurmond, I have his ear and will not say I have been entirely uninstrumental in persuading him to undertake the project in its present form. (By the way, the book title should have no honorific titles in it: no "Senator" or "The Honorable." That's the direct wish of the Senator. It'll be a title without titles, as it were.)

Please contact me at this address and I will relay to the Senator details about such things as:

   1. publicity plans
   2. advances
   3. royalties

Meanwhile, I remain, your friendly and helpful associate in all things,

Most sincerely,
Barton Wilkes
Barton Wilkes
Junior Advisor, Public Relations
The Hon. Strom Thurmond

Office of Senator Strom Thurmond
217 Russell Senate Building
Washington, D.C. 20515

April 15, 2002

Simon & Schuster, Publishers
1230 Avenue of the Americas
New York, NY 10020
ATTN: Senior Editor

Dear Sir/Madam:

In ref. to mine of the 13th inst.

Ha, ha. I'm just joking, of course. There's no need for such formality.

However, there is need for some dispatch, as the Senator always says, when telling the story about how there was only one outhouse at the school pie-eating contest when some prankster—the Senator swears, with a twinkle in his eye, it was not he—put castor oil in the blackberries that filled the pies (blackberry pie, the Senator's favorite to this day): "There is need for some dispatch, Sammy!" shouts one of the boys in line. I wish you could hear the Senator tell that one.

Of course it will not be appropriate to the project we are discussing.

Or rather, I am discussing. I sent you an inquiry one month ago and have been, you will perhaps comprehend, somewhat confused by your failure to respond.

What am I to understand?

Most cordially yours,
Barton Wilkes

Barton Wilkes
Advisor, Public Relations Department
The Hon. Strom Thurmond

SIMON & SCHUSTER, INC.
1230 Avenue of the Americas
New York, NY 10020

May 14, 2002

Mr. Blanton Wilkes
Russell Senate Office Building
Washington, D.C.
The Hon. Strom Thurmond's Staff

Dear Mr. Wilkes:

Thank you very much for your inquiry. We regret to say that the exceedingly large volume of manuscripts/proposals coming our way these days makes it impossible for us to entertain unsolicited inquiries.

We hope you will find a more receptive audience elsewhere.

Sincerely,

Simon & Schuster Publishers

p.s. If you sent a manuscript to us, we have to inform you that we are unable to return it.

OFFICE OF SENATOR STROM THURMOND
217 RUSSELL SENATE BUILDING
WASHINGTON, D.C. 20515

May 17, 2002

Simon & Schuster, Publishers
1230 Avenue of the Americas
New York, NY 10020

Dear Sir/Madam:

I can appreciate a joke as well as the next fellow, as I am sure you will discover in time.

I should begin by asking you to believe that I am whom I say I am, that I represent accurately Senator Thurmond's wishes, and that my reasons for contacting you in this heartlessly impersonal way will become clear.

Now, as they say here on "The Hill," let's get down to business, shall we?

I think you should begin.

Sincerely,
Barton Wilkes
Barton Wilkes, Advisor, Public Relations
The Hon. Strom Thurmond

Memo: Snell to McCloud

May 29, 2002

Hey Juniper!
Have a nice Memorial Day? It's my favorite holiday, Memorial Day is.
Here's who knows what. Barton Wilkes? Maybe you can figure it out. Try. Can you?
Ask the guy for a proposal, but tell him the usual about how we aren't interested. Make that emphatic. Don't leave any room for doubt.
Do you keep a cat? I find a well-groomed cat a great comfort. My ex-wife hated cats.

SIMON & SCHUSTER, INC.
1230 Avenue of the Americas
New York, NY 10020

June 1, 2002

Mr. Barton Wilkes
Advisor, Public Relations
The Hon Strom Thurmond

Dear Mr. Wilkes:

Martin Snell, an editor here at Simon & Schuster, has asked me to respond to your letter.

Please indicate in standard proposal form what your project is exactly. At that point, we can evaluate its suitability for Simon & Schuster.

Understand that this in no way indicates any interest on our part in the project. We receive many proposals and can proceed with only a small fraction of these.

Sincerely,
R. Juniper McCloud
R. Juniper McCloud (Mr.)
Assistant to Martin Snell

OFFICE OF SENATOR STROM THURMOND
217 RUSSELL SENATE BUILDING
WASHINGTON, D.C. 20515

June 4, 2002

Mr. R. Juniper McCloud
Assistant to Martin Snell, Editor
Simon & Schuster, Publishers
1230 Avenue of the Americas
New York, NY 10020

Dear Mr. McCloud,

Surely not coincidental that we are both Assistants to important people, me to the Senior Senator of All Time, Claude Pepper having died, and you to the man who is doubtless the Senior Editor there. It's a small world. "I was a child and she was a child/ In our kingdom by the sea." Do you know Poe?

Now, it's easy to see why you are being standoffish. Perhaps I would be too, though it's a matter of our inner nature, really, when the sun goes down. Don't you agree? For instance, my guess is that it is not at all your own decision to be so very formal. I know it wouldn't be mine. Neither of us is quite his own person, though, not to be presumptuous.

Anyhow, as I said, this will be <u>A History of the African-American People by Strom Thurmond.</u>

Would you need more details—like the number of pages, illustrations, that sort of thing? If not, I think this can stand as description and what you call proposal. I couldn't at this point supply such details anyhow, so there we are.

Puissant name, "R. Juniper." Are you from the Charleston McClouds? My own name is a matter of some pride to me, as yours is to you. Someone at your place called me "Blanton." Oh my.

> Yours for now,
> *Barton Wilkes*
> Barton Wilkes.
> Advisor, Junior, Public Relations
> The Hon. Strom Thurmond

Memo: Snell to McCloud

June 22, 2001

We have reason to believe that this guy is connected to Thurmond, but he doesn't seem to have very many tines to his fork, does he?

It's almost certainly a no-go, but see if you can find out more. Get him to send you a proposal.

Do NOT encourage him, by any word or gesture. Don't even hint that we might be interested—give him to understand just the reverse.

Do you wear boxers or briefs? Also, you haven't answered my question about kitty.

SIMON & SCHUSTER, INC.
1230 Avenue of the Americas
New York, NY 10020

June 23, 2002

Mr. Barton Wilkes
Junior Advisor, Public Relations
The Hon Strom Thurmond

Dear Mr. Wilkes:

We are in receipt of your letter of June 4. Please send us a detailed proposal. Such a proposal should include, but not be limited to:

--a full description of the project
--a detailed chapter outline
--an analysis of the projected audience for such a book
--an estimated time frame for completion
--a discussion of other books in the area and how this proposed
      book will meet the competition

Do understand that our receipt of such a proposal, should you choose to send it, in no way indicates any interest on our part in the project, much less in publishing it.

Sincerely,
R. Juniper McCloud
R. Juniper McCloud

OFFICE OF SENATOR STROM THURMOND
217 RUSSELL SENATE BUILDING
WASHINGTON, D.C. 20515

June 27, 2002

Mr. R. Juniper McCloud
Mr. Martin Snell
Simon & Schuster

Dear Friends,
    Much as I have come to rely on and, indeed, feel some warmth

for Mr. McCloud, I expect it is time that he evaporate from the meadow. Marty and I can take it from here.

I am trying to understand your peculiar hesitancy. I do not wish to make judgments hastily, or, indeed, at all. You are evidently not paranoid, nor are you in business in order to drive away profit-making ideas. Or are you? Here I come at you with the plan of the decade (put modestly) and you treat it as one more book on O. J. Simmons, or Mick Jagger, or Spanking. I do suppose you receive lots of ideas that are just plain kooky, or very tired, or both. But try to be alert when the real thing comes ding-donging at your door.

But I think I would be as skittish as you, perhaps, all things considered.

Strange, you will say, that Senator Thurmond did not contact us directly, did not phone, did not set up a meeting. Well yes, strange according to your way of doing business. I ask you simply to respect the fact, undoubted fact, that your way of doing business is not Senator Thurmond's. This is in no way to impugn you or your practices. It is just that the Senator has his own views on things. It is easier for me to think this way, as I am with him day and night; but now you know.

One mystery I can clear up. The Senator insisted that I convey his views in this manner for the simple reason that he is a believer in justice, equal justice. His words to me were these: "If they like the proposal, that's fine. If they don't, that's fine. That's how I see it." I think that's how I see it too. I would suppose you do too.

The proposal is this: Senator Thurmond proposes to write what he terms <u>A History of the African American People by Strom Thurmond.</u> As the history of the African American People has been, to a great extent, coextensive with the Senator's own, he will be able to draw on his own life experience (and not just in politics) for much of his material. For the earlier years in America (prior to the Senator's coming of age, let us say), he will employ books and the research of scholarly advisors.

Perhaps that will do for what you need. Kindly let me (not the Senator) know of your interest, what shape that interest takes, and where it will lead.

Sincerely,
Barton Wilkes
Barton Wilkes
Junior Advisor and Assistant Intern
The Hon. Strom Thurmond

p.s. Mr. McCloud, perhaps we can continue our discussion in a parallel fashion, running as a kind of oblongata to the main business.

SIMON & SCHUSTER, INC.
1230 Avenue of the Americas
New York, NY 10020

July 8, 2002

Mr. Barton Wilkes, Esq.
Advisor
The Hon. Strom Thurmond

Dear Mr. Wilkes:
  We received your very interesting and latest letter just this morning and thank you very much for thinking of Simon & Schuster.

Of course we believe that you are who you say you are and that the proposal you suggest is relayed from Senator Thurmond. It is an intriguing idea, or could be, and I hope you will be assured that we try to stay alert to good ideas coming our way. It's just that we are unable to determine from what you have told us whether this is a good idea. Really, we cannot quite decipher what the idea is. We can guess, but we wouldn't be quite <u>the</u> publishing house we are for long if we operated on guessing, would we?

Are you certain that a meeting would not be in order? We can assure the Senator that we will in no way compromise his belief in equal justice, a belief we fervently share, along with probably everybody else alive. It's just that a meeting would seem to us an efficient and just way to answer your questions and, on our side, to arrive at an understanding of what the Senator has in mind.

You will not be surprised to hear that we are a little puzzled by the title. The Senator's views on any number of issues are, of course, of great interest. It seems natural that he would be recording his experiences and reminiscences at this stage of his long and colorful career in public life. What we do not quite understand as yet is exactly what the Senator is thinking of when he uses the word, "History." Will the Senator be providing a continuous narrative and analysis of African-American life from the Colonial period to the present, or will he be concentrating instead on modern times and his own experience and views? Of course there are other alternatives; we are trying only to make our confusion clear. Thank you in advance for removing that confusion.

Wouldn't you like to call me or provide a number where I can reach you? Perhaps an e-mail conversation would be efficient and move things along more expeditiously?

Thank you for contacting us.

Cordially,

Martin A. Snell

Martin A. Snell, Editor

OFFICE OF SENATOR STROM THURMOND
217 RUSSELL SENATE BUILDING
WASHINGTON, D.C. 20515

July 12, 2002

Martin A. Snell
Senior Editor, Simon & Schuster

Dear Mr. Snell,

I am sure you will not suspect me of being a truculent person, one with hackles easily gotten up. Still, it would be better for both of us if we established a few ground rules, got things straight from the very get-go, as the Senator would say. (Sometimes he says, "From the first rising of my morning glory." He's a colorful one, the Senator.)

----I am not "relaying" anything. I am sure you didn't intend to insult me by referring to me as a trampoline, but things do not bounce off me. However, as we are both men of the world, perhaps we could each be more particular as to the language we are employing. I am an independent agent and a human being with ideas of my own and feelings. Perhaps you have a Mother you love, Mr. Snell? My own mother had her faults and she wasn't always there for me---don't you hate that phrase!---but she was always Mother.

----I think you should remember always that the Senator is in excellent health (and so am I). There is no need to rush, to "move things along more expeditiously." Senator Thurmond has no intention of dying before writing his History, if that's what you're afraid of, and I'm sure it is. Say what you mean, man!

---And give me the courtesy of believing me when I say what I mean and mean it. No, a meeting is not advisable, nor the use of the telephone. I said that before, and I can only wonder that you missed that point. Perhaps you are not the sharpest tack holding down the carpet there? You sign yourself "Editor." I assume that means THE editor, the boss?

Now to your questions. You raise an excellent point as to what sort of "History" the Senator will be providing. Perhaps we could leave that to him to determine as he will? That way neither of us will be disappointed, I expect. In any event, I have no idea at all what he will do. Don't get me wrong, now: when I say I have no idea it's not because I am not close to the Senator. I am as close to him as anyone has ever been. He is a private sort of man, for all his public flair. He likes to write by inspiration, as it comes to him. And it always does. Pinning him to a plan would be like stapling an eagle to a memo pad.

That should clear everything up. You send a contract by return mail and then we'll move.

Sincerely,
Barton Wilkes
Bart Wilkes

OFFICE OF SENATOR STROM THURMOND
217 RUSSELL SENATE BUILDING
WASHINGTON, D.C. 20515

July 12, 2002

Juniper:

What goes on there? Is this Snell person all he should be?

I expect you have seen the correspondence, right? If not, here it is, the latest bit. Mad, don't you think?

What a world you must live in! It's down the rabbit-hole every morning for you, little Alice, right?

Well, keep your pinafore clutched close, is my advice.

Blanton (ha ha)

p.s. Perhaps it's too much to ask for your opinion on this: should I seek out another house (as you publishers, I believe, refer to it), given Snell's unsettled state?

p.p.s. And the "R" stands for? Should I guess?

Memo: Snell to McCloud

July 14, 2002

McCloud:

See what you can find out about this Wilkes guy. I think he's a fucking psycho.

This may all turn out OK, but I can tell you that right now I am not over-pleased that you came to me with this project. It's taking up a lot of my time—and we are still on square one. I am not going to get ahead at this place if I ride projects like this one and blister nothing but my own ass! Don't forget that there is a paradox here: I am the smartest fuck here and also the youngest. I expect you are already toting up dates and saying, "Well soul-kiss your sister, he isn't the youngest at all." But you know what I mean, Juney. Don't be an idiotic literalist. I am the newest and most vulnerable. Don't take advantage of that vulnerability, please. Others have, but I thought you were different.

And if I'm fired, I'm taking you and that cute ass with me.

Cats?

Martin

July 14, 2002

From: J. McCloud, assistant to M. Snell
To: Self

Holy Shit!

SIMON & SCHUSTER, INC.
1230 Avenue of the Americas
New York, NY 10020

July 14, 2002

Barton:
Look at this, will you? I shouldn't be sending you private memos;
but Jesus Christ. Here I am just out of NYU, an English major lucky
to get a job, or so I thought, and I end up with this idiot. I don't
mean to thrust this on you, but you're the only one I know who'd
believe Snell was Snell.
He may be a lot worse than an idiot, I guess. One minute he's
leering at me, the next sneering, the next looking at me as if he
doesn't know who I am. I suppose he's insecure, being a new person
here himself, but insecurity isn't something he has a monopoly on.
I suppose you have a pretty cushy job there with old Strom? He
must sleep 20 hours a day, right? Like an old tomcat. I gather he
was just that in his day, fucking women in the office, on their way
to the electric chair, in the toilets at beauty queen contests.
Anyhow, I think you must have it pretty nice there.

As for this project on African-American history. What is it, a joke? It is so fucking moronic, it has to be—unless the old imbecile really thinks this is just the book for him. Or are you writing it? You figuring he'll never know and you can slip anything you want by the old numskull? What a great idea. It'll make you!

Well, I'm back to business---in this case, investigating you. The loonies are running the asylum!

Juney

Office of Senator Strom Thurmond
217 Russell Senate Building
Washington, D.C. 20515

July 17, 2002

Mr. McCloud:

I do not know what could have induced you to make the assumptions you have made, the ones guiding your last letter.

You must be insane. Certainly you are indecent.

I wish you well, but I must insist that you never, ever address me or one of mine in any manner whatsoever. It's a pity, but it must be so.

Love,
Bark

p.s. You seen "South Pacific"? Lovely when done properly, though nowadays it's usually profaned in dinner theaters in places like Columbus, Ohio. There's a song in it, entitled, "This Nearly Was Mine," sung by Emile when he realizes love is not for him so he may as well give his life to the cause, spotting Japanese planes, since that's what lies to hand. Except that I have no Japanese planes to spot, I could be Emile. Nuff said?

p.p.s. Renauld? Raet? Rudy?

Memo: Snell to McCloud

July 17, 2002

McCloud:

At the editors' meeting today, I had an inspiration.

It just hit me, as Sullivan was droning on about that travel series of his, that what this firm needs, and fast, is something hot. The Thurmond book came to mind as something that would be hot and that would mark me as hot.

So hold yourself at ready.

Here we go, butterfly.

Snell

Cats?

SIMON & SCHUSTER, INC.
1230 Avenue of the Americas
New York, NY 10020

May 14, 2002

Mr. Barton Wilkes, Esq.
Advisor, The Hon. Strom Thurmond

Dear Bart,

Let me say that I appreciate very much the friendly gesture: using your first name in the signature puts us on an easy and confidential basis. Do call me "Mart." I am not sure what you mean by Mothers, but I know mine was a fine one, still is. You suggest yours gave you trouble. I am sorry for that, but I realize some mothers can be downright unreasonable. Mine was too, come to think of it. Just because she loved sports, for instance, she insisted I did too. It's not that I was bad at sports or anything like that, but I didn't enjoy being pushed. Some people don't and I am one of them. Anyhow, I'm glad to see we connect on the subject of Mothers.

I also am pleased that you are so forthright in letting me know where I have inadvertently given offense through my carelessness. Good for you! If more people were as open as you, there'd be far fewer misunderstandings. I consider it manly of you.

In that spirit, let me then ask directly in exactly what position you stand vis a vis this project and vis a vis the Senator? I recognize that you are not merely a "relay," certainly not. Perhaps then you could provide for me a clearer description or term. Sending me scurrying for a metaphor to account for your relation to this project would be like sending a barnyard goose out for groceries. Are you, for instance, in regular communication with Senator Thurmond on his plans? Is he privy to our correspondence? Does he intend to start on the book right away? Does he have a projected completion date? (Please understand here that these are standard questions. We would ask them of a perfectly fit 15-year-old in just this form. We are not suggesting that they bear special relevance to the Senator or his age or health. We are very pleased that his health is fine and share your certainty that death is a very long way off. Let's hope it is for you and me as well, and for all those we hold near and dear.)

As for allowing the Senator to determine what sort of "History" he will write, of course we would not think of interfering with the creative process. However, we would be interested in learning more as the Senator's thinking on this matures. At some point, we would imagine, he will be making some decisions: is this a set of reminiscences? A scholarly history? A social analysis? A political argument? You see what we mean.

We enclose a standard contract that answers to the Senator's desire for equal justice, we hope. That is, this contract is the one we use in all cases that are not special; it is our standard mechanism in publishing.

With warmest personal wishes.

Your friend,

Mart

SIMON & SCHUSTER, PUBLISHERS

Publishing Agreement

Recitals

This publishing Agreement ("the Agreement") is entered into as of May 30, 2001 ("the Effective date") by and between **Simon & Schuster, Publishers,** 1230 Avenue of the Americas, New York, NY 10020 and Strom Thurmond, an individual, Russell Senate Office Building, Pennsylvania Avenue, Washington, D.C., concerning a work presently titled *A History of the African American People* and not described as yet to be either a factual accounting, social commentary or fictional reenactment of some era, portion of time or reflection of attitudes about or concerning people of African descent on the continent of North America.

1. Grant of Rights

Author, on behalf of himself and his heirs, executors, administrators, successors and assigns, exclusively grants, assigns and otherwise transfers to the Publisher and its licensees, successors and assigns, all right, title and interest in and to the Work, throughout the world, in perpetuity, and in any and all media and forms of expressions now known or hereafter devised, including but not limited to all copyrights therein (and any and all extensions and renewals thereof) for the full term of such copyrights, and all secondary rights therein.

2. Copyright

Publisher shall, in all versions of the Work published by Publisher under this Agreement, place a notice of copyright in the name of the author in a form and place that the Publisher reasonably believes to comply with the requirements of the United States copyright law, and shall apply for registration of such copyright(s) in the name of the Author in the United States Copyright Office.

Author shall execute and deliver to Publisher any and all documents that Publisher deems necessary or appropriate to evidence or effectuate the rights granted in the Agreement, including but not limited to the Instrument of Recordation attached hereto as an Exhibit to this Agreement.

Nothing contained in this Section shall be construed as limiting, modifying or otherwise affecting any of the rights granted to Publisher under this Agreement.

3. Manuscript

Author agrees to deliver to Publisher, not later than one year from the date of this contract ("Initial Delivery Date"), two (2) double-spaced, complete copies of the Work in the English Language ("Manuscript"), which Manuscript shall be of an undetermined length but be understood to meet the expectations of Publisher and shall be acceptable to Publisher in form, content, and substance.

4. Permissions, Index, and Other Materials

Author shall deliver to Publisher, not later than the Initial Delivery date, unless otherwise designated by Publisher, each of the following materials:

Original art, illustrations and/or photographs (collectively, "Artwork"), in a form suitable for reproduction. Subject to the mutual agreement of the Author and Publisher, Publisher may acquire and/or prepare and include in the Work additional art, illustrations, photographs, charts, maps, drawings, or other materials, and the expense for such additional materials shall be allocated between Author and Publisher according to their mutual agreement.

Author shall deliver to Publisher, at Author's sole expense, written authorization and permissions for the use of any copyrighted or other proprietary materials owned by any third party which appear in the Work and written releases or consents by any person or entity described, quoted, or depicted in the Work (collectively, "Permissions"). If Author does not deliver the Permissions, Publisher shall have the right, but not the obligation, to obtain such Permissions on its own initiative, and Author shall reimburse Publisher for all expenses incurred by Publisher in obtaining such Permissions.

Author shall prepare and submit, on a date to be designated by Publisher, an index, bibliography, table of contents, foreword, introduction, preface or similar matter ("Frontmatter" and "Backmatter") as Publisher may deem necessary for inclusion in the Work, and if Author shall fail or refuse to do so, then Publisher shall have the right, but not the obligation, to acquire or prepare such Frontmatter and/or Backmatter, or to engage a skilled person to do so, and Author shall reimburse for the costs of such acquisition or preparation.

5. Revisions and Corrections

If Publisher, in its sole discretion, deems the Manuscript, Artwork, Frontmatter and/or Backmatter, Permissions, and/or any other materials delivered by Author to be unacceptable in form and substance, then Publisher shall so advise Author by written notice, and Author shall cure any defects and generally revise and correct Manuscript, Artwork, Frontmatter and/or Backmatter, Permissions, and/or other materials to the satisfaction of Publisher, and deliver fully revised and corrected Manuscript, Artwork, Frontmatter and/or Backmatter, Permissions, and/or other materials no later than thirty (30) days after receipt of Publisher's notice.

6. Termination for Non-Delivery

If Author fails to deliver the Manuscript, Artwork, Frontmatter and/or Backmatter, Permissions, and/or other materials required under this Agreement, and/or any revisions and corrections thereof as requested by Publisher, on dates designated by Publisher, or if Author fails to do so in a form and substance satisfactory to Publisher, then Publisher shall have the right to terminate this Agreement by so informing Author by letter sent by traceable mail to the address of Author set forth above. Upon termination by Publisher, Author shall, without prejudice to any other right or remedy of Publisher, immediately repay Publisher any sums previously paid to Author, and upon such repayment, all rights granted to Publisher under this Agreement shall revert to Author.

7. Author's Representations and Warranties

Author represents and warrants to Publisher that: (i) the Work is not in public domain; (ii) Author is the sole proprietor of the Work and has full power and authority, free of any rights of any nature whatsoever by any other person or collection of individuals, to enter this Agreement and to grant the rights which are granted to Publisher in this Agreement; (iii) the Work has not heretofore been published, in whole or in part, in any form; (iv) the Work does not, and if published will not, infringe upon any copyright or any proprietary right at common law; (v) the Work contains no matter whatsoever that is obscene, libelous, violative of any third party's right of privacy or publicity, or otherwise in contravention of law or the right of any third party, or material offensive to the sensibility of any person or persons who may deem their right to fair representation compromised; (vi) all statements of fact in the Work are true and are based on diligent research; (vii) all advice and instruction in the Work are safe and sound, and is not negligent or defective in any manner; (viii) the Work, if biographical or "as told to" Author, is authentic and accurate; and (ix) Author will not hereafter enter into any agreement or understanding with any person or entity which might conflict with the rights granted to Publisher in this Agreement.

8. Author's Indemnity of Publisher

Author shall indemnify, defend and hold harmless Publisher, its subsidiaries and affiliates, and their respective shareholders, officers, directors, employees, partners, associates, affiliates, joint venturers, agents, representatives, friends, family members and acquaintances from any and all claims, debts, demands, suits, actions, proceedings, and/or prosecutions ("Claims") based on allegations which, if true, would constitute a breach of any of the foregoing warranties, and any and all liabilities, losses, damages, and expenses (including attorneys' fees and costs) in consequence thereof.

9. Review by Publisher's Counsel

Notwithstanding any other provision of the Agreement, Publisher shall have the right, but not the obligation, to submit the Work for review by counsel of its choice to determine if the Work contains material that is or may be unlawful, violate the rights and/or civil rights of third parties, or violate the promises, warranties, and representations of Author set forth in this Agreement. If, in the sole opinion of the Publisher or its Counsel, there appears to be risk of legal action or liability on account of any aspect of the Work, then Publisher may, at its sole option, (i) require Author to make such additions, deletions, modifications, substantiation of facts, disclaimers or other changes to avoid risk of legal action or liability; or (ii) terminate this Agreement without further obligation, and Author shall be obligated to repay all amounts advanced by Publisher.

10. Right to Withdraw

Publisher shall have the right to withdraw its offer of Agreement at any time prior to or after the delivery of the Manuscript.

IN WITNESS WHEREOF, Author and Publisher have executed this Agreement of the day and year written above.

Publisher   Author
Reginald Hines, Simon & Schuster   Strom Thurmond

Office of Senator Strom Thurmond
217 Russell Senate Building
Washington, D.C. 20515

July 22, 2002

Mr. Martin A. Snell
Senior Editor
Simon & Schuster

Dear Mr. Snell:

I seem to have created a great many false impressions in my time, but your response takes the cake. Still, as a man of business, I am prepared to overlook what is really a stupefying number of quite preposterous inferences you have made and proceed as if they had never reared their heads over the top of the basket, writhing baby kittens struggling to get out.

Yes, Mother was a doozey, that's for sure. She provided me with what she called "a warm breast and a sheltering wing." She meant well, Mother, but she was erratic in her breast and wing work. She would, without notice, show up at school and sit at the next desk, stroking my knee. If no desk were available, Mother would take to the floor, legs and dress akimbo. "Embarrassment" is not the word for what I felt, but neither is "comforted." By the 8th grade, mother had grown proportionately as I had, doubling in size every 5-6 years, while still offering me her warmth at, how shall I put this, inopportune times and inappropriate places: pep rallies, dances, tag-day sales, hayrides. Misplaced parental zeal, I guess you could say, though which of us is anxious to hurl that particular rock first?

You ask about my "exact position" vis a vis this project. Let me say, first, that any editor who regards "vis a vis" as expressive prose does not inspire confidence. And what is the force of "exact" in "exact position"? Do you suspect that I would give you only an approximate idea, a hint, a distant sniff? Do you suppose I would lie? Perhaps I might say I was the Senator's great aunt! You never know, do you? Well, you ought to know; and if you do not, perhaps another publishing house would.

As I have said several times, I am advisor to the Senator and deeply entwined with his inmost thoughts and passions. What's not clear about that?

The contract you send says nothing about (a) film rights, (b) an advance, (c) translation opportunities, (d) expert scholars and writers (at least some of whom must surely be African Americans themselves) to work with the Senator on this project. This will be the Senator's work, of course---how could it be otherwise? To assure that it is, we (you) will assemble a team to bore deep into the subject, as it were, and into the Senator as well. What will emerge will be of profit to you, in a sordid sense, and to the Nation, in a larger sense.

The book will be finished inside six months. You have my word on that.

So, send a new contract and some suggestions on writers and scholars (some authentically black) and we will, as you put it, "move."

Devotedly,
Button

p.s. The historical and intellectual value notwithstanding, I would be remiss not to mention the marketing opportunities screaming from the bowels of this project. For example, the promotion of a Strom doll (tasteful), a dream I have long held to and a design of which I have prepared. You should hear what it says when I pull the string.

p.p.s. I will need a number of copies, gratis as you say: I expect friends to form round me as a result of this work. Providing them with a copy, signed and free, would be graceful.

ॐ

SIMON & SCHUSTER, INC.
1230 Avenue of the Americas
New York, NY 10020

July 29, 2002

Mr. Barton Wilkes, Esq.
Advisor
The Hon. Strom Thurmond

Dear Mr. Wilkes:

Just as you say.

Here is a revised contract. You will see that it covers the issues you raise.

As for the team you wish to assemble: of course we have no objection to this, and I would think the Senator would be the one best situated to name those he would most like to work with and proceed to employ them. Are you seeking advice from us as to writers and scholars?

I assume that you do indeed wish us to provide names. To save time, I am glad to do so right here and now. Here's what we think: you need to latch onto a first-rate African-American writer, historian, or scholar. Then ask him/her with whom she/he would like to work. Perhaps one person would suffice, though it's hard to find all that in one-----a writer, scholar, and a black.

Let's take the last term first, a black. How can I put this without offending you? Perhaps I cannot, so I'll just blurt it out. Not too many eminent or even competent blacks will leap to the chance to work with Senator Thurmond on this project. As you know, those few blacks who are, like the Senator, Republicans are, not to mince words, craven, pathological, or more or less thoroughgoing nincompoops. That causes a problem.

There are, however, a few black writers who seem impervious to politics of any kind, may be more or less unaware of political energies, as I might put it. But even these will know and have some views on Senator Thurmond. No need to go into details here. But you see the difficulty. After several meetings with our full staff and the help of my advisor, whom you know, we could come up with but one name that would seem likely for your purposes---Percival Everett. He has what you want: he is experienced, virtually unknown, and black. What's more, we think he'll do it. He's at a University too, so he'll be able to call on scholarly help.

Tell us what you think and also what sort of advance you had in mind. Do you want us to approach Mr. Everett? If you do, please let us know the terms Senator Thurmond intends to propose to him for such assistance.

Sincerely,
Martin

SIMON & SCHUSTER, PUBLISHERS

Publishing Agreement

Recitals

This publishing Agreement ("the Agreement") is entered into as of May 30, 2001 ("the Effective date") by and between **Simon & Schuster, Publishers,** 1230 Avenue of the Americas, New York, NY 10020 and Strom Thurmond, an individual, Russell Senate Office Building, Pennsylvania Avenue, Washington, D.C., concerning a work presently titled *A History of the African American People* and not described as yet to be either a factual accounting, social commentary or fictional reenactment of some era, portion of time or reflection of attitudes about or concerning people of African descent on the continent of North America.

1. Grant of Rights

Author, on behalf of himself and his heirs, executors, administrators, successors and assigns, exclusively grants, assigns and otherwise transfers to the Publisher and its licensees, successors and assigns, all right, title and interest in and to the Work, throughout the world, in perpetuity, and in any and all media and forms of expressions now known or hereafter devised, including but not limited to all copyrights therein (and any and all extensions and renewals thereof) for the full term of such copyrights, and all secondary rights therein.

2. Copyright

Publisher shall, in all versions of the Work published by Publisher under this Agreement, place a notice of copyright in the name of the author in a form and place that the Publisher reasonably believes to comply with the requirements of the United States copyright law, and shall apply for registration of such copyright(s) in the name of the Author in the United States Copyright Office.

Author shall execute and deliver to Publisher any and all documents that Publisher deems necessary or appropriate to evidence or effectuate the rights granted in the Agreement, including but not limited to the Instrument of Recordation attached hereto as an Exhibit to this Agreement.

Nothing contained in this Section shall be construed as limiting, modifying or otherwise affecting any of the rights granted to Publisher under this Agreement.

3. Manuscript

Author agrees to deliver to Publisher, not later than one year from the date of this contract ("Initial Delivery Date"), two (2) double-spaced, complete copies of the Work in the English Language ("Manuscript"), which Manuscript shall be of an undetermined length but be understood to meet the expectations of Publisher and shall be acceptable to Publisher in form, content, and substance.

4. Permissions, Index, and Other Materials

Author shall deliver to Publisher, not later than the Initial Delivery date, unless otherwise designated by Publisher, each of the following materials:

Original art, illustrations and/or photographs (collectively, "Artwork"), in a form suitable for reproduction. Subject to the mutual agreement of the Author and Publisher, Publisher may acquire and/or prepare and include in the Work additional art, illustrations, photographs, charts, maps, drawings, or other materials, and the expense for such additional materials shall be allocated between Author and Publisher according to their mutual agreement.

Author shall deliver to Publisher, at Author's sole expense, written authorization and permissions for the use of any copyrighted or other proprietary materials owned by any third party which appear in the Work and written releases or consents by any person or entity described, quoted, or depicted in the Work (collectively,

"Permissions"). If Author does not deliver the Permissions, Publisher shall have the right, but not the obligation, to obtain such Permissions on its own initiative, and Author shall reimburse Publisher for all expenses incurred by Publisher in obtaining such Permissions.

Author shall prepare and submit, on a date to be designated by Publisher, an index, bibliography, table of contents, foreword, introduction, preface or similar matter ("Frontmatter" and "Backmatter") as Publisher may deem necessary for inclusion in the Work, and if Author shall fail or refuse to do so, then Publisher shall have the right, but not the obligation, to acquire or prepare such Frontmatter and/or Backmatter, or to engage a skilled person to do so, and Author shall reimburse for the costs of such acquisition or preparation.

5. Revisions and Corrections

If Publisher, in its sole discretion, deems the Manuscript, Artwork, Frontmatter and/or Backmatter, Permissions, and/or any other materials delivered by Author to be unacceptable in form and substance, then Publisher shall so advise Author by written notice, and Author shall cure any defects and generally revise and correct Manuscript, Artwork, Frontmatter and/or Backmatter, Permissions, and/or other materials to the satisfaction of Publisher, and deliver fully revised and corrected Manuscript, Artwork, Frontmatter and/or Backmatter, Permissions, and/or other materials no later than thirty (30) days after receipt of Publisher's notice.

6. Termination for Non-Delivery

If Author fails to deliver the Manuscript, Artwork, Frontmatter and/or Backmatter, Permissions, and/or other materials required under this Agreement, and/or any revisions and corrections thereof as requested by Publisher, on dates designated by Publisher, or if Author fails to do so in a form and substance satisfactory to Publisher, then Publisher shall have the right to terminate this Agreement by so informing Author by letter sent by traceable mail to the address of Author set forth above. Upon termination by Publisher, Author shall, without prejudice to any other right or remedy of Publisher, immediately repay Publisher any sums previously paid to Author, and upon such repayment, all rights granted to Publisher under this Agreement shall revert to Author.

7. Author's Representations and Warranties

Author represents and warrants to Publisher that: (i) the Work is not in public domain; (ii) Author is the sole proprietor of the Work and has full power and authority, free of any rights of any nature whatsoever by any other person or collection of individuals, to enter this Agreement and to grant the rights which are granted to Publisher in this Agreement; (iii) the Work has not heretofore been published, in whole or in part, in any form; (iv) the Work does not, and if published will not, infringe upon any copyright or any proprietary right at common law; (v) the Work contains no matter whatsoever that is obscene, libelous, violative of any third party's right of privacy or publicity, or otherwise in contravention of law or the right of any third party, or material offensive to the sensibility of any person or persons who may deem their right to fair representation compromised; (vi) all statements of fact in the Work are true and are based on diligent research; (vii) all advice and instruction in the Work are safe and sound, and is not negligent or defective in any manner; (viii) the Work, if biographical or "as told to" Author, is authentic and accurate; and (ix) Author will not hereafter enter into any agreement or understanding with any person or entity which might conflict with the rights granted to Publisher in this Agreement.

8. Author's Indemnity of Publisher

Author shall indemnify, defend and hold harmless Publisher, its subsidiaries and affiliates, and their respective shareholders, officers, directors, employees, partners, associates, affiliates, joint venturers, agents, representatives, friends, family members and acquaintances from any and all claims, debts, demands, suits, actions, proceedings, and/or prosecutions ("Claims") based on allegations which, if true, would constitute a breach of any of the foregoing warranties, and any and all liabilities, losses, damages, and expenses (including attorneys' fees and costs) in consequence thereof.

9. Review by Publisher's Counsel

Notwithstanding any other provision of the Agreement, Publisher shall have the right, but not the obligation, to submit the Work for review by counsel of its choice to determine if the Work contains material that is or may be unlawful, violate the rights and/or civil rights of third parties, or violate the promises, warranties, and representations of Author set forth in this Agreement. If, in the sole opinion of the Publisher or its Counsel, there appears to be risk of legal action or liability on account of any aspect of the Work, then Publisher may, at its sole option, (i) require Author to make such additions, deletions, modifications, substantiation of facts, disclaimers or other changes to avoid risk of legal action or liability; or (ii) terminate this Agreement without further obligation, and Author shall be obligated to repay all amounts advanced by Publisher.

10. Right to Withdraw

Publisher shall have the right to withdraw its offer of Agreement at any time prior to or after the delivery of the Manuscript.

IN WITNESS WHEREOF, Author and Publisher have executed this Agreement of the day and year written above.

Publisher
Reginald Hines, Simon & Schuster

Author
Strom Thurmond

OFFICE OF SENATOR STROM THURMOND
217 RUSSELL SENATE BUILDING
WASHINGTON, D.C. 20515

August 3, 2002

Dear Martin,

Never heard of Everett. How can his being unknown be of advantage?

$150,000.

<u>You</u> will pay the team of writers/scholars/blacks, not us.

Barton

SIMON & SCHUSTER, INC.
1230 Avenue of the Americas
New York, NY 10020

August 13, 2002

Dear Barton,

His being unknown will not prejudice the readership one way or another. Imagine Condi Rice doing the ghost-writing here. There'd be no reason for anybody to read it, as they'd know in advance what it'd say. Everett is the man. And, you know, he's not absolutely unknown, but is, rather, a kind of coterie writer, i.e., a writer who has a loyal, if small, following.

$5,000.
We'll pay Everett and one other, but on our terms.

Martin

OFFICE OF SENATOR STROM THURMOND
217 RUSSELL SENATE BUILDING
WASHINGTON, D.C. 20515

August 17, 2002

Martin,

OK on Everett. I have, for quite some time, known what coterie means, but am grateful, hun, for your explanation. $20,000.

Bart

SIMON & SCHUSTER, INC.
1230 Avenue of the Americas
New York, NY 10020

August 21, 2002

Barton,
$2,500.

Martin

SIMON & SCHUSTER, INC.
1230 Avenue of the Americas
New York, NY 10020

August 28, 2002

Dear Barton,

Thanks for the signed contracts. I think our agreeing on the $2500 presages a smooth voyage ahead. Not too much and not too little, like a well-crafted haircut. (Very hard to come by these days.) We're eager to watch as this progresses and offer any assistance we can provide to the project.

We have not yet heard from Mr. Everett but expect to soon and will relay his message to you, asking then that you establish the working relationship that seems to the Senator most efficient and useful.

Oh, one other detail. We notice that the Senator's signature is stamped in rather than signed. I expect the Senator, busy man that he is, often makes use of such a stamp. However, we really do need the actual signature on a binding legal document, you know, and I hope you will bring this to the Senator's attention. We have enclosed fresh contracts for his signature.

All best wishes.

Cordially,

Martin

OFFICE OF SENATOR STROM THURMOND
217 RUSSELL SENATE BUILDING
WASHINGTON, D.C. 20515

August 30, 2002

Dear Martin,

Here ya go, bud!

Bar-bar

* * *

IN WITNESS WHEREOF, Author and Publisher have executed this Agreement of the day and year written above.

For Cindy, With Love, Strom

Publisher   Author
Reginald Hines, Simon & Schuster   Strom Thurmond

OFFICE OF SENATOR STROM THURMOND
217 RUSSELL SENATE BUILDING
WASHINGTON, D.C. 20515

August 28, 2002

Dear Juniper,

If I am not mistaken, the ball is in your court.

I am somewhat astonished at the long delay. No, not somewhat, wholly astonished, tip to toe.

Are we rooting for different teams?

Yours,
Blanton (ha ha)

Roman? Reynard? Rilke? Raz?

Percival Everett
University of Southern California
University Park Campus
Los Angeles, CA 90089

August 29, 2002

Martin A. Snell
Senior Editor
Simon & Schuster

Dear Mr. Snell,

Your proposal is so absurd that I would not have considered it at all, but for the fact that you wrote me a letter about it and did not use e-mail or a telephone, both of which I detest. I figure any letter is worth looking at and nearly any letter-writer worth answering.

But holy Mama of God, a project by that senile orange-head Strom Thurmond? *A History of the African-American People?* I mean, it's not a bad idea for a satire, but even there it sounds more like a *Saturday Night Live* skit. And you make it clear this is no satire. I am reasonably sure you do exist. I looked you up in a directory, figuring this was a prank; but there you were.

And why me? Well, never mind that. I gather you wanted a genuine person of color. A black person giving some kind of legitimacy to the number-one racist in the last century: now there's a proposition to make me jump up and shout, "Yassuh!"

But what the hell, the idea of states' rights always interested me, and Thurmond got where he did by differentiating himself from "vulgar racists." I expect he's sincere in what he says about himself, that he has taught himself to believe he has always had the best interests of the nigra and the Constitution at heart. There's something appealing about the quality of that self-deception, that sublime idiocy. It'd be interesting to see what could be done to allow his history to proceed without condemning itself obviously from the first page.

But what sort of history does he have in mind? Does he know? If not, that's OK, as I can then shape it as I like.

You want me to get a helper. OK. I don't know any historians that would do it. A guy here, Jim Kincaid, would do it. He knows nothing of history (he's in the English Department, which tells you a lot), but he is heedless and writes a lot. Besides that, he has little on his plate, so I could count on him to do a lot of the grunt work.

So, answer a few of these questions and we'll be set. The terms are fine. You don't expect me to pay Kincaid out of that, do you? Negotiate with him separately. He'll come cheap.

Sincerely,

Percival Everett

Percival Everett

SIMON & SCHUSTER, INC.
1230 Avenue of the Americas
New York, NY 10020

September 3, 2002

Dear Barton,

Was your letter-before-last a joke? I mean, there you said you didn't want to hear another word from me "or my kind." (What the hell does "or my kind" mean?)

I supposed you were serious and so I shut up. You said to shut up and I did.

It's hard to know about tone in letters. I am an English major, graduated recently from NYU, and I pride myself on reading tone. Still, it's hard.

As you probably expected, all is as usual here. Snell pushed so hard for your project that they gave it to him, with the under-standing—or so I gather—that his ass is on the line. I never get any-thing very direct here, but I think that's the story.

As his ass goes, so goes mine. So tell me: is this the real thing?

Best,
Juniper

p.s. You asked a while back if this was the right house for you. You might as well ask your cat. I mean, what do I know? Snell is com-mitted to the project, which will be fine if it gets done before he is himself committed. So I think I'd stay here, if I were you. The way I look at things like this is: if you're someplace and it isn't too bad, stay there unless you know you can get to a place that's better.

p.p.s. Please don't make me reveal my first name.

OFFICE OF SENATOR STROM THURMOND
217 RUSSELL SENATE BUILDING
WASHINGTON, D.C. 20515

September 4, 2002

Martin,

As I mentioned many times, if this project is to blossom, it will be necessary that, at every step, you people adapt to the Senator's way of doing things and not vice versa. He did not get to where he is nor has he stayed there so long (longer, you may know, than any man or woman in the history of the world) by not knowing what he's doing. He knows what he's doing. He doesn't say you don't, but he is sure he does.

The original contracts will be just fine. The Senator is clear on all this. I am. You are. Why delay matters?

I also received your phone message—please don't do that again—telling me that Mr. Everett has agreed to consult on this project and that he has some sort of historian and scholar as an assistant. As you are paying them, as per contractual arrangement, we will abide by your decision. Let's just hope they work out. It is probably time for you to tell me how to get in touch with them, so we can get this History rolling.

Are you fond of hunting?

Yours fondly,
Barthes

SIMON & SCHUSTER, INC.
1230 Avenue of the Americas
New York, NY 10020

September 11, 2002

Dear Percival,
Just between us, I think the Senator expects you to

ghost-write this, with Kincaid's help and doubtless some input from an aide by the name of Barton Wilkes. In fact, I may as well tell you that you will probably get lots of input from Barton Wilkes, an extraordinarily strange man, I'm afraid, but one we have no reason to doubt has the ear (and maybe the mind) of Senator Thurmond. So ardent is Wilkes in protecting the Senator, that we have not ourselves been able to establish direct contact with Thurmond at all, only with Wilkes. He will probably want to know about your mother. I'd advise telling him, as it's one point on which he is truly interesting.

Be that as it may, I do not see any reason not to trust Wilkes. He'll be in touch right away, I am sure. Then you can take what he sends you, parcel out what you like to Kincaid, and go to town. We have invested very heavily indeed in this project here at Simon and Schuster, despite the uncertainty of that final shape, which we hope you will help get straightened out as soon as possible. But it's not too much to say we think this book will be the hit of the decade. My own sniffer tells me it is so, and I've never treed the wrong possum.

I wish I had a sharper assistant, but I won't trouble you with that now.

I wouldn't worry too much about accuracy and that sort of thing. After all, what's attractive (or the reverse) here is the Senator's spin on things. And we imagine he'll spin like the teacups ride at Disneyland. I'd let him. You may find it challenging to get things in order, even to make coherent the Senator's take on the past and his role in it. But don't try to make him too sensible, you know, or too reasonable. Nobody expects that or wants it either. We want a unique voice here. That's what counts. Accurate history can be got anywhere. This is different.

As for Wilkes, I'd take what he sends you and try to deal with it as seems best to you, asking him as few questions as possible. In fact, I'd try to ask no questions. He's prickly. He asked if I was fond of hunting and once signed himself "Button." I'd not fall too deeply into the personal with him, if I were you, except as regards mothers. Remember the Glen Close character in "Fatal Attraction."

We appreciate your work on this, Percival, and hope you find it challenging and, possibly, instructive. I look forward to meeting you and your assistant and talking about things. If you want to write up the Mother issue and run it by me first, that'd be fine.

Sincerely,

Martin

Simon & Schuster, Inc.
1230 Avenue of the Americas
New York, NY 10020

September 11, 2002

Dear Barton,

I enclose the contact information on Mr. Everett and also, should you need it, on Mr. Kincaid, Everett's scholar-assistant. They are both eagerly awaiting any preliminary discussion you wish to undertake or, failing that, material on the History itself.

Here's wishing you a productive and mutually rewarding relationship. We much look forward to seeing the completed manuscript.

Yours truly,
Martin

Memo: Snell to McCloud

September 11, 2002

McCloud:

I dare you to say you're overworked.

In fact, Vendetti—you know him, the depraved Italian guy? I guess he's Italian, though I wouldn't want to stereotype, just because he's fat, dark, inarticulate, and mean. I don't even know what his title is, but he acts like he's a made man on the way up that old Mafia ladder. Everybody but me just about dislocates their knees getting down to kiss his ass.

This Vendetti comes up to me and says, "Hey, Snell. That assistant of yours, the one with the funny name, Julep or something, you know who I mean?" "What of it?" I said. "Here's what of it," he said; "he have any time on his hands? Cause I got about 30 projects I need some help on and I figure he couldn't be any too busy." "Why'd you figure that?" I said. "I just figured," he said. "Well, you figured wrong, Vendetti," I said, adding, "And if you think you can figure that way about me, you got the wrong boy, that's about all that is!"

That put the swarthy prick in his place.

I protected you and now need to keep you busier, having said you were busy. Besides, I am getting a very uneasy feeling about Wilkes, not about the project but about Wilkes personally. You have that feeling too? It doesn't matter, since I have it.

Here's what you do. You try to insinuate yourself into Wilkes's personal life and find out what's what. I don't mean to get too personal or anything, nothing illegal. Just try to find out if he's a square dealer, on the up and up. Just to be perfectly clear, it's not his sex life I'm curious about. No, it's his sanity. Of course one may be entwined with the other, in which case, of course, you should collapse that distinction, using due discretion and making it clear at all times that you are acting on your own and not on behalf of the firm.

So, see if you can get a chummy correspondence going. Ask him about his mother and about hunting, two of his interests. Perhaps he will invite you there. In which case, go. Don't invite him here, though. I don't want him in the same zipcode with me.

The company picnic is next Saturday, you know. Lots of the fun comes from the paired-up games, like the three-legged race, the human wheelbarrow race, the swimming game called "wedgie your buddy," and that elaborate cosmetic and clothing game, where partners dress one another in whimsical costumes and give mutual make-overs.

It is customary for the pairings to be arranged ahead of time.

Mart

OFFICE OF SENATOR STROM THURMOND
217 RUSSELL SENATE BUILDING
WASHINGTON, D.C. 20515

September 12, 2002

Juniper:

Well, as for tone, do you know Lewis Carroll? There's tone for
you. Or Nabokov. But why am I telling this to a bonafide English
major from NYU, a credential you have now waved before me
twice. At one point, the White Queen says to pretty Alice, "I've
seen hills compared to which that [hill] would be a valley." If you
think my tone is complex, which it is, be glad you aren't corresponding with the White Queen. Or Humbert.

I see that by citing Lewis Carroll and Humbert I have laid
myself open to the suspicion that I may share their proclivities.
Well, put that in your toner, Mr. McCloud, and see what your
printer delivers!

The project is about to roll, though between you and me, we
(which includes the Senator as well as yours truly) need first to test
these boys we have assisting.

You ever heard of either of them, these writer-scholars? Your
sweetmeat Snell, the one with the extremely peculiar mother—
warped him, obviously, the mother did—picked them. You met
Snell's mother? I'd love a description.

Tell me something about yourself. I feel that I am the only one
being forthcoming.

And while I'm at it, perhaps I should just up and say to you, "Certainly, if you do not trust me enough to tell me your name, why should you? I've never been one to beg for trust. Never had to. So your given name shall be a secret known only to you, the phone company, the janitor in your building, and your whores."

Tony (get it?)

Rupert? Rik? Rodan?

ym

SIMON & SCHUSTER, INC.
1230 Avenue of the Americas
New York, NY 10020

September 12, 2002

Professor James Kincaid
English Department
University of Southern California
Los Angeles, CA 90089-0354

Dear Mr. Kincaid,

I see that I have neglected to contact you about the Thurmond project and describe our terms. I realize that you know of this project through Percival Everett and that he will assign you your duties. Whatever you work out is fine with us. It is what we call a "subsidiary arrangement," that which you and Everett have. We are not legally obliged, as I understand it.

We offer you a flat fee of $750 (seven hundred and fifty dollars) for such duties as Mr. Everett assigns, contingent on his approval of such work. The enclosed contract spells all this out clearly.

We look forward to your participation in this project, for which we have the highest hopes.

Sincerely,

Martin A. Snell

Martin A. Snell
Senior Editor

Memo: Thurmond Book
From: Arthur Sullivan, Senior Editor
To: Martin Snell
Date: September 16, 2002

Snell, I just saw the correspondence on the Thurmond project. The oddities therein are multitudinous.

I know you spoke eloquently, or at least heatedly, in support of this book. You failed to mention a few things: the absence of any evidence to suggest that Thurmond is writing this or any other book, is even aware of this project; the manifest lunacy of this Wilks character; the obscurity of the ghost-writing team. And what the fuck is this project anyway? I know you asked that question of Wilks yourself, but to have offered a contract before settling it seems to me---well, curious.

We're saddled with this now. By "we" I mean "you." If this fizzles or, worse, explodes, be sure that your first major push here will be your last.

Meanwhile, let me know how I can help.

James R. Kincaid
University of Southern California
University Park Campus
Los Angeles, CA 90089

September 17, 2002

Mr. Martin A. Snell
Senior Editor
Simon & Schuster

Dear Mr. Snell,

I have shown your letter and what you choose to call a "contract" to Percival Everett; and believe you me, we have had quite a laugh over it. I don't blame you, as I suppose you simply don't know who I am, but the idea of me working for $750 (which is worth about 10 minutes of my time) or assisting Percival Everett! My jaw drops. It's not that Percival isn't a fine person and writer, wholly deserving of an assistant, a whole damned army of assistants. But to think I would be ready to play that particular role. Really, Mr. Snell, you are droll.

I have written many scholarly books, books not wholly unacclaimed in certain scholarly circles. I also have reason to believe that my own writing abilities have not gone unappreciated and that I could, were I of a mind, write Everett's kind of fiction—or anybody else's. You'll, of course, understand my position.

Mr. Snell, I do not wish to be difficult, nor have I in mind any dulling of the sharp edge of this project, which both quickens my curiosity and tickles my scholarly funny bone. How about this? I tear up this mistaken contract and we both forget it. I have no wish at all not to be friends with you, who knows on what basis?

So, I give you a choice: $45,000 or 1% of net profits. Some equivalent combination I would also consider.

Do you ever get to Los Angeles? Next time you're here, I hope you will be my guest for lunch. I have a few other projects I'd like to waft past your nostrils.

Warmest personal regards,
James R. Kincaid
James R. Kincaid

SIMON & SCHUSTER, INC.
1230 Avenue of the Americas
New York, NY 10020

September 18, 2002

Barton:

Well, has the shit ever hit the fan here. The bosses have finally taken a look at what old Snell has committed the company to and they are all over him like missionaries on one of those bare-chested babes in "National Geographic."

You ask for something personal. You know, I guess I have told you a lot more personal stuff than you have me. And why personal stuff? I mean, I'm not averse but just curious. It's not like I'm used to saying personal things just because they're personal. After all, it's not like we're in some truth session. You ever do that in college? Stuff like, "Tell one time when you were caught or almost caught masturbating." Real personal things like that.

So, I guess I don't mind at all being personal, so long as it's a mutual thing, you know.

My sister was caught masturbating. I mean really caught. And really masturbating. My sister is two years older than me, you see, and really gorgeous, if I do say so myself. I mean, she is also pretty much a raving bitch, if you ask me, but she hides that very well around anyone except me. Others say she is warm and independent, but the truth is she's just self-absorbed and dog-dirty mean. But she can look really good, even in the morning, you know, and in ratty clothes and after a shower even. And some find her kind, I'll grant that.

Anyhow, so here I was a freshman in high school and she was a junior. I was sitting in my room one night, doing homework or something, and I hear my Mom say, "What ARE you doing? Oh my God, Reba, don't you know that is filthy? It's just filthy. And the windows are open and the blinds and you have no clothes on at all. And you are doing that filthy thing to yourself. Is that what they teach you in school now? That it's OK to do that to yourself?" And on and on like that. At first I didn't know what she was talking about, but then I figured it out and went around the corner and peeked. Now, you'd think my sister would be sobbing and howling, cringing on the floor, holding sheets up to her chin. But no. She was just standing there staring at my mother, letting her go on and on. Finally, my mother gave out one last "And what do you have to say for yourself?" My sister just stared at her, standing there beside her bed, kind of thrusting her chest out, naked as a jay bird. Then she said, "It's called masturbating, Mother. You ought to try it. It'd improve your disposition. But if you ever interrupt me doing myself again, I'll leave home." The last sentence is kind of approximate, because as soon as my sister said that about my Mother ought to try masturbating, my mother started shrieking all over again.

I know that's not personal about me, exactly. But it's still pretty personal. And it does tell you a lot about my sister. She lives in your city, by the way. Reba McCloud. She's single, but I wouldn't recommend contacting her.

Best,
Juniper

p.s. OK. It's not that I don't trust you. Of course I do, or I wouldn't have mentioned the incident above. Don't think I don't trust you. My name, though, is a matter so humiliating to me it's hard to speak of, much less speak it, the name I mean. It would be very kind of you to drop the inquiry, very kind indeed. I only use the initial "R," to tell the truth, to make myself sound more important— and also male, Juniper being one of those go-either-way names.

FROM THE DESK OF PERCIVAL EVERETT

September 18, 2002

Jim:
   Good meeting! I'm glad we got all that ironed out, as it

wouldn't do to enter into this on the back of a crawling dis-
agreement. Glad you are with me on that.

I agree too that our main problems are:

1. What exactly is this thing? A history or a set of musings? Is
it some kind of half-assed defense of his record, do you suppose? Old Strom want us to make him look good to his darkie
friends? Whatever he has in mind, we'd better find out right
off. I am with you in your feeling that it doesn't much matter,
that we can do anything we put our minds to. No doubt
about that. And it's not like either of us had any moral or
political convictions that would interfere.

2. How can we be sure what we're getting is from Strom and
not Blanton Wilkes, that lunatic advisor guy? My sense is we
should figure this out as we go. Let's first see what we get and
then worry about who is writing it. At some point, though,
we'll have to assure ourselves that Thurmond is in the mix
somewhere.

3. As to how we proceed. I know you are concerned about
this, but I don't know why. I told you repeatedly that we wait
for Thurmond or Beauregard to send us some material and
then we shape it and give it life. As I mentioned several times
in our meeting, it is not up to us to initiate the material. They
write it; we rewrite and shape. So, for right now we just sit
back and wait, unless somebody wants a conference.

Best,
P

Simon & Schuster, Inc.
1230 Avenue of the Americas
New York, NY 10020

September 19, 2002

Dear Mr. Kincaid,
   1%.
   Done.

Martin Snell

Interoffice Memo

September 19, 2002

Percival:
   Where'd you get that "From the Desk of" pad? Some ass think you'd like it? A joke?
   Anyhow, just to confirm.

   1. I think we should know before we start what genre we're in here. I mean, what if Senator Thurmond thinks he's writing a history and we cast it as informal memoir or slapstick comedy?

2. I am not wholly comfortable with allowing the mystery of the source of all this to continue. I think we should know now, as neither of us (I assume) is interested in helping Barton Wilkes perpetrate a fraud. His name is "Barton," not "Blanton" ("Beauregard" was your joke, right?). Perhaps I should be the one corresponding with him, as, from what Snell says, he is probably touchy about little things like what his fucking name is.

3. I don't know why you're thin-skinned about my concern over the exact details (and timing) of our project. I mean, I do not have the luxury of just sitting back and waiting to see what happens. I am a scholar, you know, with a position to maintain and classes to teach, though I'll grant you the latter aren't much of a trouble. I cannot, however, put my professional life (research, publishing, the many boards I am on, the conferences I attend, the calls I have on my opinions and counsel) on hold. I am surprised that you can. Nothing personal.

Looking forward to a working time together.

Jim

From the Desk of Percival Everett

September 20, 2002

Jim:

The pad was given to me by my wife. Not as a joke.

Perhaps you don't understand how these things are done. That's OK. They will become clear as we go. All this about who is writing it, what it is, when it comes to us: that's for Snell to work out. Snell is paying us, and there's no reason for us to take on the burden of dealing with Barton and/or Strom.

Calm yourself. Do some of those thigh exercises you do with that wooden massage tool you were showing me. I too am "looking forward to a working time together" and couldn't ever have put it so well.

Best regards,
P

OFFICE OF SENATOR STROM THURMOND
217 RUSSELL SENATE BUILDING
WASHINGTON, D.C. 20515

September 21, 2002

Juniper:

That's more like it.

Am I to understand that Snell is not a person of real authority? Tell me true now. I won't reveal the source of my info, but I don't relish proceeding with an underling. No offense, as I do not refer to you, of course. Snell is the subject. Stick to it. I am sure you did not ask to be assigned to him, so no shame attaches to you. Snell has always had for me an uncertain odor.

The story about your sister reveals more about you and, <u>certainment,</u> about your mother. I can say that, you know. It seems to be my curse to run into those with maternal malformations looming behind them. That she would regard your sister's shimmering, nubile body as "filthy," especially as it drove itself to the highest pitches of ecstasy, speaks volumes about Mom, doesn't it?

And you spying? Now, is that quite the thing? How often did you spy, telling the truth? Did you peek every day? Did you touch yourself as you peeked? You tell me you didn't understand your mother's meaning when she spoke of your sister giving herself pleasure. Oh sure! Hello! Were you not giving YOURSELF pleasure along with her, stroke for stroke? Did you not do that repeatedly, not to say obsessively? Did you not watch as she bathed, dressed, ran her hands slowly over herself? And what were you doing while watching? The little insert about "not understanding" doesn't take a Dr. Freud to figure out, now does it?

Did you pleasure yourself while writing to me about this episode in the past? But it's not in the past, is it, not really? It's right there in your mind, as if you could reach out and touch your sister's ripe-avocado breasts and her downy moss—but instead of reaching out and touching your sister, you reach down and touch------. Delicacy forbids.

But my own youth was not without its excitements. Though they cannot perhaps come close to your level on the perversity chart, I did play doctor with several little friends in our clubhouse. It was all very innocent, of course, and, unlike your incestuous affairs, non-coercive. Still, there was a fair measure of secretiveness and shame attached. Especially to the classic enema game; you and your sister know that one well.

I may be in New York shortly and look forward to getting together.

As for names, maybe this will help. I was not myself, at birth, christened "Barton." "Wilkes," yes; "Barton," no. I gave myself that name later on. What was my given name? John. I love that name, don't get me wrong, and that association; but it became wearisome explaining about Booth---"John Wilkes------," you know---and dealing with the misinformation about that great actor, misinformation even educated people carry about with them like papooses. There. Now you tell me. Is your first name also a go-either-way name? Robin? Regan? Ramona?

Ta-Ta!
Your American Cousin

James R. Kincaid
University of Southern California
University Park Campus
Los Angeles, CA 90089

September 21, 2002

Dear Percival,

I do apologize for the remark about your note pad. I was just feeling a little out of sorts, you know, and grumpy. I shouldn't have taken it out on you, of course, and I will do much better in the future. The truth is that I am having some trouble with my neighbor, who owns both cats and children, dueling one another to be the more distressing. The children actually come visiting, and my wife lets them in. It's not that they shit all over the place—the cats do that, outside I mean, though in the garden and so forth, and the other day I stepped in it; ever smell cat shit? They (the kids) imagine that they are interesting conversationalists. My wife lets them in, as I say, and insists I sit there and talk with them. Talk with them! It's like holding conversations with a group of sparrows, a form of wildlife they resemble—all pencil-necked and chirpy.

I see what you mean about the points at issue. Doubtless it will all work out. I have taken the liberty, however, of writing directly to Barton Wilkes—you suppose he has a middle name? He at least must be a III or IV? I add that here, as a copy, so you can see. I didn't want to bother you, as I knew you'd prefer I did it.

Did you see what our colleague _____ was wearing today? And I'm fucking sure he uses that artificial tanning cream, Man-Tan or some such.

Yours truly,

Jim

James R. Kincaid
University of Southern California
University Park Campus
Los Angeles, CA 90089

COPY FOR P.E.

September 21, 2002

Mr. Barton Wilkes, Esq.
Senior Advisor, Senator Strom Thurmond

Russell Senate Bldg.
Washington, D.C.

Dear Mr. Wilkes,

I am writing on behalf of Percival Everett and myself to say a hi to you and to inquire about a few mundane matters relating to our mutual project. We understand that you were the one initiating contact with our publisher and we are glad you did.

Just so we can all be pulling on the same wagon, let's get a few things straight. What do you say?

1. Could you tell us what the Senator has in mind, exactly, as to genre. (By genre, I mean not so much what Aristotle meant, nothing that formal, but simply what it is you have in mind.) For instance, is this a straight-line history, starting at some point and ending at some other, giving us a kind of chronicle of the life of African-Americans? On the other hand (or on an other hand), is it a set of personal reflections? Perhaps it is an account of the Senator's own dealings with African-Americans? You see our quandry. A word from you, just a word, will set us right.

2. We strongly feel that we should be connecting straight to Senator Thurmond, now that the preliminaries are over and the main feature has begun. I mean, there are certainly many details that you will be handling. I refer only to the substance of things and questions like that in 1 (see above), which will be much clearer coming straight from Senator Thurmond than filtered through an intermediary, no matter how skilled. I am sure you understand our point here, which is one merely of efficiency and trying not to get really mixed up.

3. When exactly will you be sending material to us, and at what schedule? It would help us (me, especially) to get an exact

schedule for delivery of materials (as one of us has many other projects going as well). We will reciprocate with a schedule right back to you, showing when we will be finished with our writing and shaping.

4. We need to set up a meeting with Senator Thurmond as soon as possible.

Cordially,

James R. Kincaid
James R. Kincaid

From the Desk of Percival Everett

September 23, 2002

Jim:

JESUS CHRIST!

Percival

From the Desk of Percival Everett

September 24, 2002

Dear Jim,
    You settled for what?
    1% of net?
    That's gross---ha ha. No, that's nuts!

P

Memo: McCloud to Snell

September 26, 2002

Martin:
    I need your help.
    I made the mistake—I admit it was mine—of trying to get personal by telling Wilkes a story about my sister, a true story but about my sister, with whom I am not close. As I should have known—I admit it—Wilkes turned it into a story, first about my mother, and then about me. You can have no idea how personal he made it.
    Now I feel like I am either in analysis or in a most horrible affair. Wilkes seems determined to molest either my body or my mind.
    I apologize for saying these things, but now he says he's coming to town, looks forward to meeting me, and for all I know weighs 350 pounds and is vicious.

Thanks for the card. I enjoyed the picnic a lot too. I'm sorry we didn't win any of the races. I think if we had had time to practice the running things we'd have done better, but I'm so much smaller than you, our strides didn't really match. Yes, the wedgie game was fun and, thanks for asking, I really am OK now. Didn't mean to make such a fuss.

Thanks,
Juniper

p.s. I'm glad it's all cleared up about cats and all. Let me just reiterate how fond I am of them, despite not at present having one by me. I am positive a cat would be, as you say, a comfort; but I'm pretty sure my lease expressly forbids cats. I have no idea why.

OFFICE OF SENATOR STROM THURMOND
217 RUSSELL SENATE BUILDING
WASHINGTON, D.C. 20515

September 30, 2002

Mr. James Kincaid
c/o Simon & Schuster Publishers

My dear Mr. Kincaid:

I regrettably misplaced your address, along with your letter. A quick e-mail (I hate e-mail; it is not private) to Martin (Snell, the editor at Simon and Schuster) gave me your name. He also gave me your address, but, for many reasons I won't enter into here, I think it best to correspond through him. I can only hope that you will respect my wishes in this matter. They are, needless to say, the Senator's wishes.

As for the points, as you call them, you raise:

1. The work will be ever faithful to its title. Senator Thurmond feels, and I concur that traditional ideas on genre (I can't tell you how grateful I am for your little lecture, however inaccurate) do not apply here.

2. You will regard my voice on these matters as coincident with that of the Senator. That way there will be no confusion whatever and we will all know where we are. I will not say that your way of putting point number 2 was impertinent.

3. We are glad to hear that you will be prompt. You must understand, though it is not clear from your letter that understanding of this sort will lie in your way, that the Senator is the one who is busy. He is, after all, the Senior Senator, THE Senior Senator, and thus just two heart attacks away from the Presidency. A schedule? You can take your schedule and stick it right up some dog's curly ass! I don't mean to say that this matter is not negotiable.

4. Never!

Do you ever get back this way, Jim? It is Jim, isn't it? It would be a pleasure to show you around here and convince you—I'm sure I could—that not all Washingtonians are stuffy!

Fondlely,
Blue

Interoffice Memo

October 4, 2002

Hey Percival,

Blue? Is that his nickname or something? Anyhow, look at the copy of his latest. Can he be sane? I gather you disapproved of my letter to him. You were right.

And who is this Snell guy we got as an editor? He have any authority?

You suppose this is a hoax? You seen any money yet?

I'd sort of like to get started on this, wouldn't you? I mean, this thing has me up nights thinking—but thinking about what? You know what I mean? If I knew what to think about, I wouldn't worry so much. As it is, I don't know when I've worried so much. Are you worried too?

If you used e-mail this would be easier. I don't mean to complain, but it does seem cumbersome writing notes, especially when we're right here in the same place, sort of. I could teach you how to do it—or, on second thought, somebody else could.

But that's not pressing. What is pressing is what this Blue character has in mind. Do you think I should just go to Washington and see him? Do you want to go? Should we go together? Actually, I'm not sure I want to go alone, what with him offering to show me how unstuffy he is. Maybe he'd tie me up and have his way with me or something—or kill me, maybe.

But I'd almost rather he'd do that than leave us hanging. Don't you feel that way too?

Jim

Memo: Snell to McCloud

October 7, 2002

McCloud:

The company does not have a Halloween party, but that does not mean parties are disallowed or anything. What do you say?

As for Wilkes, tell me more fully what you told him about masturbating. I don't see how I can help unless I have all the details. If you'd rather not discuss such things with me, fine; but I must say, I do not know why you would share something with Wilkes, whom you've never met, and withhold it from me, who is close to you in terms of where our offices are---if in no other way, though I rather thought . . . never mind.

When is he visiting?

Perhaps you could meet him halfway. Do your parents live about halfway? That'd be one plan. Meet him at your parents' place. Are your parents still alive? Do your parents have a cat?

Remember, the idea is for you to find out about Wilkes, not vice versa. I thought I had made that clear. You aren't looking to go half-time with Vendetti, are you?

Mart

From the Desk of Percival Everett

October 7, 2002

Jim—

Take a nap.

Didn't you mention some other project you were working on? One of those Victorian writers? Maybe you should keep that alive, vary your interests some. There is such a thing as over-dedication, you know.

All things will come to us, if we wait. I sure don't want to rush Strom. He can't stand much rush, is my guess. Wouldn't want to be responsible for killing him, not directly responsible.

So just hang tight. They'll send us some stuff when they're ready.

Did you see that student who lodged the complaint about you? Just be sure you have a witness when you talk with her, and don't threaten her or anything.

P

Office of Senator Strom Thurmond
217 Russell Senate Building
Washington, D.C. 20515

To: Percival Everett and James Kincaid (just one copy each)
From: Barton Wilkes
Date: October 14, 2002

I figured it was best to send a copy of everything to both of you. That way, it wouldn't look as if I were favoring one of you over the other. Also, it wouldn't look as if I gave a damn what your internal relations might be. Just so long as you produce results that meet the Senator's demands, I don't care if you are mortal enemies, lovers, locked in a custody battle, contenders for the light-heavyweight crown, married, operating an auto parts store together, or father and daughter. I'm both easy with and indifferent to your workings, writerly and otherwise. On the other hand, I am not made of stone.

Here are some historical materials that the Senator plans to use.

What he'd like you to do is write them up as you plan to write things up, just so he can see how you do things.

These are very short snippetty things, just so he can see. You understand.

So please write them up, using whatever methods you have worked out mutually, and send them back.

FIRST DOCUMENT:
An Address of Delegates of the State Convention of the Colored People of South Carolina to the White Inhabitants of South Carolina—1865

Here are a few points excerpted from the first official document of its kind I can locate. It was published in the New York Daily Tribune, November 29, 1865. Please notice the date and think of this remarkable document as representing the deliberate thoughts of men newly freed and thus subject to all the raptures of what they certainly regarded as victory.

This document, in other words, we can think of, justly, as representing the most elevated wishes of those colored people, flushed with triumph and set upon making what they felt they had reason to see as fair demands, demands that a bloody and most abominable war had been fought to secure.

In other words, this is what the colored people wanted. Uncorrupted by what came later, this is what they wanted. Further, these are the terms in which they expressed exactly what it was they wanted. They didn't want something else. They wanted this.

Prior to the influx of carpetbaggers and other interested scoundrels from the North, of corrupt Northern politicians and unscrupulous business-men with morals low enough to allow them to work on the simplicity and ignorance of the colored people, prior to all that, this is what colored peo-ple wanted and how they wanted it.

Think of these things.

The address from these delegates begins by saying they have met together to "devise ways and means which may, through the bless-ing of God, tend to our improvement, elevation, and progress, fully believing that our cause is one which commends itself to the hearts of all good men."

While I do not wish to bias your work, or control it, Everett/Kincaid, I do wish to draw your attention to the Senator's feelings that these sentiments, uncontaminated by revisionist lies, are such that do honor to the colored men who composed them and to all the white people of South Carolina, the vast majority, who were fully ready to join in devising ways and means tending to the improvement and progress of the colored people. The Senator's own career—though he is too modest to say this—has been directed by the very same goals announced by these newly freed slaves so long ago. The true feelings of the South, in other words, have not been the feelings of colored people or of white people but of PEOPLE. Senator Thurmond has always stressed that unanimity and worked to preserve and further it. It is only the cynical meddlings of Northerners, who used their simulated sym-pathy for the colored man to advance Northern interests, that obscured and misdirected the unity that was there from the very day the War ended.

The document, which we might as well say represents the uncontami-nated wishes of all Southern colored people in 1865, goes on:

"We fully recognize the truth of the maxim, 'The gods help those who help themselves.'"

That is, they simply wanted the opportunity to develop their domestic and commercial lives by helping themselves. Unfortunately, this was not allowed to happen, due to Northern "helpers."

Finally, they summarize their view most sensibly:

"We simply ask that we shall be recognized as <u>men</u>; that there be no obstructions placed in our way; that the same laws which govern <u>white men</u> shall govern <u>black men</u>; that we have the right of trial by a jury of our <u>peers</u>; that schools be established for the education of <u>colored children</u> as well as <u>white</u>, and that the advantages of both colors shall, in this respect, be <u>equal</u>; that no impediments be put in the way of our acquiring homesteads for ourselves and our people; that, in short, we be dealt with as others are—in equity and justice."

SECOND DOCUMENT:

This is offered without comment—it's from the Reconstruction Period—reprinted from the Montgomery Alabama <u>Daily Advertiser</u> of August 8, 1872. In this Resolution, passed by this group of prominent colored people in the city and county of Montgomery, the following clause appears. The Resolution as a whole announces the Club's support for the Liberal Republican-Democratic Party ticket, headed by Horace Greeley and Benjamin Gratz-Brown:

"Be it further resolved, that we recognize no other place but the South as our home, that the interests of the white and colored people here are one and in common and should be regarded by both in order to secure a peaceable settlement of existing prejudices."

So, please write these up and send them back as soon as it's convenient for you. Also, though I know I talked a little rough about your internal relations, I gladly offer my services to help heal any little sores that open between you. Anyhow, to it!

Bart

Simon & Schuster, Inc.
1230 Avenue of the Americas
New York, NY 10020

October 18, 2002

Dear Barton,

Sorry to be slow answering your last letter, which was certainly a fine one. It's just that things have been high-pressure hell around here. On top of everything I have to do, Martin keeps threatening to share me with this horrible guy Vendetti, who always looks like he's just been playing football for 3 hours in the broiling sun, with no shower for miles. Vendetti also weighs about 400 pounds—slight exaggeration—and has a personality to match his revolting, hulking look. I mean, one of the terrible things about working for him would be having to look at him a lot. He also handles the sleazier things we do—unauthorized biographies of the stars, inside looks at serial killers, diet books.

I don't dispute anything you so shrewdly guessed about my psyche. You got my insides right, as it were. But not my outsides. I protest against your jocular suggestions that I played with myself in time with my sister's heavings or that I did so again on recreating the scene for you. Remember, my sister, though very beautiful, was, as I recall, bitchy to me. That was quite sufficient to cool any incestuous urges, had there been any, which there weren't. You might as well suggest that my sister got caught on purpose, hoping to draw my mother into a mutual masturbation league or something.

As for "R." I don't quite see how changing your name from "John" matches my humiliation or in any way lessens it, but since you make all this a test of my trust for you and since I don't wish to be stand-offish, here is the vile truth. "R" stands for "Roba," pronounced "Robe-ah," accent on the first syllable. My older sister is named Reba, as you know. My parents evidently regarded the Reba/Roba pairing as clever. Or so I guess. Well, or so I know. But what a name! Kids called me "Rubba," and, when Terry Southern's novel "Candy" was passed among them, "Dubba" or "Give me your Hump!" In college, even friends often called me "Dis-Roba," as if that were witty. Anyway, there you have it.

But hey. Enough about me. You know, your little return for my deeply personal, my embarrassingly personal, my no-holds-barred personal revelation was—what? Nothing but a generic playing-doctor-in-the-clubhouse reference, and even that general and vague. Sure, the enema game stuff sounds disgusting enough, but details, man, details!

You talk about coming here, which would be fine. But instead of you going all that way or me all that way—I mean you from Washington to New York, or me backwards there—why don't we meet halfway? I make that Wilmington, just about. Want to do that?

Someday I'll tell you about the company picnic.

Joy

From the Desk of Percival Everett

October 20, 2002

Jim:

Don't write back to Wilkes or anybody else. Probably too late to say don't write to me. Above all, don't bother going to the library to look this stuff up.

OK. I'll read what you are writing to me at this very selfsame moment---and then we can decide what we want to do.

Be cool.

Drink some of that Old Overholt you like so much and take a full dose of the pills you say are for pain. All will be well.

P

Interoffice Memo

October 20, 2002

Dear Percival,

Well, what in Christ do you think of this?

Do they expect us to write a history based on selections from one document, representing the true feelings of all "colored people" before the North came down and corrupted them? Match what they say up with Strom's views on Strom's career, distorted by senility and dishonesty, and then before you know it, butt-fuck-your-aunt, we'll have our book?

Even in these snippets, doubtless selected from thousands of pages of documents as the only examples that would suit the Senator's sick purpose, there are the seeds of an accurate, that is to say anti-Strom, history. The South Carolina address asks for equal protection under the law, to the right of trial by a peer jury, for integrated schooling, for open housing, and for complete equity. Does Thurmond think those things came about, that he struggled to bring them about, that they obtain in South Carolina even now?

And then that pathetic thing from the Montgomery newspaper, saying that the interests of black folk and white folk are the same. Yeah, sure. Can't we all just get along?

And then—how in hell are we to "write this up"? Is this history to begin in 1865—as if slavery never happened?

Well—I say we tell Barton to take these papers and use them to set fire to the Senator's dog.

Jim

OFFICE OF SENATOR STROM THURMOND
217 RUSSELL SENATE BUILDING
WASHINGTON, D.C. 20515

October 20, 2002

Dear Percival and James (if I may),

I realize that you possibly have not yet had time to fully write up what I last sent you. But you know what? I was thinking after I sent it that, by giving you so little to work on, I was, as it were, giving you too much. You see what I mean?

You might suppose that you could take those two brief snippets and infer from them the entirety of the Senator's views or career. You might think that these two brief snippets were the SEED of a comprehensive view of the Senator's ideas on the Negro in this country. Don't think that for a minute. But I can see how you could.

I didn't give you more because I didn't want to overburden you right off and because I wanted to see a sample of how you wrote things up. So did the Senator. We both still do. My feelings for you ran wild with me and thereby caused myself and the Senator great loss of time and exertion, as I said previously.

So, here are some more things to add to what you are writing up.

The first is from a speech in Congress, made by Representative Richard Harvey Cain of South Carolina on January 10, 1874. The Honorable Mr. Cain had earlier been a minister in the African Methodist Episcopal Church—I know this church sounds like an incongruous mix, like doilies on a pig trough, but try not to become distracted by such details, as neither the Senator nor myself is—and was prominent in South Carolina politics. South Carolina is Senator Thurmond's state. Representative Cain was a colored man, you see, and in this speech he refutes the claims of a North Carolina representative, a white one. This North Carolina fellow had spoken against civil rights legislation then pending, arguing that the mixture of Negro and white would cause disturbances and citing what he called the destruction of the University of South Carolina "by virtue of bringing in contact the white students with the colored."

Here are Representative Cain's remarks on the forward-looking and successful efforts of the state of South Carolina to solve its own problems:

"It is true that a small number of students left the institution, but the institution still remains. The buildings are there as erect as ever; the faculty are there as attentive to their duties as ever they were; the students are coming in as they did before. It is true, sir, that there is a mixture of students now; that there are colored and white students of law and medicine sitting side by side; it is true, sir, that the prejudice of some of the professors was so strong that it drove them out of the institution; but the philanthropy and good sense of others were such that they remained; and thus we have still the institution going on, and because some students have left, it cannot be reasonably argued that the usefulness of the institution has been destroyed. The University of South Carolina has not been destroyed!"

Now there is testimony *by a colored man* that South Carolina was not only on the road to solving, but *had solved*, its problems on its own terms and to the betterment of all. If only meddling outsiders . . . . But the analysis is yours to make. If I make it myself, then I might as well write the book. What are we paying you for, anyway?

Meanwhile, consider the position of the Negro outside the South during this same period. We generally hear little about these people and the abominations visited upon them in the North and in the West. Why? Don't make me laugh! Because the situation for Negroes outside the South was horrible, far worse than in any part of the South. The Northern press and Northern muckrakers needed to vilify the South, to invent problems there, and often (as with carpetbaggers) to actually create these problems in order to draw attention away from the plight of the Northern Negro. Put it this way: by inventing a myth of Southern brutality toward the Negro, by ignoring the truth evident in such states as South Carolina, and by sending down to the South ruffians and brutes to stir things up, the North allowed itself the luxury of exploiting black labor and sadistically torturing black people silently and invisibly.

Item—an 1866 Illinois State Convention of Negroes noted that the "free" state of Illinois, being perfectly willing to enlist black soldiers, to slurp up the fruits of black labor, and to wallow in black tax dollars, still does not allow black equality in the courts and does not even allow black men to vote. Worse, and in direct contrast to South Carolina, the writers say, "The colored people of the State of Illinois are taxed for the support of the public schools, and denied, by the laws of the State, the right of sending their children to said schools." At that time fewer than 100 Negro children, out of the tens of thousands (or more) Negro juveniles living under the blessings of Northern liberation, attended public school. This speaks for itself—or, rather, you should speak for it. So much for Northern protests against separate but equal schools. How about no schools at all?

Item—an 1869 Convention of New York Negroes listed the following grievances:

> "[The Negroes of this state] are taxed without being represented; they are subject to trials by juries which are not their peers; they are murdered without having redress; they are taxed to support common schools while their children are denied the privilege of attending those in their respective wards; they are called upon for military service of their country without receiving proper protection from the country, and without any incentives whatever of being commissioned officers.
>
> *"These grievances belie the Declaration of Independence* by which the American people profess to be governed" [italics theirs].

Item—an 1870 memorial from colored physicians, all graduates from medical school and with experience as surgeons in the Union army, addresses the American Congress with clear evidence of the refusal of the District of Columbia to admit to membership in the medical society any colored physicians and even white physicians who favored the fair treatment of colored physicians. As membership in the Society was necessary for licensing, and licensing for practicing medicine, all these fine colored doctors were denied the right to pursue their profession *simply on the basis of the color of their skin* [italics Senator Thurmond's].

You will find nothing of this sort happening in the South and particularly in South Carolina, where black physicians were treating black patients with full sanction of the medical board. Only in the North were such systematic monstrosities recorded.

I will be sending more materials in a few days.

If you have already finished some of the work and sent it, why that is fine. It may be that your reply is winging its way to me as mine is gliding to you. Some would say such crossings in the mail could be confusing. I prefer to regard them as aviarially poetic, and I feel certain you do as well, both of you.

While we are at it, perhaps it would be as well if you gave me some means of distinguishing you. I know that Everett is a writer and James is a researcher, but I think you'll agree that doesn't tell me much. Tell me more. For instance, are you both black or only one of you? How exactly black? Do you enjoy Sidney Poitier movies? What is it that draws you together and shoves you apart, emotion-wise? That sort of thing.

Sincerely yours,
Blaine

OFFICE OF SENATOR STROM THURMOND
217 RUSSELL SENATE BUILDING
WASHINGTON, D.C. 20515

October 20, 2002

Dear Repinuj,

You now move to imagining the masturbatory coupling of your mother and sister, as if that particular spectacle left you uninvolved. I have nothing against intense voyeurism, but I don't accept for one moment the notion that it keeps you out of things, that one perversion displaces another, that you can only have one kink at a time. After all, it is you stage-managing all this, directing the scene, orchestrating the oohs and oh-Jesuses and yeses and that's-the-places and don't-stops.

You ask for more of the playing doctor. OK. I was just trying to be modest. It seems I was always the patient, carefully undressed and probed by a large hospital staff of neighborhood and visiting girls, and boys too. From the time I was maybe 8 until well into my teens I played this part. The attending physicians ranged in age from 4 to 16 at least, and several times Mr. Tolliver (my little friend Julie's father) participated. He was ever so old. I can recall all this pretty clearly and can remember only being happy to give others so much pleasure. I don't think I am lying when I say no sexual joyance came to me in all this. I felt, deeply but purely, the glow, call it altruistic if you must, that comes from being of use. I remember being very careful to present myself in a variety of comely ways, seeking out nice undergarments and, every now and then, perfumes.

I am not saying I am still available for this role. Don't get me wrong. I have graduated to other dramas.

Wilmington? DELAWARE? Have you ever left your Simon & Schuster cardboard cubicle there, McCloudiness? Certainly not Wilmington, Delaware. I have no objections to an assignation. But let's choose something with character. Veer east a little on your map and you find-------? Let's make it a game. Look and tell me.

Notnalb

p.s. I cannot imagine why you are so peevish about your name. Roba has about it a distinguished air. True, it doesn't seem a name belonging in our time and place, does it? Ringing of the names invented for grunting cavemen in films like "Barbarella" or "Cro Magnon!" or for androids in the future, it seems to bring with it, Roba does, hints of melodies lost in the breezes of yesterday or not yet played. Unhearable, unknowable, untouchable.

Memo: McCloud to Snell

October 23, 2002

Dear Martin,
    Look at this from Wilkes. What am I to do?
    If ever you felt kindly toward me, please help.

Desperately,
Juniper

Memo: Snell to McCloud

October 24, 2002

Dearest Juniper,

I don't exactly know what you're asking for.

You do seem upset. Remember our party is but a week away. If you need calming before then, I'm afraid I can't help you.

That's rather interesting, that doctor game Wilkes outlined. Wonder if he has a little brother. I don't see anything kinky or out of line in his letter. Probably you are just timid, McCloud, sexually repressed. I'm not saying you should offer yourself to him or he to you. Nor should either of you find a third party, male or female. It's not a question of gender; that's obvious enough. Besides, you affirm that you are straight, though I don't recall giving you any cause to inform me of this "fact" so often or so insistently. You are barking up the wrong shrub in the garden of gender.

What's your concern—that he will plead to give you an enema?

Martin

I see you've redacted the copy of the letter you sent me, the part that deals with the mystery of the "R."

FROM THE DESK OF PERCIVAL EVERETT

October 25, 2002

Jim:

Well, now I'm with you. What in the name of the KKK are we dealing with here?

Barton now sends us "clarification" that is about as clear as yo mama's reputation.

I can make nothing out of this, not one damn thing.

You want to cut and run?

P

Interoffice Memo

October 27, 2002

Percival:

You put me in the unaccustomed position, yes you do, of telling you to take it easy. Usually it's you telling me to take it easy but now it's me telling you. So, just take it easy and leave this to me.

It's not like you, an ex-rodeo champeen and all, to quit just because the challenges mount. I do not lay the claims to athletic accomplishment that you devise, but I do remember my days on the intramural basketball team. I played both guard and forward, even, when Jimmy Canton didn't show up once, center. We called our team "The Klondykers," because we all, apart from one guy, came from a part of town called Klondyke. I really enjoyed all that, you know. I'd give anything to be back there right now, though just between you and me, it'd be better to go through high school again a whole lot better looking. It wouldn't hurt to be a cool guy too. I wasn't cool back then, were you? I mean, I wasn't the worst geek or that sort of thing, but not really cool. I can say that now. Why is it we don't have a chance to just fold time over like a sheet or a piece of legal pad paper and live it all over, only good looking and cool? I'd give anything. You ever think of that?

Don't you get some feel from this latest material? I get some feel from it. Look again and tell me.

You're a good friend.

Jim

⌒

FROM THE DESK OF PERCIVAL EVERETT

October 29, 2002

Jim:
    You OK?

Percival

⌒

SIMON & SCHUSTER, INC.
1230 Avenue of the Americas
New York, NY 10020

October 30, 2002

Dear Barton,

I figured out that backwards spelling. Very clever. Did you do that on purpose?

Thanks for the details on the playing doctor experiences. That all sounds delightful, and of course I understand when you say your motives were altruistic. It's just that I cannot myself ever remember acting altruistically—certainly not when my clothes or anybody else's clothes were off. I once told the most obnoxious girl in our (or anybody else's) high school not only that she had a great personality but that I loved her. And you know what that bought me— simply the right to remove her bra and suck on one nipple. I don't know why one, but she guarded the other as if it were the Hope Diamond. Maybe she was saving that one for marriage.

You are much more outward-thinking, I see.

OK—east of Wilmington. Got it! Philly. Not my favorite city but certainly easy to get to. Right? And I don't mean to suggest I know Philly well enough to have an opinion really. Who knows? I expect you do. Is it sort of like Paris? Anyway, Philly it is.

Duolccm

p.s. Tomorrow's the Halloween party Snell has cooked up. As far as I know, I'm the only guest. He says he'll supply costumes. Pray for me.

From the Desk of Percival Everett

November 1, 2002

Jim:

I didn't mean to ignore your other letter exactly. It did have a strange calming effect on me. Like dribbling bourbon between my toes and strummin on the old banjo.

Really, though I got lost in the story about how much you enjoyed basketball and sex in high school, I did do what you said. I went back to this second batch of stuff from Wacko Wilkes and tried to see if there isn't something there.

What do you think? All these petitions from Northern blacks do hint at something that is a partial but important truth: the South functioned as the North's convenient Other, allowing the North to do very little toward establishing equal schooling, housing, and voting rights by presenting a whipping boy. Focusing on the demonic South allowed the North to keep its attention away from itself, certainly away from the plight of actual black people right there on the other side of the tracks.

That's true enough and it may hint at a stronger truth for us. What do you think? The North operated this way, constructing the South so as to deflect its attention away from its own defects and establish a kind of automatic virtue it could always draw on. The simple fact of living in the North allowed any asshole to feel righteous without doing a damned thing. The automatic quality is what strikes me. And maybe there's an automatic quality too in Strom's alliance with things like States' Rights. I haven't got it figured out yet, but maybe we will find that he is, for all his political smarts, less a calculator than a guy operating day by day within a set of assumptions he never questions, that are there for him in the air he breathes and come to him automatically. I guess we just have to be careful that we don't breathe in the same air---or at least mix it with some L.A. smog.

What do you think?

P

Interoffice Memo

November 3, 2002

Dear Percival,

I see.

Maybe so. Maybe old Strom just was there and acted on being there, kind of like a weather vane? Well, that makes him too passive, but I see what you mean. The North never really thought much about equality for blacks, just found itself in the pleasant situation of being able to feel real good by pointing out how unjust to the blacks the South was. That was certainly easier than doing anything themselves.

But I see what you're saying: it's like both sides are battling windmills, setting up caricatures of the other and tilting away at them. Blacks simply define the field; they are of themselves of almost no importance.

That's too cynical, right?

But you're thinking Strom is less an independent force than a reflector of positions that are, somehow or other, always there for him---really there before him. He doesn't wake up on Tuesday and think things through; he wakes up on Tuesday to find things thought through for him.

J

OFFICE OF SENATOR STROM THURMOND
217 RUSSELL SENATE BUILDING
WASHINGTON, D.C. 20515

November 5, 2002

Joy---

What was the name of the girl who gave you her breast? Maybe I knew her. You ever think that maybe her other breast was deformed and she was ashamed of it, trying to protect it and save her dignity? Maybe it was wizened, marked with lines or strange circles, equipped with multiple nipples. Who can say? I'm rather glad you cannot, as it would probably have supplied you with more fuel for mockery. Not everything about sex is funny, you know. Women are not simply objects with tits and pussies and so forth either, just there to be manipulated and lied to so you can---- AH! Mother enters the picture again, right?

Philadelphia? Are you mad? That's North. Look further east and a little south.

Baa

p.s.   Oh, Roba! Roba! Roba!

Now please do not say No—bah!
Let's grab our bags and go—bah
To the land of E.A. Poe—bah;
Where we can pitch and throw—bah,
Woo with our little Lo—bah;
Then jump a boat and row—bah
Away from cops and woe—bah,
Lie low, low, low, low, low—bah;
Then back to Lo, shouting "Yo—bah!"
Until the heat doth go—bah.

FROM THE DESK OF PERCIVAL EVERETT

November 5, 2002

Jim—Let's draft a letter right away to Wilkes, laying out the grounds of our confusion and trying to get him to tell us what the fuck he's doing. You want to draft it and THEN SEND IT TO ME (not Wilkes, until I see it)?

SIMON & SCHUSTER, INC.
1230 Avenue of the Americas
New York, NY 10020

November 8, 2002

Dear Percival and James,

Well, our project is attracting some attention, you'll be glad to hear, and it's attention from the highest quarters. Because my dealings with those in high positions, elected and appointed, would be damaged, perhaps irreparably, were I to bandy about names, I must leave you to guess, or, rather, not to guess but to quiet your curiosity on this point.

In any case, I received a phone call this morning from a Senator—I think I can say that much—asking about our project. This senior and highly respected Senator said that he had heard talk (in the corridors of the Senate and the Senate dining room) about our project. (He also said he had heard wonderful things about me, which I pass on just for completeness sake.) I might add that, in addition to having his ear to the ground, he is a person who has fought back against calamity and, even worse, the calumny of the vicious press in reporting an accident he had years ago. I can't use names, but it is a tribute to his fighting spirit and that of his family the way he has stood solid and large against those who would be willing to turn a mere accident into something more.

I'll add only that he is not even of Senator Thurmond's party and thus is speaking out of concern for the dignity and democratic forms of the Senate. To quote him, "I wouldn't even call it 'concern,' Martin, confident as I am that a friend like you—may I call you a friend? [I said "certainly"]—will do the thing right. I know I can count on you and won't insult you by asking."

So, I think that's wholly reasonable. And I'll just repeat the luminous Senator's words: I know I can count on you to do this thing right and won't insult you by asking. I mean I can count on you not to mock Senator T or anything like that, right?

Yours truly,
Martin A. Snell
Martin Snell, Editor

SIMON & SCHUSTER, INC.
1230 Avenue of the Americas
New York, NY 10020

November 8, 2002

Barton,
   Atlantic City?

Juniper

Interoffice Memo

Percival—This OK?

* * *

DRAFT

November 9, 2002

Dear Martin,

I enclose here material received from Wilkes.

What in God's name are we to make of it? I mean, he says we are to work it up. What the hell does "work it up" mean? Here we are waiting patiently for real material FROM THURMOND and we get what are apparently writing exercises from this Barton person. Who is he? How are we to deal with him?

Is he mad? Are you?

The material also. For fuck's sake, it leans toward the most absurd apologetic I've ever seen. We supposed to say that all was peachy for Southern darkies, that the only ones suffering were those who went North? It gets worse, as you will see.

We are serious writers, Snell, and we sure as Christ cannot proceed without knowing what it is we are to be doing. I can tell you what we won't do:

> --write some cockeyed history designed to make salmon-head look like a friend to man
> --sit around for months playing hide-the-hankie with Wilkes
> --put up with much more crowshit from you

So, with all respect, do clarify things for us. We don't mean to cause difficulties. We mean to work. We are dying to work. We work well, you'll see. Let us work!

Cordially yours,

Percival and Jim

FROM THE DESK OF PERCIVAL EVERETT

November 10, 2002

Jim:
I altered the tone a little and sent it on.

OFFICE OF SENATOR STROM THURMOND
217 RUSSELL SENATE BUILDING
WASHINGTON, D.C. 20515

November 10, 2002

Juniper:

Atlantic City is fine by me. Good suggestion. Next weekend?

How was Halloween? Strange you didn't mention it. Did you get to feed from anyone's breast? Was Mother there in the flesh? Big Sis?

Barton

Office of Senator Strom Thurmond
217 Russell Senate Building
Washington, D.C. 20515

November 10, 2002

Dear Percival and Jim,

Should it be "Jim and Percival"? Or should I alternate? You let me know, if you would, as I cannot be expected to guess and do not want to hear, somewhere down the road, "Barton, you have caused a rift." But why put it negatively? I wish not to avoid disharmony so much as to conjure concord.

Enough of that, though you must understand that I have no wish to be impersonal. Tell me more about yourselves. Which one is black? Forgive me if you've already said this, but I sometimes forget some things in the rush of doing other things. Only one of you is black, right? Neither name is much of a giveaway, is it? But then they seldom are. Jackson, perhaps, or Johnson, but then you can get into serious troubles by making such assumptions, believe you me. Now, if one of you were named Shumoonunu

Ackabawka, then I wouldn't have to ask. But neither of you is, so I must.

Anything else you'd care to add in the personal line, do.

I think the reason you haven't sent me anything is that I haven't given you enough to chew on and work up properly. So here's some more. Part of it is a little lengthy, but just take a deep breath and go at it, working it up.

First comes an excerpt from a little-known speech by the greatest Negro of his time and probably any other time, Booker Taliaferro Washington. This is a speech given in 1884. This is not the celebrated speech he gave later. That was in 1895. Don't confuse the two, as I will give you some of the latter later in this message. But they are different.

> "Any movement for the elevation of the Southern Negro, in order to be successful, must have to a certain extent the cooperation of the Southern whites. . . . The best course to pursue in regard to the civil rights bill in the South is to let it alone; let it alone and it will settle itself. Good schoolteachers and plenty of money to pay them will be more potent in settling the race question than many civil rights bills and investigating committees."

Let me just add here that it is common for certain historians (all from guess where?) to dismiss Washington as an "Uncle Tom," a leader who would sell his people for the humiliation of vocational education and some patronizing. I know this, but I will warn you two that history is never so simple. Neither are men. Neither is Stowe's Uncle Tom, for that matter. He's actually a tough old bird and resists to the death. That's another issue, though. Don't confuse me.

Note this. In the crucial year of 1904, just twenty years later you will note, Washington published in the important magazine, The Outlook, an essay, "Cruelty in the Congo Country." I can send it to you if you like. In it, Washington brilliantly shows how the United States government, having

established Liberia as what it regarded as an African showcase, then coop-
erated with Belgium to ensure the existence of the Congo under Leopold's
vile rule. Moreover, our government had done nothing to halt the abuses in
the Congo, abuses that Washington outlines with grisly clarity and with his
wonderful, judicious acumen. He was no dummy. He showed how King
Leopold of Belgium worked by using one tribe to police another, taking a
small portion of the "tributes" he was collecting to pay off those he was
inciting to acts of horror. King Leopold, Washington says, is not really <u>cap-
italizing</u> on the native savagery and brutality; he is <u>instilling</u> these qualities, <u>importing</u> them from Europe. The heart of darkness (cf. Conrad) beats
not in the African but in the European who transplants it there—with the
blithe cooperation of the United States of America.

Mix that in with your liberal acid and shoot it up.

Second is a short bit from M. Edward Bryant of Alabama, writing in <u>The
Christian Recorder</u> (Philadelphia), January 19, 1888. Now M. Edward Bryant
was a well-known Selma radical, both an editor and a minister. He was a
firebrand, you might say, capable of such Malcolm X-like outbursts as "Let
the world know that we prefer death to such liberty as we have today." But
here's what he really intends to say:

> "The Negro needs to learn how to use his power wisely. We want to
> live in peace with all mankind, and especially with the whites of the
> South. Our interests are identical. But we do not want the peace of
> the lamb with the lion. Give us our rights, not social equality, and we
> will die by you, for you, and with you."

I don't want to presume to guide you much, but do note that, apart from
all that flapdoodle about dying, these sentiments echo the Senator's his-
toric position.

Two short pieces follow.

First from the North Carolina [Negro] Teacher's Association report,
1886, offered without comment. You'll see for yourself the significance
here and the representative quality of these two sentences. (The second

sentence is curtailed, but nothing of importance is left out, you have my word.)

"To have separate schools seems to be a part of the political organism of the South; and we would not have it otherwise, but there should not be any wide disparagement in favor of or against either race. This would be out of harmony with the genius of American institutions. . . ."

And then from the Virginia Readjuster Party statement in 1883. I confess I do not know a lot about this Party. To be candid, I know nothing at all, though I'm sure the following statement, once again, represents the good sense even of what we would call, anachronistically but inescapably, THE FAR LEFT of Negro sentiment IN THE SOUTH:

"We are not as intelligent, nor as strong, financially, as any other people. We are just out of slavery; we are struggling upward, we need friends."

I don't know what you make of that remark about inferior intelligence. I can speak for the Senator in saying that he (nor I) never supposed anything of the kind. Why they said that is something for you to work out.

Finally, the Atlanta Cotton Exposition speech of September 18, 1895 by, of course, Booker T. I wonder why so many things happen in September? Apart from the days dwindling down to a precious few, I mean. Is it so with you? I know it is for me. In early September I met _____, who has, despite some recent idiocies, meant almost everything. Almost but not---well, you know. Also in September I learned to have a good personality, as we called it then. I set myself a rigorous course of training, all through the month. When done---well, you know the result. Or rather, you don't yet. Not really.

Heeeeeeeeeeeeeeeerrrrrrre's Booker!

"It is in the South that the Negro is given a man's chance in the commercial world. . . . You can be sure in the future, as you have been in the past, that you and your families will be surrounded by the most patient, faithful, law-abiding, and unresentful people that the world has ever seen. . . . In all things that are purely social we can be as separate as the fingers, yet one as the hand in all things essential to mutual progress. . . . The wisest among my race understand that the agitation of questions of social equality is the extremest folly, and that progress in the enjoyment of all the privileges that will come to us must be the result of severe and constant struggle, rather than of artificial forcing."

If you are not familiar with the striking metaphor of the bucket Washington uses in this speech, do look at it. I can supply it, but I find it a little long to reproduce here. Perhaps, as one of you—the black?—is a researcher, you can find it yourself.

Well, ta ta for now.
Do either of you have a sister, younger?
Go Diamondbacks!

Bisto

Interoffice Memo

November 12, 2002

Percival:
    Well, suck off your dog, isn't this the limit? Here we haven't

written a word—right? you haven't written anything, have you?—
and we get this warning to do the right thing. I take it the whole
fucking letter is a tribute to Snell's intimacy with fatso Ted
Kennedy, who has obviously never heard of Snell before. "May I
call you a friend?" indeed. I didn't know anybody used that line
except vacuum-cleaner salesmen. I tried it once in picking up a girl,
back in my inexperienced days, and you can imagine what she said!
What she said was, "You can call it as you see it, dumbo, but that
doesn't mean I gotta do it!" She wasn't the brightest, I guess, but
then neither was I for using a line like that. I sometimes think I'm
not very bright period. That ever occur to you? About me, I mean.

The last line in the letter is what Snell wants from us, I think. "I
can count on you not to mock Senator T or anything." That after
he's just said he needn't mention what it is he wants. Thinks better
of it and decides he has to spell it out to dummies like us.

Why do you suppose Ted Kennedy is worried about us mocking
Strom Thurmond? For all I know, Strom Thurmond is dead and
we'd only be mocking assface Barton Wilkes, if we even mocked.
And mocked what? What is it we have to mock?

Where is the source of all this? What are we doing?

I bought a new shirt today—on the net. One of those Eddie
Bauer real big ones that go over other shirts.

FROM THE DESK OF PERCIVAL EVERETT

November 13, 2002

Jim:

You seem a little disoriented. Try to get your gyroscope spinning up and down again.

Snell's letter is really something, isn't it? I wonder who'd win in a loony contest, Snell or Wilkes?

I think we should give Snell about as much attention here as Teddy deserves. Imagine trying to stroke Snell so he'll not embarrass the Senate by publishing anything untoward, even about Thurmond. Makes you wonder if there's a dime's worth of difference between any of those old boys. Fuckers.

Anyhow, I have a short response to Snell. If it's OK with you, we'll send it. It's attached here.

Don't you have a whole bunch of those big shirts?

Percival

Percival Everett
University of Southern California
University Park Campus
Los Angeles, CA 90089

November 13, 2002

Dear Martin,

You mystify us, Martin. Who could that Senator be? All we know is that he is an old and valued friend of yours who knows he can trust you, and you him, right?

Wow. Neither Kincaid nor I know a single Senator, not one. You probably know a lot.

As for keeping things warm and cozy inside those chambers, hey, why would we want to disrupt that? It's august, that's what it is.

Tell your chubby buddy—is he about to explode?—from us that we'll treat the subject and his reflections on the subject with all due respect and courtesy, camouflaging as best we can the Senator's bigotry, manifest shallowness, self-aggrandizing nonsense, and overwhelming ignorance. We agree with Tubbo, and you can say this with confidence, that such attributes are a vital and long-standing Senatorial feature and that we are glad to see today's Senate embracing them with patriotic fervor.

Can you get us any autographs?

Love,
PE and JK

SIMON & SCHUSTER, INC.
1230 Avenue of the Americas
New York, NY 10020

November 15, 2002

Dear Percival and James,

On an entirely different matter—concerning yours of the 10th, in reference to material sent to you by Mr. Wilkes.

I do very much appreciate your eagerness to proceed

with this project, proceed perhaps more rapidly than Mr. Wilkes, according to your lights, is allowing. That sort of chomping is a good sign, but it can go too far, you know. A certain amount of eagerness, even impatience, is a good thing; but too much—. You know what I mean?

Academics tend to be quite impatient. Perhaps it comes—you'll excuse me—from having so few demands on your time. I know you are all doing research and the like, but how many hours a week do you actually work, maybe 5? I think it's all that vacant time, that sense of hours stretching out before you with nothing to fill them, that gets on your nerves so. It's understandable, but it's not always the best thing.

I think Mr. Wilkes is not sending you "writing exercises," as you put it, but fodder, preliminary fodder perhaps, but who's to say? I can tell you that Mr. Wilkes is indeed connected to Senator Thurmond. Why else would this forthcoming book be THE topic of conversation in the cloakroom and dining hall? Of the Senate, I mean.

My best advice, and I speak here for the project as a whole and the interests of the United States Senate, is "cooperate." Cooperation and patience will pay big dividends when all the dust settles and the checkered flag comes down. Trust me.

If I can be of further assistance, do not hesitate to contact.

Your friend,
Martin

SIMON & SCHUSTER, INC.
1230 Avenue of the Americas
New York, NY 10020

November 16, 2002

Dear Professors Everett and Kincaid,

I don't know where to turn, certainly not to my family or to anybody here. I don't know either what you can do for me or why I am writing exactly, but, as I say, I have nowhere else to turn.

I am Juniper McCloud. I expect you know already who I am (see letterhead) and how I am connected to this project, but maybe not, as Snell tends to represent himself as the whole firm, the whole publishing industry, eclipsing everyone beneath him (i.e., me) and pretending there is no one above him, when in fact everybody but me is. In short, I work for Snell. In that position, I am largely responsible for the Strom Thurmond project, so-called, though I have seen no evidence to suggest Strom Thurmond is even aware of this book, assuming he is aware of anything at all, of course. But I am the key man on that, or the set-up chump, as the case may be. Snell either takes credit for everything or blames me, depending on whether the project blows hot or cold around here. There's this guy named Vendetti you wouldn't believe.

But I'm getting astray, and I wouldn't blame you if you were right now saying, "What a madman!" I would myself, I suppose. But please bear with me. I really need help or at least advice.

Barton Wilkes. That says it all. Unless he's calling himself Button, Blanton, Billie, or Bubbly. He's a puff-adder is what he is. You've been dealing with him, right? You doubtless know what I mean, but you can't know it up close and personal like me.

Well, Snell ordered me to get close to Wilkes, really he did, to fish some personal details out of him, all presumably to see if he was on the up and up but really because Snell is a very nosey guy with odd personal habits and, between us, pretty much an unregulated libido. I think Snell was not using me to pimp for him but maybe he was. Who's to say? Probably he didn't know what he wanted, just wanted to see what might happen. He's extremely nosey, king of the noseys. Some day, if you're interested, I'll tell you about the company picnic, which itself wasn't as bad as the Halloween party he threw, just the two of us.

But it's Wilkes that's the problem here, not Snell, though Wilkes would never have been a problem for me, had it not been for Snell. Trying to worm details out of Wilkes, as ordered, I ended up somehow learning nothing of him and disclosing a lot about myself, very personal stuff. Whether what I disclosed was always entirely true is beside the point here; but a lot of it was true and very personal. Do I have regrets for disclosing? Well, duh. But I did. That's my fault. As a private dick, I am a bust.

But what was I to do? And, in any case, I did it.

So, in the process of getting personal, Wilkes started insinuating that we meet, insinuations quickly turning into outright demands for a meeting time and place. I turned to Snell, which was like eating anchovies to cure a heartburn. Snell said I couldn't meet him here in New York but HAD to meet him somewhere.

I should have quit my job right there, you are thinking. I guess so, but look at it from my point of view. I am young, just out of NYU (major in English), and here in my first job, which is a good job, but for Snell, who constitutes pretty much the entire material world of my job and that's rotten fucking luck. How could I quit? I mean, maybe Snell will be fired and I won't. Maybe he'll die or that Vendetti will kill him. Maybe he'll kill Vendetti and I can rat on him anonymously and get him sent up the river. You see.

So, this Wilkes pins me down to Atlantic City last weekend. Here's where I need help and advice. But first let me give you a brief glimpse of what happened. If you need more details, I'll give them. They're humiliating, but what the hell. I've compromised my dignity so deeply now, the only thing worse would be to jump onto the field at Yankee Stadium, shake my dick at the crowd, wave a sign saying, "I went down on my sister," and try to dry-hump the second baseman.

OK, Wilkes gets there—I mean, to the hotel lobby where we arranged to meet. He gets there. Have you seen him? Probably not. It's not a sight you'd want in your scrapbook or in your mind, believe me. You remember in The Silence of the Lambs where Jack Crawford tells Clarice not to let Hannibal Lecter inside her head? Well, it's the same with Barton's body.

You seen Blue Velvet? You know the smarmy piece of ugly blue velvet Frank keeps stroking? OK, think jump suit. Tight. Here comes Wilkes, like a slut from Caligula's court, trailing two rolling suitcases and pretending not to see me. Makes me say, "Barton?"

"Yeaaaayus?" he says in what I can only call a cross between a bray and a purr. If he'd had a cigarette holder, he'd have been Tallulah Bankhead. Not that he was effeminate exactly.

Well anyhow. You're thinking I'm going to tell you the details of our sophisticated sexual adventures. Think again. They weren't sophisticated. They weren't even sexual, to my surprise. I could have handled that. I'm not gay, though I have nothing against being gay, it just happens that I am not, I guess. Still, I have a good relationship with my body--I don't give a shit about it--and wouldn't have made a fuss about almost anything Wilkes had in mind. I mean, that's not a problem. You'd think it would be, but it isn't. That isn't even the problem with Snell and his Halloween plunges into hell.

With Wilkes it wasn't sex. It was, to start with, talk and board games. Then carnival rides. Then we cooked together. Then more talk and board games. Then we put on winter clothing and played "Twister." That sounds sexy maybe, but it wasn't. We slept in separate beds. Didn't even undress in view of one another. He talked half the night. Insisted we cook all the next day, when we weren't playing board games or riding the calmer carnival rides. You're wondering how we cooked in a hotel. I would be too. It seems Wilkes carries his kitchen equipment with him. It folds up and such.

So, here's my problem. All the talk. Somehow, I ended up not only telling him secrets I didn't know I was keeping, but, I swear, telling him things I'd thought and done I'm not entirely sure I really did do or think. How can that be? Too many board games, perhaps. Still, I ended up weeping, not once but on several occasions. Once I was clinging to him and sobbing, right outside the "Dungeon of Doom," a funhouse ride that takes you past lunging goblins and through spider webs, all in the dark.

I tell you this because I have nowhere else to turn. You see, he wants me to meet him again in two weeks. He wanted to do it immediately, but I invented obligations to my sister---like I'd ever really want to see her!---but couldn't postpone things any longer than two weeks. What should I do? Can you help me by inviting Wilkes to come out there for a two-month stay or something--- you know, get material for this fucking book? Short of that, can you advise me? You know him and may be aware of the terrifying power he can exert. I am not ordinarily impressionable, but this is different. If he has another go at me, I am not sure what I might do or what shreds of self I may be left with.

Help me and maybe I can return the favor. Perhaps I can use whiteout and change the figures on your contract, for instance? I'm up to anything.

Your friend,

R. Juniper McCloud
Juniper McCloud
Assistant to Martin Snell

OFFICE OF SENATOR STROM THURMOND
217 RUSSELL SENATE BUILDING
WASHINGTON, D.C. 20515

November 18, 2002

Dear Percival and James, James and Percival, Jacival and Perames,

Martin Snell, who is a caution don't you think?, sent along to me your letter of November 10. In that letter, you (which of you? both?) raised points of clarification—don't you love people who raise their hands in meetings and say "point of clarification" when what they really want to do is get their two cents worth in and achieve anything but clarity? But your points of clarification really deserve a careful review and, as you are saying right about now, responses that drill right to the mother lode.

You see, I know you better than you suppose, know and sympathize. But I have trouble keeping you apart. You are two separate people, right? One of you writes and the other grubs facts? But which of you thinks? I don't mean that as an insult exactly. It would help if you answered my previous question: which of you is black? I ask not because I assume that knowing race I would know all. I wouldn't be the one to suppose that if Kincaid were black, for instance, he would be able to play for the Washington Wizards (a basketball team), that he would have children scattered all over the West Coast, or that he would have a huge dangler of a tommywhocker. Nor, to continue this, would I assume that Everett, if white, would be insecure, inept on the court, and hardly able to find his equipment when doing the old hobble and gobble.

I am, you see, no racist. None of my best friends are black, but that's a matter of accident and what you might call geography. The black people who are in my immediate world, that is the Senator's office, are numerous but not quite my thing, if you follow me. Were they the right thing, they would, some of them, be my best friends. I thought perhaps Juniper McCloud, who works for that Snell person, was black. But I've seen him and he is not. Well, to be honest, I never supposed he was. "Stop dissembling, Bub!"

But if I knew which of you was black—you couldn't send photos, could you?—I could form a mental picture. Once I have a mental picture, that's all I need. I dwell on it and I know. Are you aware, either of you (perhaps the fact-finding one?) that Thomas Carlyle wrote his celebrated lectures "On Heroes and Hero Worship" by gazing at pictures of heroes like Cromwell and Luther (not exactly a hero in my view) and Napoleon (who is to argue with that choice?) and letting his mind burrow into the soul of the image? Then he wrote. Just wrote from inside. He didn't do mundane research; he stared and depended on his own inner resources to supply the rest. Did you know that? Anyhow, that is the process I would like to follow with you two, Percival and James. Hey, do you have nicknames? Should I create nicknames of my own? I mean, Percy and Jim, which is likely what you have now, don't inspire much soul-gazing, now do they?

I suggest Spike and Panda.

So, without knowing exactly whom I am addressing, but still knowing what I know, I will move to your concerns. I gather that your concerns fall into three areas:

--the form, that is, what kind of history is it?
--the position to take, that is, how political is it and what is the political brand?
--the flow of information and authority, that is, who feeds whom?

In order:

--My view is that it should be a rather informal history, factually accurate without being dull. It should be relatively discontinuous, not concerned with filling in every little nook and cranny, but concentrating on those areas the Senator regards as vital, which are generally those in which he has played a part. It should emphasize the Senator's role in the shaping of this country and the strong position now enjoyed by African American people. In that sense, it is what we might call a history of a man, which enfolds the history of a race, which charts the history of a country. I have no objection if you use that sentence early on in the book to explain what it is, though of course I expect full credit.

--Politics will play a part. I don't want you telling me that there is no such thing as objectivity, since I've heard all that post-structuralist stuff and heartily embrace it. Of course the history will be political, through and through. The Senator is, as you know, a Republican, was the leader of the powerful third party movement in the 40s, and was previously a Democrat. But it's not politics in the sense of party that we're talking about. You don't need to tell me that. I know it. We are talking more about what I like to call "ideology," and that is harder to get at and more pervasive. The Senator's ideology is, for the time being, my own. That is a bald statement but true, which leads us to--

--the question of the flow of information. Since I have adopted the same set of assumptions and operating procedures (that's what "ideology" means) as the Senator, there really is, as I keep saying, no need to getting panty-wads over dealing with me. I don't <u>represent</u> him. I AM he, in this sense, the only sense that, one might say, makes sense for us. Of course our experiences have been different and our life spans vary considerably, as do our families, hobbies, and taste in modes of outdoor recreation. Still, when it comes to writing a history of the African-American people, as an overflow of the Senator's life and times, I think you will get from me exactly what you would get from him. I have tried to be patient on this point, but I do not know how many different ways I can say this and do hope this is the last time we will have to do karate chops on the loins of this tiresome subject.

Not wanting to ignore anything in your letter, from the most important obfuscation to the faintest whine, I move now to the questions you raise about the materials I have been kindly supplying you. It seems that you—both of you? just the white one?—resent what you regard as "writing exercises," as if I were a high-school composition teacher and you were both 16-year-old studs in low-slung baggy pants with your undies showing above. Please understand that these materials are just that—materials for the history. They are not meant as a test. If it helps, I am willing to say that I trust you—either or both of you—to know what you are doing as regards research and writing a rough draft. Polishing is another matter, but we'll even waive that for now.

So, do know and wholeheartedly believe that I am not testing you. Find calm and peace and stop fretting. Go to a Japanese garden if there is one close or, if not, buy yourselves two of those little gray sand things that come in a box and are complete with the tiny rakey wooden scratchers and take them home and make lines and curvy patterns. Very restful, I hear. If you cannot afford two, buy one and share. I think, though, they are quite reasonable. You do have Japanese where you live, if I'm not mistaken. Tidy people.

Don't forget the photos and try to find happiness. Do you two take Thanksgiving dinner together?

Love,
Baabaa

FROM THE DESK OF PERCIVAL EVERETT

November 20, 2002

Jim:

Well, the mails are working fast—or Wilkes misdated his letter. You got it too, right? And the one from Martin? And the one from McCloud?

I hope you aren't all red in the face and yelling. Assume that I share your feelings on all this, which relieves both of us from exposing them.

Martin's letter we should ignore, I think, as it tells us nothing.

Wilkes's letter, if you look close and stop fuming, is by far the clearest thing we've gotten. It isn't clear at all, you'll say, and that's true. But compared to what he spread on us before, it's heavenly sunshine. Besides, don't you think it's as good as we're going to get from him? I'm not saying it gives us an indication of what to do; I'm just saying that there's no point hammering Wilkes about it. He's got nothing more to give.

McCloud now. That poor bastard interests me in a petrifying way. Frankly, I'm afraid of him. Why don't you make him your project? You could handle him in your special way, privately. See if you can rescue him from Wilkes, give him some of your good advice.

Where do we go from here? You don't want to hear this---but

wait. Wait and see. Too bad we aren't working with McCloud as, hysteric that he is, this weeping child seems to be the steadiest of the lot. But Snell will never loosen his grip on the project and Wilkes will keep doing what he's doing.

BUT, Jim, there is a publishing house involved. Sooner or later they will sort this out and get us moving. Nothing we can do.

I see you're strongly in favor of remodeling the faculty lounge. There's a surprise.

P

Interoffice Memo

November 20, 2002

Percival:

I don't think you need to take such a patronizing tone with me. I just got your note in my mailbox, and the first thing I noticed: its patronizing tone.

If you'd waited until I wrote to you, you'd have seen that I think we should wait too. I believe I said that some time back, and didn't need you instructing me. It was my idea to begin with, Polonius!

So we'll wait.

I'm not ashamed of supporting the idea of shifting money from grad student stipends to give us something decent in the lounge department. I mean, why should grad students live in luxury while faculty have ratty old couches and not enough magazine racks?

You really think I can help McCloud? It was a heartrending letter. He has no place else to turn. OK. I'll see what I can do, though not for a few days. I have that student hearing, the one who filed a complaint against me that I told you about. Just between us, I may have told that joke in class, but I am confident I can show that only a paranoid witless idiot would regard it as in any way offensive— "racist and obscene," the student said. My ass!

November 20, 2002

Juniper:

Hi honey. I've been missing you so much and wondering how you're doing. No, I don't want money, and no I'm not in trouble. I don't know why you always think that.

You're so cute, you know, and I think I have found just the dolly for you. She's more subdued than the one you didn't like, Michelle, you remember, that I introduced you to. Michelle was a little wild, I guess, or just not too mature. But you have to admit she was a lot of fun, in her way. But her way was not your way, and maybe not any sane person's way. Michelle was not the one for you. Sorry. She's engaged now, by the way, and you should see the place they have picked out for the wedding. It's an old garage—I mean the kind where they fix cars. They are going to have themselves lifted on one of those racks that go up when they change your oil, along with this Justice of the Peace or something, and read their own vows from that perch. So—my mistake.

Anyhow, this other girl is named Ritzi, which does not indicate anything about her, as I know how quick you are to judge people, especially on names. Her Mom and Dad named her Ritzi because they had parents, her Mom and Dad did, who liked the comic strip Ritzi Ritz and they, Ritzi's parents, wanted to pay a sort of tribute to their parents. But Ritzi is quiet and very well educated. She's pretty in a different way from Michelle.

So, Juney, who is this Barton Wilkes? He says he works for a Senator and that he, Wilkes, is your dearest friend. That's how he puts it, your dearest friend. Somehow that doesn't seem likely. Anyhow, this Wilkes calls and I answer (the first time) and he goes on and on, real pleasant but without making a lot of sense that I could figure out. He says he'd like to get together and "see if we can get our Jell-O in the same mold." What does that mean? I have no objections to clever talk, but I'd like to be more at home with it. Suppose I say my Jell-O will fit in the same mold with his Jell-O? What then?

Anyhow, this Wilkes guy scared me a little, so now I've been screening my calls until I could check with you. I've been avoiding him, except for once, when I picked up without thinking and there he was, asking if I didn't think you were very cute, did I look at all like you, and did I ever get to Atlantic City. He also said some stuff about Risk, which I thought was him propositioning me but which turned out to be some kind of game. He said you two played it? I am an easy-going person, but I don't want to go out with a guy who is going to gaze at me and see YOU! But more than that, I just get a funny feeling about this guy and hope you are safe. Don't be mad at me, please. I know you don't like me meddling, and I don't mean to. I just hope you are OK with this guy and not in any danger. If you need help, please call me. I know you'll hate me saying that, but I don't want you needing help and not having anywhere to get it. I can't stand to think of that.

Please tell me what's what, little brother. I promise not to bother you any more than I can help, as I know it annoys you and you don't like me very much. I wish you did.

All my love,
Reba

SIMON & SCHUSTER, INC.
1230 Avenue of the Americas
New York, NY 10020

November 20, 2002

Dear James and Percival,

Just a brief follow-up.

I acknowledge receipt of your humorous comments on the Senatorial buzzings re the book and am pleased that you are willing to play ball.

Was my letter to you regarding your various confusions and concerns fully adequate? I didn't receive from you an acknowledgement of receipt, so I assume it was fully adequate.

Yours faithfully,
Mart

Office of Senator Strom Thurmond
217 Russell Senate Building
Washington, D.C. 20515

November 20, 2002

Dear Percival and James,

Now that we are all clear on the nature of this documentation, I am providing material for the book and not a "writing exercise"— I think I can give it to you straighter, as it were. Without so much commentary, I mean.

Here is some more material, then, meant to aid you in the development of the writing, which I assume is proceeding apace.

I think, really, I shall give you but one piece this time, from a John Merrick speech in 1898. Mr. Merrick, as you see, is from North Carolina. Since there is only one bit this time, I will give you a little more to swim in, though still not a whole lake.

"There has been lots and lots said about the Negro and his condition in North Carolina. So much so that I think that the least of us have a perfect right to give vent to our feelings if we wish; and on these grounds, I take the privilege to say a few words about me and my people the way I see it.

"We are here and we are going to stay. And why not stay? We have the same privileges that other people have. Every avenue is open to us to do business as it is to any other people. We are allowed to own homes and farms, run farms, do banking business, insurance, real estate business and all other minor businesses that are done in this Commonwealth. . . . Now to show you why we have not been benefitted [sic] by politics and why we ought to let them alone: In the first place, our good men and lots of our best men have turned their attention to party and office. A man goes into politics a good man and he goes to pulling the wires and soon is classed a politician. This naturally makes him lose interest along business and industrial lines; then he has to stick to it for protection, and that settles him as a businessman. This happens with very few exceptions . . . . What difference does it make to us who is elected? We got to serve in the same different capacities of life for a living . . . . We got to haul wood, and don't care who is elected.

"Now let us think more of our employment and what it takes to keep peace and to build us a little house and stop thinking we are the whole Republican Party and without us the whole thing would stop.

"Now don't the writers of the race jump on the writer and try to solve my problem. Mine is solved. I solved mine by learning to be courteous to those that courtesy was due, working and trying to save and properly appropriate what I made.

"I do think we have done well and I think we could have done better. Now let us make better use of the years we have left than we have the years that have past, as we have the past to look back over and see the many mistakes."

Add this to the recipe. Stir and make a sunshine cake!

Toodle-oo,
Beeuuttee

OFFICE OF SENATOR STROM THURMOND
217 RUSSELL SENATE BUILDING
WASHINGTON, D.C. 20515

November 22, 2002

My dear Minty Juliper,

Just a note re our weekend.

Don't regret a thing. I know I don't.

And you know what they say about what comes to those who wait.

Atlantic City will always hold for me a special---well, you guess.

Never let it be said that I gilded a lily.

Puss-puss,
Big Blan

SIMON & SCHUSTER, INC.
1230 Avenue of the Americas
New York, NY 10020

November 22, 2002

Dear Barton,

I opened my suitcase and out fell several game pieces. I enclose them, not recalling with any confidence which of your many games they came from. I also had $1000 of play money in my shirt pocket. I meant to return that, but it got all gummed up with other stuff. Sorry.

My sister contacted me, saying you were calling her and asking me about you. I just want to say that I warned you about her. She is EVIL. That's my opinion. But you are certainly welcome to get scorched by her, if you like.

The one thing I will not tolerate is getting into the middle. Should you two get involved, fine with me. Just keep me out of it, hear?

Hope all goes well there in Washington.

Yours truly,
Juniper

FROM THE DESK OF PERCIVAL EVERETT

November 23, 2002

Jim:

Let's keep our focus here, lest we become adrift in a wide, wide ocean far out of sight of land.

The latest from Wilkes—that speech. Can you tell me if it's accurate and who John Merrick was? Wasn't that the name of the Elephant Man?

Percival

p.s. Has the hearing been held yet? You need a character witness?

Interoffice Memo

November 23, 2002

Percival:

Way ahead of you.

I found out where Wilkes is getting his stuff—from a famous anthology of documents compiled by Herbert Aptheker. Anyhow, according to Aptheker, John Merrick of Durham, North Carolina "had been put in business by two Southern millionaires, Julian S. Carr and Washington Duke." "The speech," he adds with acid spraying, "is fittingly 'reasonable.'"

That's interesting about the Elephant Man, whose name was George Merrick, not John. The physician attending him and writing about him, Frederick Treves, always called him John, which says something about the quality of his concern and compassion, I've always thought. Anyhow, the book and the plays and movies about the Elephant Man all call him "John," so it's understandable that you'd make that mistake, egregious as it is. For accuracy in information, consult a scholar.

Happy to oblige.

No. They postponed the hearing in order to "gather more information." What information?

Office of Senator Strom Thurmond
217 Russell Senate Building
Washington, D.C. 20515

November 23, 2002

Dear Percival and James,

A little bird tells me you two are not working as expeditiously as you might.

WHOA now! I'm not saying you are unindustrious, Perkal and Jimby. Far from it. I am saying that you are confused by two things:

1. The paucity of the material I've sent you.
2. Despite everything, some lingering distrust.

As a result, I am conjuring up a picture of you two sitting in your racing cars, revving up at higher and higher speeds, but not able to see that flag that says "Go" or even to make out the track.

I can handle #1 and send more (see below).

As for #2, well, pufferbellies, I think I can only hope you will grant me the trust I am granting you. Let's be clear about this. I am granting it. Grant it in return. Do not dissemble. Let's curl pinkies on this: spit and swear.

Has the Senator seen this material? Yes and no. Have we talked in detail about it? Yes and no.

<u>No</u> in the vulgar sense of two separate and distinct corporeal presences getting together over brandy and flapping their lips. <u>Yes</u> in the meaningful (the only meaningful) sense of things in which essences leave the calm chamber of the imagination, holding in their arms the agency of the sublime. In other words, this is the

Senator, Senator Strom Thurmond of South Carolina, Senior Republican and Senior Senator, and Senior Lawgiver.

If that doesn't convince you, I despair. Or, rather, I would despair, were despair in my blood.

Belief, gentlemen, belief!

So—here are some more materials, giving what I now regard as the full picture. The first represents the tiny, but undeniably present, number of African Americans who urged unspeakable violence. I'll give that first and then tell you about the second. The first is from an Address to the U.S. Congress in 1896 from "The National Association of Colored Men," a fortunately and significantly short-lived group of radicals (I use the word advisedly) from the North who were furious at and jealous of Booker T. Washington and sought to gain notoriety by advocating violence. (You will not fail to see the parallels to such later groups as The Black Panthers, the followers of Malcolm X; as well as individuals like Cassius Clay, Reggie Jackson, and Al Sharpton.)

> "We mark the opening of the militant period of our race in this country. . . . We hail and accept the burdens of the new time without fear and without favor. . . . That time [for militant action] we conceive to be now. Our calm, deliberate advice is for every member of the race henceforth to employ every weapon of every kind of warfare legitimately and courageously in the demand for every right."

I gather one of you is a literary type, or both of you? Which one? The black one? Anyhow, it doesn't take a literary scholar to see at work in this passage the sort of rhetoric Communists used a little later. Words like "calm," "deliberate," "legitimately" try to mask a howl to "every" Negro man, woman, and child to use "every weapon of every kind of warfare" any way they wanted. Any thuggery, murder, looting, raping would be, you see, "calm" and "legitimate."

The next is from the much misunderstood W.E.B. DuBois. Here Dr.

DuBois writes a Negro schoolgirl and reveals attitudes toward racial advancement that I am proud to say (and DuBois would be too) anticipate the Senator's own. The letter is dated 1905, written when the Senator was only 4, so it is remarkably anticipatory. Now, DuBois was sometimes unable to resist in his oratory a certain self-indulgent and undisciplined rhetorical flair, but here he speaks his heart.

"I wonder if you will let a stranger say a word to you about yourself? I have heard that you are a young woman of some ability but that you are neglecting your school work because you have become hopeless of trying to do anything in the world. I am very sorry for this. How any human being whose wonderful fortune it is to live in the 20th century should under ordinarily fair advantages despair of life is almost unbelievable. And if in addition to this that person is, as I am, of Negro lineage with all the hopes and yearnings of hundreds of millions of human souls dependent in some degree on her striving, then her bitterness amounts to crime.

"There are in the U.S. today tens of thousands of colored girls who would be happy beyond measure to have the chance of educating themselves that you are neglecting. If you train yourself as you easily can, there are wonderful chances of usefulness before you: you can join the ranks of 15,000 Negro women teachers, of hundreds of nurses and physicians, of the growing number of clerks and stenographers, and above all of the host of homemakers. Ignorance is a cure for nothing. Get the very best training possible & the doors of opportunity will fly open before you as they are flying before thousands of your fellows. On the other hand every time a colored person neglects an opportunity, it makes it more difficult for others of the race to get such an opportunity. Do you want to cut off the chances of the boys and girls of tomorrow?"

Just copying that makes my heart sing.

There's a character in Dickens, one Dick Swiveller, who says to a friend, "Why should an uncle and nephew peg away at one another, when all might be bliss and concord? Why not jine hands and fergit it?"

Substitute for "uncle and nephew," "Bunny, Perkal, and Jimby," and you see the application. All might be bliss and concord. All will be bliss and concord.

Here's my hand—jine it!

Ever,
Barton

James R. Kincaid
University of Southern California
University Park Campus
Los Angeles, CA 90089

November 24, 2002

Dear Juniper,

Percival and I have read your letter with deep concern and sympathy. We are protected from Barton's flesh and jump suits by distance, and he has not yet sent any pictures, though I suppose that's next; but we can have compassion for anyone who has to spend weekends with him, cooking and playing Parcheesi. (What sorts of things did you cook?)

You seem like a nice young man, and I think I can help. Percival asked me to write to you, as he is less skilled than I at such things. Perhaps I should say that he is simply less experienced. He does not extend to his students the same degree of personal warmth that I radiate almost against my will. I extend warmth to my students and they feel it. (I know this from student evaluations.) The mind is only a small part of the whole person, Juniper. I am sure you know that, having encountered at NYU professors you took to. (Probably some like Percival too.) My students do come to me for help. I find that most student problems have to do with (a) parents, (b) room-mates, (c) sex. The last is by far the most prevalent topic of concern to students these days, and in other days too. It just doesn't go away, and I try to help. Percival says my students talk to me about sex because I steer them in that direction. But you'll notice his students don't talk to him at all, except to complain about grades. Grades, you observed, are not on my list at all.

Parents, I find, are ill-equipped to deal with the problems of comely youth. Obviously. They are themselves a problem. I try to get my students to detach themselves from parents, without at all interfering. It's simply a part of growing up, and I am happy to play a useful role in a natural process. You may have tried consulting with your own parents about Wilkes. Were they of any help? You see my point.

As for Wilkes, do not see him again. Here is the direct advice part. I have decided that both Snell and Wilkes are unreliables. Do not lean on them. Tell Wilkes that Snell has ordered you not to interfere in the proper flow of information, that dating a client is forbidden, that you are so attracted to him (Wilkes) you need to withdraw for your own sanity, that you are moving in with Sister and adopting a child together, that you have but three weeks to live, that you are entering rehab for prescription pain killer abuse, that you are Roman Catholic and can't bring yourself to sin like that any more. Anything!

Don't tell anyone you have cut it off with Wilkes. If he complains to Snell, tell Snell that Wilkes is obsessed with him (Snell) and really wants to see him, not you. You are seeing Wilkes, you say, on a regular basis, just as ordered. Tell Snell Wilkes is just using you to get at the boss, that all he ever talks about is "Martin this" and "Martin that." That'll satisfy Snell's ego and convince him you are indeed seeing Wilkes. Of course there's a chance Snell will go after Wilkes himself, but, believe me, if he does, your name will never come up between them. It'll be Parcheesi passion all the way.

Get it out of your head that Wilkes has hypnotic or Svengali-like powers. What it is, Juniper, is that you are a nice young man and simply need somebody to talk to. You have dilemmas, of course, but who doesn't? That they are sexual dilemmas, by and large, should not make you feel ashamed.

I know I am far away but I am here.

Very glad I could help you.

Sincerely,
Jim

November 24, 2002

Dear Reba,

Your letter has upset me a lot. You don't just meddle but ask personal and insulting questions.

What you and Wilkes do is nothing to me. I just don't care.

Sincerely,
Juniper

November 24, 2002

Dear Reba,

I mailed a letter to you about 2 hours ago. If ever a letter got lost in the mail or somehow destroyed, I hope it was that one. It was a monstrous letter. Please throw it away.

Your letter caught me off guard in a variety of ways. Maybe I should say it slipped by a lot of my guards. But that is no excuse. I did a shameful thing.

When I play through all my memories of you and me, Reba, I somehow can't find a one that doesn't make me ashamed of myself. Was I ever kind to you, even as a little kid? I hope so, since you have been nothing but kind to me. When I read the part of your letter where you ask about Wilkes and me and then start worrying about me and then you ask me not to be mad about you "meddling"---I can't tell you how shocked I was. I don't know why, but all of a sudden it came on me like a swarm of yellow jackets that I had spent so much time being embarrassed by your attention to me, your good humor and social inventiveness, when I was the embarrassment, always.

Let me say it out loud, Reba, no matter how bad it sounds. I was ashamed of you, Reba. I thought I was better than you and didn't want anybody to know you were my sister. That is so awful, I don't know how I can say it. But it was much worse to be it and do it. I know I am hurting you, but I also know you have realized all that and remained, despite all the hurt and humiliation, not only loyal to me but loving.

Reba, please forgive me. You are a thousand times the better person.

I promise you that I will be a good brother to you and honor your fine qualities and try to give you someone you can rely on. I do need help. I'll tell you about it later in this letter or in another.

But please tell me about yourself. Naturally (unnaturally), I know almost nothing about even the outer details of your life. I am sure you have a million friends, that you are busy working and partying and volunteering in the lousiest neighborhoods. Please tell me.

As for me, I am trying to make good decisions in a maze of confusion, much of it brought on by people around me but much of it inside me too. I was lucky to get a wonderful job, or at least a job I wanted really bad (and didn't deserve) with a terrific publishing house. That part's good, and I keep reminding myself of it. But my boss is insecure, a lunatic, and, in his paranoid and frightened way, eager to have sex with me. He's a man. You can't believe, Reba, what narrow escapes I've had—and only partial escapes, sex not really being the issue even. I'll give you details later, but I want to get on to other things.

Namely Wilkes. Reba, don't have anything to do with him. I don't know if he's dangerous at all, but he is even loonier than my boss, Martin Snell, and that's like saying—well, it's like saying he's King of the Loons. I have no idea what he is up to, and I'm pretty sure he doesn't either. He sends the most jumbled letters and I had to spend a weekend with him.

Here's the details. Martin Snell, my boss, is in charge of this project, a book putatively by Strom Thurmond. Now Wilkes has been the contact person for Thurmond, in fact he says he speaks for the Senator, as if he were the Senator. Very suspicious, of course, but he does work for Strom; we've checked. He bombards us and the ghost writers (named Everett and Kincaid) with deranged letters and shields us from Thurmond. We aren't sure that this isn't really Wilkes's book, which is one problem. But Mad

Martin Snell has staked his job on this project and uses me as a fall guy, dirty-work guy, and office sweetie. He ordered me, Snell did, to get close to Wilkes and try to determine what his game was. What a disaster. First, Wilkes wormed stuff out of me and revealed nothing himself. I felt like Rosencrantz or Guildenstern with Hamlet. Compared to me, they were super sleuths. Then Wilkes insisted on a weekend together, insisted and insisted, and Snell made me go. It turned out to be a weekend of cooking in the room, playing board games, and blah-blah-blah. Odd as hell, but not the end.

So stay away.

But about me, honey. I don't want you messing with the Wilkes business, but I hope I can talk with you about the job that has me in such a mess. I've appealed to Everett and Kincaid for help, but they haven't had time to answer yet.

I am going to write you soon about my inside problems, problems inside me, I mean. But I've gone on too long. Please throw that last letter away and keep this one please.

Forgive me. I won't stop drawing on your kindness; but if I have so much to ask for, perhaps I can muster up some to give.

Your loving brother,
Juney

November 24, 2002

Dearest Reba,

Just ran down and mailed the letter, came back, sat down, and remembered I had rudely ignored your suggestion of Ritzi. If you still think you wouldn't be mortified to have me take out a friend, I'd be awfully happy to meet her and ask her out.

One other thing, while I'm talking about how fucked up I am, I shouldn't hide anything about what a fuck I am. One of the secrets Wilkes got from me, and I can't honestly say he wormed it out; I just blurted it, was about Mom catching you masturbating and you telling her she ought to try it.

But I love you and promise to do better---and promise not to weigh down your life with three letters a day!

Love,
Your brother

Memo: Snell to McCloud

November 25

McCloud:

Under the guise of an office memo, I transmit to you material that is <u>PERSONAL IN NATURE, HIGHLY</u>.

First, tell me how Wilkes is behaving. I mean, what have you gleaned as regards his motives and plans? I am sure his interests include you, as I am unable to imagine a sensibility that would be immune to your boyishness. (As I told you, one of your appeals, though by no means the only one, is that you could be passing papers, just riding by on your little bicycle with the bell and throwing papers onto porches, your little butt in those cut-off jeans bouncing on the seat, with your shirt riding up and revealing a little skin and just a hint of those cute whitey-tighty undies, the waistband part, so one could make out only the tops of the letters and have to guess at the word (Hanes? Jockey? JC Penny?), just as they would have to guess at how soft your butt might be, what sensations might be imparted by molding and smacking those little cheeks.)

So, what is the story on Barton?

Thanksgiving, of course. I am a hopeless traditionalist as regards Thanksgiving. I put up cut-outs in the window of Pilgrims and the helpful Indians. I play the merry songs of the season. I thank the Lord. I prepare a hell of a turkey "cum gin." You'll be there. I won't mention the costumes, just hint (as with your undies). Priscilla, Squanto, the stern Cotton Mather, the lovely John Alden, Pocahontas, Hester Pryne, the Rev. Arthur Dimmesdale, Edgar Alan Poe. As always, you'll get to choose the first round.

We need to get cracking on the project. I can't in conscience bother Kincaid and Everett yet. But what does Wilkes say about the progress? Give me an exact account. And, as they say in bad movies, have it on my desk by 9 in the morning. I am not kidding. This is no movie. This is life, McCloud!

M.S.

Memo: McCloud to Snell

November 25, 2002

Dear Martin,

As for the progress of the book, Wilkes has, candidly, not said a word. You told me to get personal with him, worm my way inside his head. That's what I am doing. Give me a little time, though, and I'll be so deep in his head I'll know everything about his motives and plans.

As for Thanksgiving, Martin, I'd love to. You know that. The costumes sound delightful, as does the food. However, I'm tied up with Wilkes. Following your orders, you know, even on holidays.

I never had a paper route.

Best,
Juniper

Simon & Schuster, Inc.
1230 Avenue of the Americas
New York, NY 10020

November 26, 2002

Dear Barton,

You know without me saying it that I would like nothing better than a weekend with you. I got your message inviting me and I at once promised myself I would do it. All this is plain as day to you, and I won't insult you or me by insisting on its veracity.

The problem is—you guessed it—my boss and his way of making my attendance at his maniacal private get-togethers unavoidable. I could resign my position, of course, but that is what it would take; and I needn't tell you that I am not situated in such a way as to make resignation a realistic course.

And then my sister is making demands for after Thanksgiving, and I must see her at some point, crone that she is. I'm telling you, Barton, you'd be happier and safer cozying up to Jeffrey Dahmer than to my sister. Not that you would, of course. I'm just expressing how lethal she is.

Have a great holiday!

Juniper

OFFICE OF SENATOR STROM THURMOND
217 RUSSELL SENATE BUILDING
WASHINGTON, D.C. 20515

November 29, 2002

Dear Juniper,

Do you realize that you signed your last epistle "Juniper." Not so much as a "Yours truly" or "Love." You just slam the fucking door without so much as a by your leave. I would think decent manners would have made you more gracious, even if heart-stirring feelings couldn't.

Obviously they couldn't.

I don't believe a word you say about your sister, especially not now. You have probably subjected her to some of the torment to which you have subjected me. Do you derive pleasure inflicting torture on innocents? Oh sure, as children we all set dogs on fire and ripped turtles from their shells, but most of us, MOST of us, graduate from such things.

Not you.

Reba and I will find much in common and will be able to grow whole together.

Notice that I will not sign off as if I were talking to the IRS or Count Dracula.

My fondest wishes,
Barton

Oh Roba, Roba, Roba
How could you be so low—bah?

SIMON & SCHUSTER, INC.
1230 Avenue of the Americas
New York, NY 10020

November 29, 2002

Dear Professor Kincaid,

I can see why your students respond to you as they do. You do indeed radiate much warmth. I wish I had been lucky enough to have taken a class with you or someone like you at NYU.

I thank you very kindly for your shrewd counsel. As for playing Wilkes and Snell off against one another, I don't think I have the skill for that. I can see the wisdom of your advice and appreciate it deeply. I know someone as skilled in these things as you could mastermind it adroitly. Me, I'd probably just tangle things up badly, like the snarls you used to get in your fishing line. Knowing me, I'd probably get them both clawing at me just by trying to get away. Like running from a couple of killer bees. Incites them.

Again, I cannot thank you enough for your generosity. Please let me know if there is any way I can be of assistance in this project. My abilities may be limited; but they are at your disposal.

Your friend,
R. Juniper McCloud
Juniper McCloud

November 29, 2002

Dear Mr. Wilkes:

I have received your address from my brother, by way of the publishing house.

I am not sure how you got onto me or even how you determined my phone number, though I guess it is in the book. In any case, I am afraid I must ask you not to call me any more. I am sorry to be rude and I do not like to hurt you or anyone else. However, I am not now at liberty to complicate my personal life, much less to be spending Thanksgiving with you.

As for your questions about my brother, I, again not wishing to be rude, must ask you not to go on to me about him. Your messages are sometimes almost violent in tone. I do think, though, that you have no reason to be so angry. Without knowing the details, I do know Juniper and am quite sure he is incapable of a mean or hurtful act. Please do not threaten him or attempt to relay your threats through me. It is an odd way to persuade me to spend time with you anyways, don't you think? As I say, circumstances absolutely prevent me from doing so.

I wish you well, Mr. Wilkes, but trust you will not pursue me or my brother, as you are surely not the person to give pain wantonly.

Thank you.

Sincerely,

Reba McCloud
Reba McCloud

November 29, 2002

Dear Professor Kincaid:

You cannot possibly know who I am, and I apologize for intruding on you. I just wanted to thank you for your kindness to my brother, Juniper McCloud. (He showed me your letter.) It is not everyone who would take the time to write such a wise letter to a forlorn stranger.

Whether or not Juniper is able to take your advice, it is nonetheless a rare and fine thing you did.

I am as grateful as he.

Warmest wishes,

Reba McCloud

Reba McCloud

From the Desk of Percival Everett

November 29, 2002

Jim—
    What is this latest shit from Barton?
    What should we do?

Percival

Interoffice Memo

November 29, 2002

Percival:
    What is this latest shit from Barton?
    What should we do?

Jim

Interoffice Memo

November 30, 2002

Percival—

Glad we talked. I agree that we should write directly to Strom—
or try to. The only sane one in this whole mess seems to me
McCloud's goddamn sister. Lot of fucking good that does us.

You go ahead and write Strom. You got that South Carolina
touch.

By the way, the hearing was a fucking farce. I'll tell you more
when I'm less depressed about it. The upshot is I have to go to sensitivity training, apologize, and "watch my step." Can you believe it?
And can I appeal or anything? No! Of course not. Maybe I should
have brought character witnesses, but the thing was stacked from
the beginning. You get the picture—young woman and middle-aged
man (albeit distinguished professor with unblemished record).
That's all she wrote. (What does that phrase mean? Where does it
come from?)

Anyhow, go ahead and write to Strom.

Fuck!

Jim

p.s. What will they train my fucking sensitivity to do? Fetch? Roll
over? Ha ha!

**Percival Everett
University of Southern California
University Park Campus
Los Angeles, CA 90089**

December 2, 2002

The Honorable Strom Thurmond
Russell Senate Office Building
Washington, D.C.

Dear Senator Thurmond:

Only the most extreme desperation sends us coming straight to you. I hope you will excuse us and, when you look into matters, agree that we are justified in horning in on your valuable time.

We are the writer/research team assembled by Simon and Schuster (Martin Snell is the Editor in charge there) to assist in the completion of your HISTORY OF THE AFRICAN-AMERICAN PEOPLE. We are eager to proceed with this work and have been, often frantically, trying to worm out of Snell, the Editor, and especially one Barton Wilkes, your Assistant, clear directions on how to proceed.

I don't know if you'd believe the smoke which has been blown in our faces (and, excuse me, up our skirts) when we've tried to get a view of the terrain. I append here copies of all the correspondence, along with the materials Mr. Wilkes has sent us to "write up." You will see for yourself.

Believe us, Senator Thurmond, when we say that we are not habitual complainers. We simply want to help you in your project and have arrived at the conclusion that we cannot possibly do that when everything is reflected in the funhouse mirror that is Barton Wilkes, Snell, and (so says Snell) Ted Kennedy.

A word or two from you on what you want would set us straight, I am sure.

We write with respect, with eagerness to proceed, and with frustration amounting to frenzy.

Very sincerely yours,

Percival

Percival Everett

James Kincaid (who signs but has not read)

SENATOR STROM THURMOND
217 RUSSELL SENATE BUILDING
WASHINGTON, D.C. 20515

December 6, 2002

My dear Mr. Everett and Mr. Kincaid,

Yes, by Jesus, I see what you mean.

That Wilkes seemed a nice boy, and very likely he is. Don't seem to have all his apples from government inspected orchards, though, does he? As my dear mother would say, he's a caution. You boys probably have stronger language to shit-swipe him with. Don't blame you.

I do most sincerely apologize to you for not keeping an eye on this. It has always been tough for me to keep my eyes from wandering, as you may have heard. I should have been more vigilant.

Why don't you boys come down to Edgefield and have lunch with me? I'll have an assistant call you and see what you'd like to eat. And when you can come of course.

The assistant calling you will not be Barton Wilkes. He the one who wears those light blue outfits? You wouldn't know, I expect.

Over lunch, we can work all this out.

I hope you boys enjoy bourbon.

Sincerely,
Strom

LUNCH

The following is a transcript of a lunch attended by Senator Strom Thurmond, Professor James Kincaid and Percival Everett. I am Percival Everett. You can tell because I appear last in the list of attendees. That is the polite thing to do, list one's self last. Courtesy is a curious business at best, and one of the businesses of the American South, however little obvious profit is in it. I was taught that it is always best to be courteous and fair, even when others are not, that there is no better way to irritate your enemies, that a kind word is often appreciated and never hurts. So, it was that I put my assumptions and knowledge of history aside to share a meal with a person whom I had previously once called the Reddest Neck. I am, by nature, more polite than my associate,

Mr. Kincaid, who often says to me "fuck you" when we disagree. But perhaps I should hear that as a nice thing, as Lenny Bruce suggested. Kincaid also says "get fucked," but he says it in a friendly, jovial, brotherly way, which is troubling in and of itself.

This transcript was going to be a straight reporting of what was said, with no description whatsoever. But a glance through a couple of books of quotations worthy of repeating changed my mind, as I realized that I not once found anything uttered by the good Senator worth repeating. This will be dry enough, except for those really tedious historian types who pore over archives page by page counting the number of times a certain person refers to another person in a certain way to substantiate something most of us knew all along about the way one person felt about another. "See, Humphrey really didn't like Nixon."

Edgefield, South Carolina. I spent years five through seventeen in South Carolina. My parents said I was growing up. I did grow up. Apparently, South Carolina did not. Jim and I drove from the airport in Charleston to Edgefield on a Saturday. Still, I will attempt to stay with my original transcript idea by not describing much, or anything, for that matter. Just let me say that the Edgefield we drove into, in our turquoise subcompact rental (publisher's expense), was probably no different from the Edgefield young Strom walked through when he was ten.

THE TRANSCRIPT:

THURMOND: Gentlemen, I'm glad you could join me for lunch.
EVERETT: Thank you, Senator.
KINCAID: Thank you.
THURMOND: You're Mr. Everett.
KINCAID: How could you tell?
EVERETT: I am. I'm pleased to finally meet you.
THURMOND: No, the pleasure is mine. And Mr. Kincaid.

KINCAID: Senator.

THURMOND: Come on out and join me on the porch. You know, sitting on the porch is a Southern thing. Not that people in the North don't enjoy their porches as well, but down here it's special. Yes, porches are as Southern as mint juleps or kudzu. So is the enjoyment of cold drink. Hollis!

HOLLIS: Sir?

THURMOND: Hollis, what kind of refreshments can we offer our visitors?

HOLLIS: Would you gentlemen like iced tea, lemonade, a soft drink or something a bit stronger?

KINCAID: Lemonade, please.

THURMOND: Mr. Everett.

EVERETT: Just water, thank you.

THURMOND: And Hollis, I'll have my usual.

HOLLIS: Yessir.

EVERETT: You have a lovely home.

THURMOND: Thank you. And Hollis?

HOLLIS: Yessir?

THURMOND: I'll have my usual.

HOLLIS: Yessir.

THURMOND: This is the very porch on which my father and my dear mother would sit and watch us children at play out in the yard. There were six of us finally. Bill, myself, Gertie, George and the twins. I taught Gertie to dance out on that lawn. More than once I beat the tar out of my brother Bill. Bill's a doctor now. History, there's history here on this porch. On all porches, I suppose.

KINCAID: Senator, that's why we wanted to actually meet with you. We'd like to understand what you mean by history vis-à-vis our current project.

THURMOND: That's getting right to the point. You're from the Midwest, aren't you?

KINCAID: I am, indeed. Ohio.

THURMOND: And Mr. Everett, you're a fellow South Carolinian?

EVERETT: I was born in Georgia.

THURMOND: You're the one who gave that speech at the State House.

EVERETT: That was a long time ago.

THURMOND: Would you look at those clouds? We're going to have a storm this afternoon for certain. My dear mother hated thunder and lightning. She'd sit on a chair in the foyer for the duration of any storm, said it was the safest room in the house. She never gave any reason for thinking that, but she believed it.

EVERETT: About the book.

THURMOND: I have to confess that the book project was not my idea, though I have grown rather fond of it. Barton Wilkes, a staff member, concocted the idea and I let him move with it. He found a publisher and now it appears the two of you are involved. I hope things are going smoothly.

EVERETT: Your reference to Mr. Wilkes doesn't suggest the closeness that he has led us to believe exists between the two of you.

THURMOND: No?

KINCAID: No, to hear Wilkes talk, he's in constant contact with you, you're best buddies.

THURMOND: Perhaps in his mind I am. He's an odd man. I think his family is from Florida. Do you know what Rhode Island and Florida have in common?

KINCAID: No, what?

THURMOND: Neither state counts in a national election.

EVERETT: That's very funny. That aside, how do you see this project?

HOLLIS: Sirs, here are your drinks. Your lemonade, Mr. Kincaid. Your water, Mr. Everett. And your usual, Senator.

KINCAID and EVERETT: Thanks.

THURMOND: Thank you, Hollis. Hollis, isn't this a fine day?

HOLLIS: Yessir.

THURMOND: And Hollis, isn't this a fine porch? We've sat out here often in the evenings, haven't we?

HOLLIS: Yessir.

THURMOND: We've slapped our share of mosquitoes. They seem to favor Hollis, don't they, Hollis?

HOLLIS: They do indeed, Senator.

THURMOND: Okay, Hollis, you can go see to lunch.

KINCAID: We've been wondering when the history is to begin. With slavery? The Civil War?

THURMOND: When I was a child we referred to the war as the War of Northern Aggression. [laughs] I'm not sure where the book should begin.

EVERETT: I was thinking that you might comment on the shaping influences of Reconstruction. Though I assume you didn't live through it, I imagine the effects were still quite evident when you were young.

THURMOND: That's true. You boys know that I don't pretend to be a historian. However, I consider myself part of the history of the land you two know at present. I lived most of the last century and participated in running this country for three quarters of it. Does that sound like bragging to you, Mr. Kincaid?

KINCAID: Why, yes.

THURMOND: And to you, Mr. Everett?

EVERETT: It depends.

THURMOND: Depends on what?

EVERETT: Whether it's finally true.

THURMOND: You understand of course that I'm not seeking to write this thing in order to clean up my image. I don't think my image is in such bad shape, however much the liberals vilify me.

KINCAID: That's refreshing.

THURMOND: I'm more concerned with addressing what I see as the unfair treatment of the South.

EVERETT: You're not still bitter about Reconstruction, are you? You're not out to get those carpetbaggers?

THURMOND: [half laugh] No, I'm mostly over that. No, I mean the image of the South right now, how the media chooses to paint it, the endless fun-making and stereotypes.

EVERETT: Say more.

THURMOND: You know when you get old your toenails get yellow and harder than the shell of a Brazil nut? You know what we used to call those nuts?

KINCAID: What?

THURMOND: Back to the South thing. You remember when those New York

City Police shot that African boy in that doorway? Why, they shot that poor colored boy over forty times and media and the country jumped all over the policemen and the NYPD, calling them racists and pigs and such, but no one suggested anything about the character of the city of New York.

KINCAID: Your point being?

THURMOND: Well, when those rednecks, those dumbass peckerwoods down in Texas dragged that poor boy to death behind that pickup, all you heard was how awful Texas and the South remain.

EVERETT: And you disagree with that.

THURMOND: To tell the truth, I don't. But why not offer the same judgment about the Northeast? Can you imagine the outcry if that African had been shot down dead in that fashion on a stoop here in Edgefield?

EVERETT: So, this whole project is an attempt to set the record straight, a forum for you to say that the South isn't as bad as it's cracked up to be. Or maybe you're about pointing out that the whole country is as racist as ever.

THURMOND: Maybe, maybe not. I'm an old man. I just want things to be fair to the South.

KINCAID: To rewrite history.

THURMOND: That sounds awfully fancy.

EVERETT: Nonetheless.

THURMOND: You know, this is the very porch on which I first met Pitchfork Ben Tillman, former governor of this state. I walked up to him, like my daddy told me to, and I shook his hand. He glared at me with that hard face and said in that high voice of his, "Boy, if you're gonna shake a hand, then, by God, give it a shake!" That was my first and most important lesson in politics and one I've never forgotten.

KINCAID: Did you have servants when you were young?

THURMOND: Why, yes we did. We had a sleep—I mean, live-in maid. Her name was Hattie. There was a yardman. I don't remember his name but I remember he was always trimming the hedges. And there was a driver, Beau. He lived in the shed out back. He was a terrible driver. I'm not certain he had a license.

KINCAID: All African-American?

THURMOND: As I recollect, I believe they were, now that you mention it.

EVERETT: As you recollect?

THURMOND: It was a long time ago.

EVERETT: Do you recall whether Hollis is white or black?

THURMOND: Oh, Hollis, he's a good man. He's been with me going on forty years. He's been with me longer that my wife. We've shared everything except sex.

EVERETT: Do you remember if your wife is white?

THURMOND: I'm pretty sure she's white. She sure looks white. You know, my brother Bill used to stutter something terrible. He couldn't say grace and have his food be hot. That's why Daddy sent him off to a military academy.

KINCAID: Because he couldn't say grace.

THURMOND: No, because of his stuttering. He's a doctor now. He lives in Georgia. Well, he did anyway.

KINCAID: Is it true your father killed a man over Ben Tillman's politics?

THURMOND: As I recall the story, Daddy was defending himself.

EVERETT: And was named a US Attorney for his trouble on Tillman's recommendation.

THURMOND: Politics is a funny business.

EVERETT: Since we're talking about Tillman, what will you have to say in the book about his revamping of the state constitution in 1895 instituting residency requirements, a poll tax and separate schools.

THURMOND: Those were different times.

KINCAID: So was yesterday.

THURMOND: Tillman was a hard man in hard times, but he wasn't a racist or a bigot like that Vardaman in Mississippi.

KINCAID: Tillman's the one who called Teddy Roosevelt a "coon-flavored miscegenationist."

THURMOND: You boys do your homework. Well, if you gentlemen will excuse me. I have to go relieve myself often these days. My physician tells me my prostate is the size of a pimple on a flea's ass.

Once Thurmond was out of the room, Jim bolted from his chair, took a couple of steps and turned back to face me.

KINCAID: Is he a piece of work or what? Can't recall if the servants were black.

EVERETT: I should have asked if the slaves were black.

KINCAID: I think it's going to take us awhile to dig through this stuff and figure out what he wants.

EVERETT: To hell with what he wants. I say we just lampoon the fuck out of him and have some fun. Still, I'm kind of intrigued.

KINCAID: By what?

EVERETT: By what it is he expects from this book. By the fact that he doesn't sound as stupid as I thought he would sound. I guess he sounds pretty stupid.

KINCAID: He's a walking balloon.

EVERETT: You don't think this room is bugged, do you?

KINCAID: That's a hell of a thought. What do you think of him?

EVERETT: I don't know. He's old. He's real old. He's the oldest person I've ever seen in person. I don't know if he's nuts or charming or patronizing or just a son of a bitch.

KINCAID: I vote for nuts. What have you gotten me into? I'm not even sure we're safe here. What if the Klan is on the lookout for a turquoise rental with an ugly black man and a distinguished-looking gray-haired white man a few years his senior?

EVERETT: Then we're pretty safe. But I feel sorry for those guys you just described.

KINCAID: He's coming back.

THURMOND: No matter how much you wiggle and dance.

EVERETT: Senator, what do you think of Barton Wilkes? I ask because we've both found him to be, shall we say, eccentric.

KINCAID: Loony.

THURMOND: He is a strange child.

EVERETT: He's given us the idea that you want to publish this book because you believe you've had a great impact on the lives of African-Americans. He suggests that you believe you've had more influence over black people than any living person.

THURMOND: I've never said as much. But as I think about it, I would have to agree with the assertion.

KINCAID: Impact being not necessarily a good thing.

THURMOND: I guess that would be correct, Mr. Kincaid. Have you ever had sex with a woman forty years younger than you?

EVERETT and KINCAID: No.

THURMOND: I do every third Tuesday of every month. With the lights on. What do you think of that?

EVERETT: We're impressed.

THURMOND: I caught holy hell when I married my wife, do you realize that? I heard the jokes. How many times does sixty-six go into twenty-two? Ask Strom Thurmond. They were all jealous.

KINCAID: I see. Why don't you tell us, what do you think of Brown versus the Board of Education?

THURMOND: I think this country was founded on the principle of separate but equal facilities for all sorts of different people. Why, you don't expect Jews to go to a Catholic church. Of course not. So, why should colored children have to be in a school with people different from them?

EVERETT: So, you want to do the "colored" children a favor.

THURMOND: Well, anyway, it should be up to them.

EVERETT: Do you think black people might choose to have their own restrooms and water fountains as well?

THURMOND: We were talking about Pitchfork Ben when I left.

EVERETT: Let's forget about him for a while. Let's talk about education. You were actually considered a progressive in the thirties and forties. I read that you offered to teach reading and writing to anyone who cared to come by. Is that true?

THURMOND: It is.

EVERETT: Did anyone take your offer?

THURMOND: A few.

KINCAID: Were any of them black?

THURMOND: The offer was extended to everyone, white and black.

KINCAID: But were any of the takers black?

THURMOND: I can't say I recall any black students. You have to remember the times. I did make the offer and I was serious, but my house was my house and, generally, colored folks didn't feel that comfortable in a white man's home. It's a large home.

EVERETT: You supported "separate but equal" schools.

THURMOND: You gentlemen forget that I did vote for the Civil Rights Act of 1964.

KINCAID: That's not altogether true. You were entirely against the public accommodations section of the House bill.

EVERETT: Title two.

KINCAID: You said that it was not about public accommodation, but an invasion of private property.

EVERETT: You said it led to integration of private life.

KINCAID: You said that the Constitution says that a man shall not be deprived of life, liberty or property. "We should observe the Constitution."

EVERETT: "A man has a right to have his property protected."

KINCAID: This was on *CBS Reports*, a debate with Hubert Humphrey.

EVERETT: But finally it was about white control. You claimed that it was OK for a Minnesotan to consider integration because there were only seven blacks per one thousand whites, but in South Carolina, there were four-hundred blacks per one thousand whites.

KINCAID: You, in fact, called the passage of the bill "a sad day for America." I think you claimed it would increase racial tensions.

THURMOND: Well, I remember supporting it. We're used to it all now though, aren't we? Where is Hollis with my drink? Hollis! Excuse me, gentlemen, but I must again relieve myself.

EVERETT: Maybe we went at it too much like an interrogation.

KINCAID: Could be. You think we should be more low-key?

EVERETT: I'm not sure. Do we want to write this book? I mean, if he thinks we're out to crucify him, he might bail.

THURMOND: Well, boys, where were we?

EVERETT: You were telling us your views on education.

THURMOND: I'll come back to that. First, let me tell you what the secret to politics is. It's got nothing to do with issues or even rights. It's got to do with people and what they believe. Not even what they think. Hell, they don't know what they think. But they know what they believe. The great thing about beliefs is that you can convince people they have them. I'll tell you a quick story. This happened a few years ago when Barton Wilkes first came to work for me. I think it was Wilkes, anyway he looked like Wilkes. They all look alike. [laughs] So, Wilkins comes into my office in Washington and sees me writing a card to one of my constituents down in Aiken. This ol'boy down there lost one of his sons in a car wreck and I was writing him a sympathy card. Wilkie comes in and tells me that I shouldn't be wasting time on little matters like that. I told him I was just a dumb old Southern boy, but I knew how to get elected. He said my time was precious and I just nodded. About six month later, I was over in Columbia and that ol'boy from Aiken came up to me on the front steps of the State House and introduced himself. He said, "Senator, suh, me and my whole family appreciated the card you sent when our Raymond died. We couldn't believe that an important man like you would take time to do that for us. My whole family will vote for you forever." He actually said that and Willies was standing right there to hear it and couldn't believe it. I didn't know that ol'boy from Adam, but I read the obituary in the Aiken paper and I sent the card. He believes I care about his family. That's what he believes. Nothing wrong with believing a thing. By the way, that man was colored. [pauses] What people believe. I think he worked as a groom at one of those horse farms down there. He had great big hands, I remember that. But I was supposed to be talking about education, wasn't I?

When I was a boy, my daddy forbade me to go over to the town square to watch a lynching. There had been others and I understood that some colored man had raped a white woman and that the common folk had to make him an example. You know, my daddy was troubled by the whole thing. I could tell. But I was young and I wanted to see and so I went anyway. I saw that man hanging there and that was gruesome enough, but to this day the ugliest thing I remember seeing was the smiling faces of my own people. Fact was, I learned later, that Negro man hadn't done anything but frighten a white woman, probably by coming around a corner or something. But all my life I heard of raping and lynching all tied together and it was hard to separate the two. I know that the poor crackers around here used it as an excuse, but they really believed it too. How'd I get on that? I guess it's the belief stuff. That hanged man had big hands too. Maybe that's it.

After I finished Clemson, I came back here to Edgefield and after one week I was teaching a Bible class. I didn't know my scriptures all that well, but I was teaching. Then I got a job teaching farming in a school over in McCormick. I used to ride over there on my old Harley. A lot of people back then thought that education just ruined a colored man, just turned a good field hand into an educated fool. I never believed that, but I have to admit that back then I never gave a single thought to how unequally resources was allocated to colored and white schools. You have to remember, Reconstruction was not that far in the past and it wasn't until 1921 that there were more white people in the state than Negroes. Back then I was a real ladies' man too. Did I mention that? Anyway, in 1928 I ran for county school superintendent and beat some in-law relative. What I did was call for free health examinations, medical and dental, for colored and white children. Poor people are poor people. This state has always had its share and more. We have a lot of honeysuckle down here as well. Have you ever smelled honeysuckle?

EVERETT: I have a question.

THURMOND: Please.

EVERETT: You've carried on the tradition started by John C. Calhoun with the nullification doctrine by continuing to insist on states' rights. Given that, how do you reconcile this state's support of Roosevelt in 1932 and the embracing of federal relief and solutions?

THURMOND: The grass out there in that yard needs to be mown twice a week. Can you believe that?

KINCAID: You were a New Deal Democrat yourself.

THURMOND: Roosevelt was elected because he was a Democrat. Lincoln was a Republican. South Carolina belonged to the Democratic Party.

EVERETT: That aside, don't you see the hypocrisy?

THURMOND: I don't think I do.

EVERETT: That was the same year that Cotton Ed Smith was re-elected to the Senate by claiming he would keep black people in their place.

KINCAID: Like James Vardaman, he even called for lynchings.

EVERETT: Did you find that unacceptable back then?

THURMOND: Of course I did. You know, I have never said a negative thing about a black person because of his race. I have never tried to do any black man any harm because of his color. Cotton Ed was a product of his time, a simple country man with some shortcomings, but still a loyal South Carolinian.

EVERETT: A shortcoming being a willingness to hang a black man.

THURMOND: If you'll excuse me.

KINCAID: Way to let him talk.

EVERETT: Yeah, well.

KINCAID: This guy sure pees enough.

EVERETT: I don't know about this whole thing.

KINCAID: Want to go back to Charleston and eat some seafood?

EVERETT: That's not a bad idea. You know, I halfway want to like the guy. Is that weird or what?

KINCAID: It's weird, but I know what you mean. Are we going to let him talk again? You were so good at it last time.

EVERETT: Listen, he rambled for a while. Would you say he's about the whitest person you've ever met?

KINCAID: Should I be offended by that?

EVERETT: You know what I mean?

KINCAID: Yeah, that's what I'm talking about.

THURMOND: No matter how much you wiggle and dance.

KINCAID: Senator, maybe you can tell us again why you want to write a book about African-Americans.

THURMOND: Well, for one thing, I may have already said this, I repeat myself a lot these days. I didn't used to do that, not so much anyway. About the colored people, I reckon that more than any other living political figure I have affected the lives of these people. I honestly believe that any progress that the Negro race has experienced is not due to the efforts of emancipators, but to the kind of decent and honest white Southerners. It doesn't bother me that coloreds can stay at white hotels and go to white theaters and eat at white restaurants. Not now. Now white people are accustomed to their presence, but back in 1950, we weren't. I have to tell you that I was against the North forcing the South to desegregate. Especially when the North was more segregated than the South. You have to admit that the South has been the national whippin' boy. I have never in my life used the word "nigger."

EVERETT: Back in 1948, you invited William Hastie, governor of the Virgin Islands, to dine at the governor's mansion in Columbia. As I understand the story, you didn't know he was black and when you learned this fact, you said if you had known you never would have invited him, that such an invitation would have been ridiculous.

THURMOND: The man had been a federal judge and the dean of a law school, why would I have thought he was black?

KINCAID: He was dean of the Howard Law School.

THURMOND: I guess I didn't put two and two together.

EVERETT: Why would the invitation have been ridiculous?

THURMOND: For one thing, what would we have talked about? It would have been cruel to bring a man into such foreign surroundings.

EVERETT: Dinner with you would have been so foreign?

THURMOND: He would have felt out of place.

KINCAID: Well, then, you were awfully generous.

THURMOND: Thank you, Mr. Kincaid.

EVERETT: Back to the meddling North and the emancipators, why do you think they want to destroy the Southern way of life?

THURMOND: The war never ended. We just don't shoot anymore. If one man is going to be rich, then somebody has to be poor. That's the way of the world. If the North is going to be superior, then we down here have to be inferior.

EVERETT: Four of the last eight presidents have been from Southern states.

THURMOND: Liberals.

KINCAID: The present Bush?

THURMOND: Well, he's not really from Texas now, is he? He's just a Connecticut boy in a cowboy hat. But he's a good states' rights conservative, I'll give him that. [pause] A colored man wrote in to a magazine some years back, it was that *Ebony* or *Jet*, and the fella said that I had never stabbed the colored community in the back, that I had stabbed it in the front, but never in the back. At first, I was hurt by that, but then I started to think about it. Colored people knew what to expect from me, they knew where I stood and I think they appreciated that.

EVERETT: Why do you insist on saying colored instead of African-American or black? Why not say negra the way you did in the seventies?

THURMOND: I'm an old man. I'm not always sure what I'm saying.

KINCAID: You weren't old in the seventies.

THURMOND: On really hot summer days down in South Carolina, we like to go sit in the shade by a river and fish for catfish. When I was a boy I used to keep me a trotline strung across the river and I'd check it every couple of days. I'd bring the fish home to our cook. She was a great big colored woman and she'd clean the fish and fry them up for lunch. She used to dip the fish in beer batter and boy was that good. Anyway, one day I caught this fish that was darker than the rest and she looked at that thing for a long time and finally said, "This here fish you shoulda throwed back." I asked her why and she said, "This here is a negra catfish and it din't know where it belonged and that's how it come to be caught. You see, it ain't fair."

EVERETT: That's a great story.

KINCAID: Yes, indeed.

THURMOND: Yes, I have always loved that story. I tell it often. I told it at a dinner at South Carolina State College, that's a colored school in Orangeburg, and nobody seemed to get it. Funny, that. Anyway, I love that story. As far as education, I was a progressive, that's true. I have always believed in the importance of a good education. But you have to be smart about education. My friend, Henry Hyde, likes to say that an intellectual is a person whose education has exceeded his intelligence. That's the problem in these colleges.

Separate-but-equal was always good enough for me. I think it's a natural, even wholesome desire on the part of a people to want to educate their children among their own kind. You have to admit that bussing, everywhere, North and South, was a miserable failure. I'm not saying that funds weren't split unfairly back in the first half of the last century, but now I think we can do that part better. But it ought to be up to the people who live in their communities. You know, slavery was an awful thing, but it was a thing of its time. And slaves weren't treated so badly.

EVERETT: Jim, what time is our flight?

KINCAID: Oh, yeah. If we're going to make it, we should leave now.

THURMOND: What about lunch?

EVERETT: You've been so kind to us that time has just slipped away. We'll grab a bite on the road. Can you recommend a place where we can both eat?

THURMOND: There's a nice rib place at the edge of town.

[silence]

EVERETT: Well, thanks for everything.

THURMOND: Wait, I want you boys to see something.

EVERETT: Jim, that's not a . . .

KINCAID: A headstand.

EVERETT: Is it good to stay upside down like that?

KINCAID: Well, we have to be going.

THURMOND: Hollis!

EVERETT: We can see ourselves out.

HOLLIS: Senator, you know what the doctor said about blood getting to your brain.

THURMOND: That's "rushing to my brain," Hollis. Have you boys ever seen anything like this?

KINCAID: I should say not.

EVERETT: Not today.

THURMOND: Hollis will see you out. Hollis, see our guests to the door. And give them some clear directions to that rib shack. You know the one, just outside town.
HOLLIS: Certainly, Senator. This way, gentlemen.
EVERETT: Thanks, Mr. Hollis, but we don't need the rib shack.
HOLLIS: I should say not. It was burnt down thirty-five years ago.

SIMON & SCHUSTER, INC.
1230 Avenue of the Americas
New York, NY 10020

January 3, 2003

To: Percival Everett
From: Martin Snell

Dear Percival:

This is to acknowledge receipt of your alleged expenses, all itemized and put in columns, pertaining to what you say was a trip to talk with Senator Thurmond. Kincaid's too.

I am very glad to hear that you are meeting and talking. That's good. Very promising.

Twice burned is once _____. [I can't decipher this word.]

Of course meeting and talking is not reading and writing, now is it? Writing is what we want here at Simon & Schuster. I suppose you know that but you don't always act like it.

As a friend, I am cheering you on and am delighted at what is probably (or at least maybe) good news. As an editor and a professional, I am about as interested in these preliminaries as I would be in the news that you had found relief from chronic constipation and were able once again to resume gardening.

We can correspond as friends. I never said we couldn't. Birds of a feather, you know. But as editor and writers, our correspondence is different. For instance, the news that you are talking to the Senator and have incurred expenses thereby is of interest, though mild, to a friend. To an editor, it is—how shall I put this?—inexpressibly annoying.

If you are concerned about being reimbursed, I suggest you contact your university or withdraw funds from the stock previously supplied to you by Simon & Schuster for your work. As we have yet to see any work at all, I am sure you don't expect us to pay extra for expenses you encountered in the pursuit of what, for anything we know, is not writing at all.

Now that should put us on an equal footing, with everyone on a level playing field and shooting the same caliber rifles. Instant gratification is the curse of the X generation. [I may have got this wrong. Please check.]

Love,
Martin

Dictated to Juniper McCloud

SIMON & SCHUSTER, INC.
1230 Avenue of the Americas
New York, NY 10020

January 4, 2003

Dear Percival and Jim,

I just noticed that Slime Snell sent out <u>as if it were a letter</u> the rough copy I typed out from my notes. He thinks I take dictation.

It'd be one thing if he told me what he wanted and let me write the letter, but instead he says to take down precisely what he says. "Every word, every emphasis, every little gesture, Juniper!" When he said that, I swear to God he started singing, "Every little movement has a meaning all its own-----" and then he started kind of dancing. And I was alone in the office with him. He only knew that one line of the song and kept singing it over and over, each time to a different tune. Every time the word "meaning" got more and more elongated, until I thought he'd get apoplexy. He started brushing his hand across my head and then my brow as he went at it-- "meeeeeeeeeeeeeeeaaaannnnnnnnnnnnnnnnnneeeeeeeennnnnnnn nng" with this clammy finger-brush across my face as he sashayed by.

Should I shoot him?

Anyhow, excuse the incomprehensible letter you got from him. Or don't.

My guess is that the burden of the letter is this: we ain't paying.

Yours faithfully,

Juniper

Interoffice Memo

January 4, 2003

Dear Percival,

Happy New Year!

How is it I missed you at MLA? You didn't even come to the department reception you were hosting. Nobody noticed. And that's good.

I sat in on lots of the interviews. Between you and me, it'll be blind luck if we get good people. The other people interviewing, our colleagues, mostly didn't like the smart people and asked them such assy questions they wouldn't come anyhow even if we made them an offer. The dumb candidates they of course liked. No threat. Some of the minority ones were good. Too bad you weren't there to show them we aren't all white. I said maybe we could prop up a cardboard cutout of you and set it over aways from the candidates, by the toilet, so they'd see how we welcome blacks and all. Ha ha.

Anyhow, we haven't talked since the Strom lunch, really. I was hot to talk right afterwards, but you had that friend to see, so you said, and then you slept all the way back on the plane. It's my view that we should have been talking then, while everything was fresh. But never mind. I do tend to get things a little mixed together in my mind as time goes by, as we retreat, as it were, from the actual event. But you made a transcript, right? You wouldn't tell me. Did you tape it? The meeting, I mean.

Anyhow, I am really hot, still hot, to get to this. We may not have gotten much clarification or material from Strom, but that's OK. I sorta like him, and I don't think that's a racist thing to say. You admitted you sorta liked him too. There was that quasi-headstand, of course, but think of it as pathos. He's just trying to find his way back to the light as all the windows are closing on him. That's a good line we can use in the history.

Maybe we can start with that.

Anyhow, let's start putting pens to papers! That's how I feel.

Best,
Jim

⁂

FROM THE DESK OF PERCIVAL EVERETT

January 5, 2003

Dear Jim,

I was hoping I'd get this off to you before you chirped in with your views. Unfortunately, I missed.

Sorry we didn't hook up at MLA. I didn't go.

I'm sorry to say, Jim, that I do not share your enthusiasm for this project or your glowing memory of our meeting. It was perhaps interesting in a bizarre way, but I think we got as much from Hollis as from Strom. Not one damned thing.

But I did get the sense that I want nothing to do with this project or with anything I can see coming from it in the way of a book. You heard Strom: he's politely unrepentant, twisting everything so as to make himself seem not only fair and understandable but a fucking champion of the "negra."

All the fun has been drained from this. Right now I can't imagine how I ever thought it would be fun. So I'm quitting. No more.

I am sorry that you feel differently, but there's no reason you can't go it alone, if you want. You can have my share of the dough, if it's OK with Snell and all.

Speaking as your Chair, colleague, and friend, I would advise you, though, to drop out of this too. It couldn't be good for your career. And you do need something good for your career right now. Don't get all defensive either. You know it as well as I. And kissing Strom Thurmond's baboon ass in print wouldn't be good.

Best,
Percival

Interoffice Memo

January 6, 2003

Dear Percival,

Now here's a switch, but not for the first time. Not for the first time do I find myself playing the role of wise counselor, seasoned pro, cool vet to your part as headstrong youth, jumpy hysteric, rank amateur. But in a team such as ours, and I think you'll agree with this, we both play all the roles. Like a repertory company. We have one of those repertory companies in our little town, not a good troupe, but a troupe all the same; and they all take turns playing different parts. At least I think they do. I only saw them once. It was a production of "The Innocents," you know, the Deborah Kerr movie thing, based on Henry James's "The Turn of the Screw," which you may have read but probably not. The most talented actors were little Miles and Flora. The others ranged from barely mediocre to shut-your-eyes awful. And there was a problem even with the kids. Flora was just fine, but Miles, for all his talent, was costumed in a nightgown, which was appropriate for a kid who is often supposed to be in bed but is actually prowling the grounds, but Miles (the actor) was quite fat, really awfully fat (though I know we shouldn't say such things without acknowledging that we may be encouraging anorexia), and his nightgown kept creeping up over his thighs, very unseemly.

Anyhow, Percival, please don't quit. I am really interested in this project. But that's not the point, really. It's the first project I've had in years, the first real project and not just something I've invented a title for and never done. I mean, this I can do, but only with your help and not just because they wouldn't do it with just me because I'm white. It's because you're black, see?

I messed that up. What I mean is, I think this may be my last chance and I plead with you as a friend not to take it away from me.

Jim

egm

SIMON & SCHUSTER, INC.
1230 Avenue of the Americas
New York, NY 10020

January 6, 2003

Dear Percival,

My Juniper, I refer to my assistant Juniper McCloud, just told me, after an unconscionable amount of hemming and hawing, that he was responsible for a rough draft, really what we call "dictation copy #1," being sent to you as if it were a letter.

My apologies. If the burden of that letter—its gist—is unclear, do let me know.

Do you know the song, "I get no kick from champagne! Mere alcohol doesn't thrill me at all! So tell me, why should it be you? So come do the trick, la la loo"?

This is the last straw with that Juniper. Whatever his virtues, and I won't say he has none, so don't spring to his defense, are beclouded by this impertinence. I'd call it insubordinate, wouldn't you?

Warmest personal regards,
Martin

From the Desk of Percival Everett

January 7, 2003

Dear Jim,

Of course I'll carry on. I hear what you're saying and we won't have to mention it again.

I enclose here a copy of a letter from Snell about expenses. I think you got the one from Juniper clarifying the Snell letter. But without the Snell letter, you must have been pretty confused.

So, here we go. You be little Miles and I'll be Flora. But please don't wear a nightgown.

Percival

p.s. We do have to find a way to guard ourselves from Strom heavily revising what we write. He strikes me as still partly, if not functionally, literate.

~

OFFICIAL NOTICE

From: Martin Snell
To: Juniper McCloud
Date: January 8, 2003

I hate to be official here, as it sounds so impersonal. However, as what I am about to say, even to you, is really, in its way, not a personal issue, this seems the best format. By "format" I refer to the memo form. What I mean is that it's personal but it's not. You and I are persons, and I am writing to you. That makes it personal. It is not "personal" in the sense people use when they say to someone they have accidentally insulted or spilled food on, "nothing personal." Often, of course, that's just an excuse, when people say that, and what they mean is, "This is personal as all hell." But not with me.

As you know, McCloud, Vendetti has been putting great pressure on me to release you to him so he can make use of you. I do not know what use he has of you or what uses he expects you to fulfill. It did not seem quite right for me to inquire. In any event, I have withstood his pressures for a superhumanly long time, considering his tenure here and mine and what a loudmouthed son of a bitch he is. I can no longer withstand them. A lesser man would have caved in long ago. I am sure you appreciate that.

None of this will, I dare say, alter in any way the social side of our arrangement. You know: the busy-buttoned-up-executives-by-day-larking-playboys-by-night duo we have become. I mean, why should it?

Now, you will be thinking that your gaffe, your latest gaffe I mean, wherein you sent a rough draft to Everett and that other fellow, Kindy? You will be thinking that you are being punished for that. Don't let yourself dwell on such imaginings. After all, you signed on with Simon and Schuster, not with Martin Snell. Try to keep that straight. Of course, I am not going to put up with shoddy work and with such egregious and embarrassing sloppiness. That just stands to reason.

You see now what I mean by it being nothing personal. Be assured that I can always be counted on to do the fair, the just, the kind thing.

SIMON & SCHUSTER, INC.
1230 Avenue of the Americas
New York, NY 10020

OFFICIAL NOTICE

To: Percival Everett
From: Martin Snell
cc: Jane Kinkade
Date: January 8, 2003

Hi!

I trust you are making good progress, but this notice does not concern that point, though you might say while IT doesn't concern your progress, your progress IS it for me.

What isn't of any real concern to YOU is the subject of this memo, i.e., notice. However, it's best to let everybody in on everything. That's an excellent rule of business management, when it's used with discretion: it's best to let everybody in on everything, which is much like letting nobody in on nothing.

Somebody stop me. I'm rolling today.

As of this inst. R. Juniper McCloud (I didn't know there was an "R" until I looked it up in personnel records. Did you? Anyways, in the records it's just "R." Frustrating. What does it stand for, not that it matters, but is it Randolph? That's my guess) is no longer assigned to your project. He is no longer assigned to me. He remains under Simon & Schuster's warm wing, at least for now, but he will be working for a Ralph (call me "Ralph") Vendetti. You don't know him (Vendetti), but he makes Woody Hayes (remember him?) seem cultivated and suave by comparison. It'll do McCloud good to work for him, and if it doesn't, fuck him. Fuck McCloud, I mean; though for that matter, Fuck Vendetti.

So, for now, I will be handling this project myself. Let me assure you that I remain hotly convinced that it is a

winner and look forward to seeing the completed manuscript in short order.

OFFICE OF SENATOR STROM THURMOND
217 RUSSELL SENATE BUILDING
WASHINGTON, D.C. 20515

January 10, 2003

Dear Perce and Jim,

Barton here. Your friend or used to be.

I know about the lunch. I knew about it before it happened, by
way of a friend who keeps me in touch with the Senator's social
calendar. I am not involved with that sort of thing, with schedul-
ing those meetings where the Senator can give out awards and
look up the skirts of Brownie Scouts. I am what you might call his
non-social secretary, the guardian of his intelligence, the protector
of his positions, the paladin of his integrity and consistency (making sure that he says today more or less what he said yesterday).

But the lunch. I just hope you are satisfied, fully satisfied, with
the fruits of that little get-together.

Don't say I didn't send a little birdie to sing in your ears a little
tune: "Tweet, tweet, oh lovely day, don't try to see Thurmond, oh
wail-a-way." I told you it would be a miserable waste of time.

You thought you could get straight to the horse's mouth. But
you have to turn the horse around first.

Why did you do it?

I am not sure I can go on walking under the dark clouds of distrust, wetted by your suspicions and petty qualms. Do you suppose you're the only ones with qualms? Well, think again. You suppose I don't have qualms, what with never seeing any write-ups of that rich material I have sent you over and over. Oh yes, I have my qualms.

The difference between us is that I would never have farted them, those qualms, in your faces. It's a matter of honor and charity. I have them; some don't.

You know, I am trained in the deadlier forms of martial arts, the kinds that make no pretense about being for self-defense. No, mine are of the attack mode exclusively. No oriental occultism, no spiritual enlightenment, just ways to splay noses over seven counties and drive bone into brain.

I mention this in a friendly way, just to lighten a letter that might seem to be veering into the heavy. I expect we all have our little hobbies and harmful happinesses. You do too, I am sure. They make life so much fuller, I feel. In my case, they also provide me with a certain aura and a reputation. Both the aura and the reputation I can back up, not that I mean any part of that as a threat.

Do send me your impressions of the lunch with the Senator and any notes or memorabilia you compiled or carried away with you.

What do you hear from Juniper?

I have reason to believe that one or both of you is (or maybe are) dating Reba. You know very well who Reba is, so don't waste our time by saying, "Who is Reba?" Two (or more) can play at that game.

I am considering taking up archery.

Devotedly,
Barton

OFFICE OF SENATOR STROM THURMOND
217 RUSSELL SENATE BUILDING
WASHINGTON, D.C. 20515

January 10, 2003

Martin,

What are that Kincaid and Everett doing? What do they mean by it?

Did you put them up to this?

I tried to call McCloud (my Juney) but he doesn't like phones, so I hung up after a few rings (and several calls), honoring his little whims. We all owe it to one another to do a lot more respecting of whims than usually gets done.

So, you tell me. There's an interesting phrase, agree? I mean, depending on how it's inflected, it can mean so many things. "YOU tell me" or "you TELL me" or (my own favorite) "you tell ME." The last is friendliest, unless it's snide.

In any case, I feel I should get information on this point. Surely I deserve it—who is more deserving, I'd like to know?

Do you date much, Martin? I can tell from your letters that you are currently unattached. I picture you as having an oblique sort of restless attractiveness to you. Oh sure, you have a complexion nobody'd bid on, and that slouch, and hair you've always despaired of. Still......... Am I right?

Barton

January 14, 2003

Dearest Reba,

There is some good news. I haven't heard from Barton Wilkes in several days, maybe weeks. I don't know.

Hope you are equally blessed, and not just in that negative way, for sure. I hope your life is filled with wonderful times and lovely people. Whatever happened to Fred—I can't remember his last name—you went with for so long? He seemed to have a lot to offer and certainly was fine looking.

I guess I have more good news. I'm out from under Martin Snell—no pun there. He got me reassigned or maybe was forced to reassign me. I still have a job, but it's with this Mafia type, Ralph Vendetti. Only he's not really a Mafia type, Reba, at least not the movie Mafia type, quiet and ominous. That might not be so bad. It's more like he's a male Sicilian version of Leona Helmsley. That's bad. Vendetti does about 60% of the company's business, I expect, seeing as how he's in charge of trash: cookbooks, self-help books, true crime, and unauthorized biographies.

And let's not forget diet books. That's what he put me on. Diet books, Reba, can he believe it? The one I'm assigned to "work into shape" is called The Butter Bliss Diet. I want to change it to the Yogurt-Plus Diet, but Vendetti, when I mentioned it, said, in his bull-bellow tenor, that the first title was better. What he said was, "Go suck your hemorrhoids, Julep! Don't you know any fucking thing?" Then he smiled and said, "That's OK, kid." I was slinking out of his office, when he stopped me with this real soft, mocking, girlie voice: "Oh and Julep. Don't hesitate to stop by any time you have an idea I'll like. Kissy-kissy." Then he smiled again and gave me a friendly wave. I can't tell about him, really.

Anyhow, this diet book I'm supposed to work into shape, as I say, is—get this—based on the old-wifey premise that we are all healthi-est as babies (not true) and that such health is given us by cows (not true) and that we can all regain the vigor, the fitness, the sylph-like figure, and the creamy complexion of babies, if we return to our cow home. Thus the butter bliss. The diet is based on cream and ice cream, milk and yogurt, butter and cheese. It also features a lot of beef, for the simple reason that cows are . . . . Well, you know the rest. Since nobody's going to buy a diet book that doesn't proscribe something, this one sets strict rules on the amount of water one can drink, on yellow vegetables (disallowed altogether, I think), on all green vegetables that are not leafy (such as the sort cows might fancy), on Chinese food generally and anything soy based (tofu especially). Anything fried in butter is excellent, as are sweets (a staple of any cow's diet), breads (especially in the form of doughnuts and muffins), and most alcoholic beverages, rum excluded. I think I can steal a copy for you when it's out. You can give it to an enemy.

But Vendetti at least doesn't seem to want to undress me or pat my butt. That's a step up. And he hasn't started marking each holiday and festival by having me to a party. I think I'm safe there. So far as I can tell, he detests me, or maybe just includes me in his all-round contempt for the world and its creatures. I don't think it's anything personal, as he doesn't know my name even. Thinks I'm Julep, though possibly he regards that name as an amusing attack on my man-hood. Well, attack away, I say. I'm not defending. And he did stop by my desk to ask if everything was OK. Now and then he smiles.

Still, dear Reba, it's an impossible situation: doing sub-stupid books for publishing's own Mike Tyson. I'm lonely and useless and feel more lost than I ever have. Strom's book wasn't much and nei-ther was Martin; but both sure beat this. I haven't got so I miss Wilkes, but that'll be next.

And then, my sister, I think of what Mother would say: "Remember there are people in the world much worse off." I do think of that. But I don't find it cheering. It simply adds shame to my list of woes.

All in all, I am going to think of what I might do next and then quit—or vice versa. Please tell me if I whining. I always seem to be coming to you for help. Just being able to tell the truth and know you listen to it means that I can think. During the course of writing this letter, it came to me that being bounced back and forth here between King Kong and Godzilla didn't make any sense. So I'm quitting. Thanks, dear Reba.

Much love,
Juniper

Memo: Snell to McCloud

January 15, 2003

Juniper, my Juney,

Miss you.

Keep an eye on Wilkes. Just between us. Keep an eye on him. He's not a person I feel safe about. Do you? Anyway, I look to you to have your feelers out.

We still work for the same company, remember. And there's so much else we share.

Wilkes said he was thinking of taking up archery. Everett told me that over the phone. What do you suppose that means? I know what archery is, of course. I don't want you to explain to me what archery is. I want to know whether anyone can kill someone or cause them great pain with a bow and arrow. Can they? I suppose so but would like to be sure.

I think Wilkes must feel threatened by Everett and Kincaid going straight to Strom. Feed that. Sic Wilkes on them. Don't you agree?

Miss you.

Marry-warry

p.s. Less than a month until Lover's Day

Interoffice Memo

January 17, 2003

Dear Percival,

I figured you'd want me to respond to Barton Wilkes, as I am much better than you at sizing up a difficult personality and dealing with it tactfully as it flows. I don't mean that I understand Wilkes. It's not a matter of understanding, you see. That's where you make your mistake. You try to understand difficult people and then deal with them according to that understanding. That's a mistake.

Like with Strom. I was adjusting to the flow, making little alterations in my manner and speech, trying to make him hum to our tune. I was playing him like a violin. It's not that you didn't raise good points, all through our lunch. You did. It's just that you didn't make those adjustments.

It's simply a people skill, Percival, and probably not one that can be learned. Knowing you, I expect you wouldn't want to learn it were that possible, which it isn't.

So here's a letter to Barton. I send it to you as a courtesy, seeing that your name is attached. But I knew you'd like this letter; so, in the interests of time, I sent it on to madman Wilkes. (Who in hell is Reba?)

* * *

January 17, 2003

Dear Barton,

I want you to know how very much Percival and I enjoyed receiving your letter and how appreciative we are of your energy and courtesy. Both are alike impressive and gallant, just like you.

You are a very busy man. You are an important man. You are a man with much on his plate. Many demands. Decisions. Staff (none too competent) to supervise. The Senator to manage and to act, as you say, as paladin to. (I confess: you had me there. I didn't know what paladin meant----needless to say, neither did Everett---but it was the perfect word.) Busy, busy, busy.

We knew that and know that.

And so we didn't bother you ahead of time about our little visit to the Senator. We intended to get in touch with you afterwards should anything come up worthy of your attention.

Nothing did, nothing that we can see, anyhow.

Another reason, Barton, is that the purpose of our visit was less substantive than atmospheric. You see? You are around the Senator daily. You know him. You are, so to speak, inside him. We needed to get a feel. We needed to sort of sniff him, let him exude, get into our head and senses and let us experience, let us BE, the man we are writing through. Why bother you with that?

No need for qualms, you see. We have none. You are too busy and important to have them. Qualms are for others, not you.

Let me turn to your hobbies. Martial arts and archery. I know that archery was, at the time you wrote the letter, simply on your list, your list of things to master. "Barton's List of Things to Master: archery, calligraphy, opera (baritone), deep-sea diving." Am I right? By now, you have mastered archery, I dare say. Several days have gone by, and I am not so dense or so unfamiliar with your brilliance as to suppose that you have not yet mastered it. Rome wasn't built in a day, perhaps, but Barton Wilkes can master anything in two or three!

I assure you that we are not dating Reba. I won't pretend to be ignorant of who she is. Why should I? When I say WE are not dating her, I mean that neither of us is. Actually, we are both married, securely and blissfully.

No word from Juniper McCloud. Martin Snell told us McCloud had been transferred to another editor.

Let us know how we can make your job, indeed your life, easier and more pleasant.

Affectionately,
Perce and Jim

From the Desk of Percival Everett

January 18, 2003

J

I see what you mean about your skills in diplomacy. It's a remarkable letter. I've never seen prose that puckered and sucked simultaneously.

You got anything else you're signing my name to?

P

Memo: McCloud to Snell

January 20, 2002

Dear Martin,

I think archery is dangerous.

In some parts of the South, bow-and-arrow season had to be canceled. You know why? Because the archery guys (and gals) were killing the deer at such a rate. They were also winging each other a lot, causing, in every case, a slow and certain and agonizing death. They stopped it and brought back guns, since guns are so much safer.

This is in response to your question about what one might have to fear from a skilled archer with his quiver full.

Faithfully,
Juniper

Simon & Schuster, Inc.
1230 Avenue of the Americas
New York, NY 10020

To: Ralph Vendetti
From: Juniper McCloud
Date: January 20, 2003

This is to give you notice of my resignation, effective immediately, though I will of course remain on the job for two weeks, unless that is not enough time for you to find a replacement, in which case I will stay longer.

I don't think you know who I am, but I'm the one working on the Butter Miracle Diet book. I'm the one you call Julep when you yell at him.

In leaving, I want to thank Simon & Schuster for giving me this opportunity and indicate how sorry I am that I have disappointed both editors to whom I have been assigned. I can only say that I have tried to do my best, with full awareness of what a loser's slogan that is.

Simon & Schuster, Inc.
1230 Avenue of the Americas
New York, NY 10020

January 20, 2002

Dear Mr. McCloud,

Your note touched me deeply and made me reflect on a manner that I have come to regard as gruff, perhaps, but wholly professional. I see that it is sometimes simply rude and that I have caused you pain and, worse, a feeling of inadequacy.

I sense in your note that your decision is final, but I wish it were not. There is nothing about your work that seems to me amiss. Of course, it would be dishonest of me to pretend that I know anything at all about your work, one way or the other. But that's good. If you were fucking up big time, I'd know.

Can I induce you to stay? I will try to be more considerate, though even as I write this, I suspect that any modifications will be slight and short-lived. There are reasons why I act as I do, reasons that I suppose I could plumb and perhaps understand, change. But I know I won't. Clearly I am devoting much energy to avoiding any battle with those reasons, and that avoidance won't be abandoned.

But if you could work for me, I'd appreciate it. It's just that, were I you, I wouldn't. There's the one virtue left to the vile: bitter candor.

I will arrange for you to have two months severance pay. You should consider yourself free to leave at the end of work today.

I may not be able to change, but I can feel regret. And do.

Sincerely,
Ralph Vendetti
Ralph Vendetti

SIMON & SCHUSTER, INC.
1230 Avenue of the Americas
New York, NY 10020

January 20, 2003

Dear Mr. Vendetti,

You are a man of such skills that I wish I had it in me to live with your way of expressing them. But I do not.

Thank you for your generous offer regarding severance. I will vacate this afternoon.

With all best wishes,
R. Juniper McCloud
R. Juniper McCloud

January 21, 2003

Dear Professor Kincaid,

I am sorry for the formality, but the truth is I cannot remember what we had grown to in the way of addressing one another. I am not in the office and have no access to the file, which would tell me. Also, I feel a little ruffled, bedazzled actually.

Not to burden you with my problems, but I have left Simon &

Schuster. There is no earthly reason you should care about that, but you seem like kind men, both of you, and you're the one I had the correspondence with. You have helped me before, and I hope you don't think ill of me for turning to you once again.

As I think you know, Martin Snell shuffled me off the project and out of his office. I think it was because that idiotic draft got sent to you (though the truth is he was the one who sent it, but never mind). Anyhow, he booted me down the hall to a strange guy who had me working on diet books—how to live better with butter. It was the worst of both worlds, since Snell had clearly not cut me out of his social life, making little buzzing noises about Valentine's Day.

I feel as if I've escaped from Bedlam. But I've escaped into something of a void.

Any chance you two might be able to use me as a research assistant? I know the project, can take the research off your hands, and do any of the writing you'd like. I come very cheap, cheaper than any grad student you might have working now. You see, I have a friend in L.A. I could live with and I could do some waiting tables and maybe get into grad school or something.

As I say, there's no reason you should help me; you just seem so very kind. Kindness attracts those who need it badly.

Cordially,
R. Juniper McCloud
Juniper McCloud

January 21, 2003

Dear Professor Everett,

You don't know me from Adam, and you probably think I'm going to try and sell you time-shared condos or aluminum siding. Actually, I'm Juniper McCloud's sister, Reba. I know you have been working with Juniper on a project involving Senator Strom Thurmond. I also know that he speaks very highly of you. He has read all your novels and sent some to me, which I found both hilarious and shocking.

Most important, he says you are witty and kind. So's Juniper, as you probably know or have guessed.

But he has found himself in a position there at Simon & Schuster that's intolerable. It would be for me, I think, judging from what I know of the people involved in this project. One of them, a Barton Wilkes, went on a campaign to date me or something. As best I can tell, he is not securely balanced, though I hesitate to say that about a man I have not even met. (Still, it has been one of the triumphs of my last months that I have avoided meeting him.) I realize Wilkes is not at Simon & Schuster, but you probably know that Juniper was ordered to distract Wilkes and go with him on a weekend outing of some kind, maybe more than one.

The man issuing the orders was Juniper's immediate supervisor, Martin Snell. Mr. Snell recently transferred Juniper to an editor named Vendetti, who set my brother to work on diet books connected to dairy products somehow.

The situation does not appeal to reason. But it may appeal to feeling. I hope so. Juniper is surrounded by these three—Wilkes, Snell, and Vendetti—none of whom seem to be just or even sane. Juniper doesn't whine, he really doesn't, and I know he wouldn't even be letting me in on this were the situation not desperate.

He is thinking about resigning. He told me so. I believe he is likely to do just that, and I must say I cannot discourage him. But he has no prospects that I know of. Is there some way you could help him or point him toward somebody who could do so?

Please forgive my ignorance in contacting you. I do not know the ways of publishing or the ways of the university. But I do know something of the ways of the human heart.

Sincerely,
Reba McCloud
Reba McCloud

FROM THE DESK OF PERCIVAL EVERETT

January 24, 2003

Jim---See attached from Reba---Percival

Interoffice Memo

January 24, 2003

Percival---See attached from Juniper---Jim

From the Desk of Percival Everett

January 26, 2003

Jim—
   OK, here's what we do.

1. You write to Reba, who is more in your line. You and she have lots of feelings.

2. I'll write to Snell, forcing him to take McCloud back.

3. I'll write to McCloud, telling him we can't use him, stay put, Snell wants him back.

   I'll send you copies of 2 and 3. Please do not send me a copy of 1.

P

Interoffice Memo

January 27, 2003

P:

So "here's what we do," is it? Couldn't you be a bit more preemptory?

I could have told YOU that we couldn't use McCloud as a research assistant and that he had better not count on that. No need for You to tell Me.

It is as much my idea as yours to force Snell to take him off diet books and put him back on our project. I am of the opinion that I could figure out Snell's weak points and how to attack them better than you, but you find it hard to listen to anything but that little personal cheering squad you transport inside your head. Write him, by all means.

And you're writing Juniper too, I see. Correct me if I'm wrong here, but I was under the impression that Juniper turned to ME, not YOU. It was Reba who wrote to you, as the fucking man of feeling. Why this switcheroo?

I know you were hired first on this project and I have never said it was simply an affirmative action hire and that I was added on as the scholar, historian, academic, fact-guy, writer. I have never said that. Give credit where credit is due.

I am a little sore about all this. I think I have every right to be. You probably don't. You probably think I have no right to be sore. Now look, I don't think it's a racial thing. I never said that. But Jesus Christ, look at the facts. If you can.

J

Percival Everett
University of Southern California
University Park Campus
Los Angeles, CA 90089

January 27, 2003

Dear Barton,

We have been making, shall we say, extraordinary progress after our meeting with the Senator. You were right about how little of substance we got. That we get from you. What we got from Strom was, as Kincaid said, no more than atmosphere and encouragement. Now, if you're with us, we can really roll.

However, we are unable to continue without Juniper McCloud. His judgment, good cheer, and dependability are essential to this project.

We count on you to force Snell to get him back.

Tell Snell, if you would, that it'll be a crackerjack book, as he's said all along. It will bring great credit and justified advancement to him.

But there will be no book at all unless he hires McCloud back.

We are dead serious about this and would address Snell directly. But we know you carry much more weight with him.

As one pro to another, I depend on you----and now owe you one.

Sincerely,
Percival Everett
Percival Everett

Percival Everett
University of Southern California
University Park Campus
Los Angeles, CA 90089

January 27, 2003

Dear Juniper,

We're on the case, old friend.

Wish we could employ you here, but there's no money and less work.

Stay there. We're getting Snell to rehire you, put you on the book with us. We can also protect you there, even from a certifiable like Snell.

We like you. Trust us.

Best,
Percival

p.s. Jim says Hi.

FROM THE DESK OF PERCIVAL EVERETT

January 27, 2003

Dear Jim,

Yes, that's so.
But remember, I love you.

Best,
Percival

⁂

OFFICE OF SENATOR STROM THURMOND
217 RUSSELL SENATE BUILDING
WASHINGTON, D.C. 20515

January 30, 2003

Dear Martin,

I think you will agree that, when all is said and done, continuity counts. I know there are those who disagree. You are not one.

Continuity does not mean stagnation; it does not mean always planting the same crop in the same field. There is no opposition between continuity and sound ideas on crop rotation. I am not ashamed to say that I know something about these matters. There is not that much difference, to an alert mind, between life in Washington and life on the farm. Know crops and livestock, the world of modern agriculture, and you know politics.

We have a team here, a team that is working very well together. Oh sure, we have had our little bits of static, a few interruptions of our program for announcements that were nothing more than personal vanity. I don't deny it. But if you, Martin, were not expecting this, then you're nothing but a little boy showering after his first gym class (usually Grade 7), worried that people will see his pecker.

Continuity is to us what the Pentecost was to Babel.

Take steps immediately to reinstitute continuity. Just do it, Martin, no questions asked. You'll be glad you did it.

You didn't respond to my telepathic guesses as to your social life and personal bearing. Are you cooling?

Call me Lars,
Barton

James R. Kincaid
University of Southern California
University Park Campus
Los Angeles, CA 90089

January 30, 2003

Dear Reba,

You don't mind me calling you "Reba," do you? I feel that I know you, and know you not distantly either, having come to understand and admire your brother so. He often speaks of you. I think I can say that, distance aside, I know you both well, as if you were my own brother and sister. I never had a sister, but still, the heart is a lonely hunter, as Carson McCullers once said.

You may be wondering why I am answering you and not Percival. It's not that he doesn't like you; let me assure you of that. He likes you a lot. It's just that he thinks my people skills are more advanced than his, that I am what we might call more sensitive. It's not that Percival doesn't have his virtues. He'll be glad to hear you like his novels, assuming you do. And I'm sure you do, as you say you do. I know you would never say one thing and mean another. I can tell that instinctively. I have very good instincts in these matters. Percival does not.

As for your brother, what we're doing is, we're contacting Senator Thurmond's office directly so as to put pressure on Martin Snell there at Simon & Schuster to rehire Juniper. He's resigned, as you know, but he was so badly treated we wouldn't be wrong to say he had no choice. But trust us: we know Senator Thurmond and can call on his influence. Whatever you think of him---and believe me I have my thoughts too---he does have influence. And he knows how to use it.

So, Snell will rehire Juniper and treat him well. Count on it.

Of course, we would have loved to employ Juniper ourselves and get to know him even better close up. Maybe you would have moved here too. But those are pipe dreams, better left to waft away in the breezy ocean air we enjoy out our way. We didn't really have the occasion to offer him suitable employment, you see, nor, to be frank, the funds.

This way we can keep a fatherly eye on him. And on you too.

Very cordially yours,

James R. Kincaid

James R. Kincaid

OFFICE OF SENATOR STROM THURMOND
217 RUSSELL SENATE BUILDING
WASHINGTON, D.C. 20515

February 3, 2003

Dear Marty,

Have you rehired Juniper yet? I have heard nothing.

Is it possible that you did not see the application of my last letter? No, it is not possible?

Yes it is.

By "continuity," I meant rehiring McCloud. You wouldn't have fired him in the first place had you understood continuity. And don't tell me somebody else fired him, or he quit, or some such.

I don't care.

Just give him a raise and get him back on this book.

Look, Martin, Juniper may have his oddities, but who of us do not? I may be odd myself, but I do not like to see good people hurt. Juniper is a good person and probably deserves much better people than you and me around him. I know I don't exactly provide for those I love an easy passage over life's rough spots. Sometimes I am one rough spot myself. And so are you.

So do a decent thing for once and give McCloud back his job and treat him better.

If you don't, I'll get you fired. I'll send a letter signed by Strom that will have such rock-in-the-water resonance you'll never work in publishing again—anywhere.

So do the kind thing.

Love,
Barton W.

OFFICE OF SENATOR STROM THURMOND
217 RUSSELL SENATE BUILDING
WASHINGTON, D.C. 20515

February 3, 2003

Dear Juniper,

I have these moments when things are clearer for me, though they are not always welcome. They let me see the wrong things.

I cannot imagine you are very happy to receive a letter from me. I just hope I haven't hurt you somehow over the past months. God knows I might have.

This is to let you know that a cabal of your friends—me, Kincaid, Everett, and probably your sister—have put pressure on that Snell to rehire you, to lure you back with more money and promise of kindness—by which he probably means personal attentions you could well do without. But maybe not.

Anyhow, things will be better. You'll be working on the book. Everett and Kincaid are good sorts—at least Everett is.

You'll have to deal with me too. I can only say that I right now see what a grim prospect that must be. I have no right to ask it, but if you could summon the graciousness of heart to tell me it won't be so bad working with me, it'd mean much. I don't ask for the truth; a lie will do fine.

Your friend,
Barton

SIMON & SCHUSTER, INC.
1230 Avenue of the Americas
New York, NY 10020

February 10, 2003

Dear Barton,

Let me say at once that you and I are on the same page. There is nothing at all separating our thinking on this point.

Enough said? Well, certainly, considering how quick you are, how deft. Still, it may be as well to spell it out in a little detail, unnecessary as that also is. I have offered R. Juniper McCloud a reinstatement at an improved salary, under what, I think we both would agree, are improved conditions. I mean by that last point that he will be protected from Vendetti. By me. I won't trouble you with details as to how that unfortunate transfer of our Juney was forced on me. I could see how he drooped and withered away from me. I was helpless to fertilize his leaves, water his roots.

Consider my situation.

But all that is changed. Believe me, as I know you must.

You refer also to friendly questions you raised a while ago (January 10) about my social life. I had not answered, Barton, as it would have seemed to me presumptuous. You understand, of course. Who am I to thrust personal details on such as you? I mean, of course you asked, and that would be grounds enough for some to load on you the most personal, the most embarrassing of revelations. Not me.

Now I see that you have repeated your gesture, so I will tell you that my dating life is and always has been---well, not quite always, of course, but since the time, and I was precocious, when I graduated from playing doctor and hide-the-oreo to what might justly be called "dating"--- highly inventive. That's a hard sentence to follow, isn't it? My dating life is, I am happy to say, creative and unbounded by rules or public declarations. I am not one to say, "I will only date people who do A, or people who eat B, or people who are proficient at backyard C, or people who----." You see. Your comments on my complexion (poor), slouch, and bad hair are fine jokes. Very manly. That's just one thing I like about you. I think we are the sort who could, if we liked, have some beers, eat peanuts, watch football, insult one another, and pee on the floor. That is, if we wanted to, if you wanted to. I mean we could do that, not necessarily that we would or anything like that. It'd be up to you.

As always,
Martin

Simon & Schuster, Inc.
1230 Avenue of the Americas
New York, NY 10020

February 10, 2003

Dear Juniper,

I come to you extending the hand of remorse and contrition. The average person would likely say that these words both mean the same thing. But you are not an average person.

I'd like to think I too am not an average person, but I am not able to deny that in my treatment of you, I was average. I know that your generous nature—shall I call it a generous heart?—will spring to deny this, to bring succor and comfort. But allow me this one moment of valor.

I was wrong. I was average.

The project on which you and I have, together, prayed and bled and perspired needs you. I need you too, but I make this plea in the name of the project, hoping you cannot but respond to that call. Knowing you cannot but respond.

A 20% increase and protection from Vendetti. What do you say to that?

Your dear friend,
Martin

p.s. I have the most ingenious welcome back present. I won't tell you what it is (or they are), but I'll give a hint. Zippers must be zipped (or Unzipped, as the case may be) to reach them, to display them.

February 15, 2003

Dear Barton,
    You have always been kind to me. I hope you don't think I imag-

ine otherwise or suppose that I harbor anything but good feelings and good memories. You are a friend, and I hope never to feel anything but gratitude and a kind of wonder toward those who wish me well.

In your case, you not only have wished well, but done well.

Thank you, Barton. I look forward to resuming our work.

Your friend,
Juniper

꼬꼬

February 15, 2003

Dear Percival and Jim,

I just talked with Reba, who confirmed what Martin Snell had told me. And Barton Wilkes, in a letter so sweet it made my eyes water. Snell's letter didn't, since it was his characteristic prose and manner.

But I am back, thanks to you two. I know you threatened Snell, and I gather Barton did too. Imagine that. I am still dazed and even a little shaken by the kindness of you, who have never met me and have little to go on except my griping. You must be good on principle.

Whatever it is, my heart is touched and I am so grateful.

Yours,
Juniper

SIMON & SCHUSTER, INC.
1230 Avenue of the Americas
New York, NY 10020

February 16, 2003

Dear Percival and Jams,
   I am doing my ow typing these days, what
with Juniper nott back as yet and not quite
realizing how to use the spell-checker thing.
But things like typing stay with you, don't
you thik? I went bowling just last week.
Hadn't been in oh a dozen yeart and you know
what? I bowled 196. I don't know if you juys
bowl, but that is a fine score. And I think
typing is just like bowing.
   Wanted to let you know right off, tthought,
that all is well. Juniper is back on boar and
will be in tomorrow I think. We did it. I
credit you just as much ws me in gettinf him
his job back after Vendetti and all. I won/t
say it was exacrly easy, you know, but I
pulled it of.
   Now we're back in business!
   I drink a typewritten toast to both of yoi.

                    Your fiend,
                    Martin

OFFICE OF SENATOR STROM THURMOND
217 RUSSELL SENATE BUILDING
WASHINGTON, D.C. 20515

To: Martin Snell, Simon & Schuster
From: Amos Jackson, Assistant to The Hon. Strom Thurmond
Re: Barton Wilkes
Date: February 25, 2003

Be advised that Barton Wilkes is no longer Public Relations Advisor to Senator Strom Thurmond. He has now no connection whatever with the Senator. It obviously follows that he will not be connected in any way with the book project.

That project will proceed uninterrupted.

OFFICE OF SENATOR STROM THURMOND
217 RUSSELL SENATE BUILDING
WASHINGTON, D.C. 20515

February 27, 2003

Dear James and Percival,

Hey there! There is a person in the office who, when I do not manage to evade him, brightens his eyes, narrows his lips, tenses his ungainly body, and then uncoils with a pert and jaunty, "Hey there!"

Some people would say, "So what? What does it matter how he greets you, when it's all just conventional anyhow." "Precisely," I say; "it's for that very reason that one should take the greatest pains with these matters." "Why?" they say. "Because they are conventional!" I say. "Tell us what you mean, Barton," they plead. "I will," I say; "it is by conventional compasses that we navigate this world. Convention allows us to rub together without galling one another. Convention is, when you think of it, how we live." "And?" they are prone to say. "And," I respond, "it follows that, since we get through life relying on convention and not originality, we should respect and nurture that convention."

"So what should he do, this hey-there man?" "It's plain as those little pimple things at the corner of your nostril: say, 'Hello, Barton.' Then, if he sees me a few minutes later, he should nod, kindly but mutely. Is that so difficult? That's what convention dictates, and convention never makes unreasonable demands."

"Would you say the same principles apply in areas other than bidding good-day one another?" they continue. "Not exactly," is my answer.

You know, I was thinking that it is a mistake to confine your discussion of this History and Senator Thurmond to political and public matters. That is to say, Senator Thurmond feels that his engagement with the human beings around him, including blacks, has always involved a great deal more than legislation, public policy, and picnics. He has entered into the people's spirit by way of what one might call an enthusiastic participation in their culture, the full culture and not just part of it.

You see where this is going. What is African-American culture? Is it just some marches and riots and rapes, leading to legislation? No. It is singing and dancing very well indeed in a certain way and basketball and jazz. But I am sure you two know nothing about any of those things. (I mean that as a compliment.)

What you undoubtedly know about is the literature, right? I mean you are in English Departments, so I'm just saying.

So, while you're getting the historical materials I sent you some time ago to write up in the mail to me, I will send you some matter more to your liking. These are, of course, the Senator's ideas, comingled with mine, as our lives have been. I don't know about you, but I haven't had all that many close ties in my life. Funny, isn't it? Consider who and what I am, and you'd say, "Barton has friends clinging to him like moss on a vine." But that's really not so. I could of course say I choose not to be close, that I could have friends if I wanted them. But none of that's true.

But that's a menu for another meal. For now, please write up some of these.

--Frederick Douglass. Don't forget the extra s. What the Senator is interested in is his book: <u>Narrative of the Life of . . . .</u> Not his speeches and such like. What strikes us especially about the book is what he has to say about violence and Christianity. He seems to us very smart and very courageous, you know, when he points out how Christianity was used as a cover for cruelty, how it did not combat but encouraged the false equation of slavery with outright ownership, irresponsible ownership. As the Senator sees it, slavery was a contract, with rights and obligations on both sides. You'll say it was an unequal contract, but waive that. What the Senator zooms in on here is the way Christianity allowed the worst in the South (and we had some, though not a monopoly!) to forget the contract. Now, look at Douglass's book and write that up.

And don't mince words. Christianity and irresponsible violence. Douglass said that the worst masters were always the most Christian. The Senator finds that telling, especially insofar as the Abolitionists cloaked themselves in THE VERY SAME DOCTRINES. Doesn't this suggest that the abolitionists were attracted by the very torture and torment they pretended they wanted to end? I mean, what would they have done without it? They loved the violence and took not only their cause but their identity from it. They were like anti-pornography crusaders who want to think of nothing BUT pornography.

The Senator says the issues were all territorial (geographic) and economic. As soon as they got muddied up with morality, the Negro people were lost in the shuffle. Nobody gave a good goddamn about them.

In this, he is with Douglass and has learned much from him. So write that up.

--Booker T. Washington. Up from Slavery. Now here's a rich field to plow. The Senator feels that Northern people who criticize Washington for being an accommodationist simply do not understand the situation. Senator Thurmond has known the KKK, has known real redneck terror. Washington knew it too and was trying to find a way to make some slow progress in the face of unreasoning brutality. It was very easy for DuBois, with his white boy education and know-it-all Northern safety, to mock Washington. But it was cowardly of him to do so. Did DuBois know what a lynching was? Did he have the lives of others in his care? Washington did. When Washington made his "Atlanta Compromise" speech, how many lynchings were there in Georgia and South Carolina that year? Add in Alabama and Mississippi and you see what he was up against. Washington was in a real world, trying to save real lives. DuBois was in a comfy world of self-flattering tough talk that pumped him up and accomplished nothing. Well, that's not fair. It might have done something. It might have got a few hundred Negro men lynched.

--Zora Neal Hurston. Look at how she was treated. She strayed from the party line and got jumped on by the totalitarian males in the Harlem Mafia. She wasn't writing to advance "the cause," they said. Well, Langston and Co., who are you to define "the cause"? Stalin? They managed to ruin her career, kill her. And why? Because, as she said, she refused to see black lives as simply a defensive formation forced on them by whites. She didn't think black people were no more than what white people said; she didn't think black people could exist only by battling the definitions foisted on them by white people. She didn't think black was the opposite of white. She thought black was a world and a people that could make themselves, tell their own stories, form their own lives.

I hope you agree with me, James and Percival, Percival and James, Permes and Jacival. This is the Senator at his best. You may have imagined he didn't have it in him, this subtlety and thoughtfulness. "I like to think outside the box," he often says to me.

He is so much more than the labels slapped on him. Those who do that use him as an excuse, a person to hate so they won't have to hate themselves. For my part, I can find it in my heart to love him. To tell you the truth, I don't think I admire him exactly. Still, for all his short-circuiting and conniving, he has struggled not to be defined by the circumstances in which he found himself. Of course he has not succeeded, but he has never stopped trying.

Which of us can say the same?

I'm not feeling as well as usual, so I will close this short letter. Ordinarily, I am like a dandelion: not much to look at but not likely to wilt on you. I don't know exactly what it is now, but I feel like Wordsworth: The things which I have seen, I now can see no more.

Affectionately,
Barton Wilkes
Barton Wilkes

SIMON & SCHUSTER, INC.
1230 Avenue of the Americas
New York, NY 10020

March 1, 2003

Dear Juniper,

I write this in letter form and not as a memo, since the material I intend to present to you (as a gift) is not at all memo-like. You understand. This is a voyage of discovery for me, this letter.

Barton Wilkes has been fired. I showed you the memo from Thurmond's office. You remember? I hope so. I need your memory, among other things. He has been fired, and you and I both know what his twisted mind will do with this. He will sit in his bare room (a much-befouled bed, a lamp, a cheap bureau, a desk with pictures on it—of movie stars and Senator Thurmond and those he broods upon). On whom does he brood? Yes, I'm afraid so. Me. And I'm very afraid his brooding will turn to thoughts of vengeance. He will want to hurt me in the worst way. I just know it. He will want to stick things in my ears and eyes and tongue and anus. You feel I'm right, don't you?

Of course I had nothing whatever to do with his firing. You may have, but I didn't. But will that matter? Ha! Might as well tell the Voyager Satellite that blew up that you were sorry you decided to come on board as tell Wilkes he is mis-directing his rage. He is obsessed with me, I know. Now he will be thinking of blood. What is it Macbeth says? Something about wanting blood. Anyhow, he needs distracting. Wilkes, not Macbeth. Once started, both are like loco-motives on a straight track. It's Macbeth's wife I'm thinking of, come to think of it, and that just makes it worse.

I count on you renewing your physical association with Wilkes. That way you can discover what is on his mind (or minds) and also act to deflect his passions, as it were. Try domestic animals.

Whatever you do, tell no one he has been fired. Tell no one. If it spreads, he will come after me. He will come after me anyhow, but if he thinks I'm the one who spread it, he'll come after me—well, indeed he will.

Tell no one, especially not Everett and Kincaid, that Wilkes has been fired. I'm almost sorry I told you, except that you know already and I need you to help me.

What'll I do when you are far away and lonesome too, what'll I do? You know that song. It's very apropos. Please.

St. Patrick's Day. Party at my place. The theme will be "concealed green." We'll each wear (or adorn ourselves with) green in places—well, you know. There will be prizes for those who can most successfully search out the other's green pastures, so to speak.

Love and I mean it,

Martin

SIMON & SCHUSTER, INC.
1230 Avenue of the Americas
New York, NY 10020

March 2, 2003

Dear Barton,

I have just heard from that horrible Snell person—can you imagine a world in which Snell presents the best alternative available?—that you are no longer an associate of Senator Thurmond. I hope and trust this is an excretion from Snell's diseased brain. You seem to me to be the one who provides all the energy there, certainly the one, according to Kincaid and Everett, providing the material and guidance for the book.

Say it ain't so, Barton!

So or not, I realize that you are in a position far worse than mine. You are forced to disguise your talents and, I suppose, your views. I cannot, certainly, say that such is the case with me. I simply have to be around Martin Snell's mad insecurities and uncertain lusts. I don't really think Snell is possessed by ill will.

But are you in such a situation? Madness is one thing, but active and informed plotting is something else.

I am writing a very bad letter here, Barton, struggling to sympathize with you without knowing anything about the circumstances.

What I should have said was that I am your friend and hope you will tell me how I can help, if help is needed.

Fondly,
Juniper

March 5, 2003

Dear Juniper,

I think there's an old saying that goes something like: when you're down and out, lift up your head and shout, "There's gonna be a great day!" Actually, it's a song. You will hear his horn: rooty-tootin.

Well, your letter came rooty-tootin to me, Juniper. It's extremely noble of you to reach out your hand to such as I. To tell you the truth, I don't think I've ever had a friend. God knows I've tried. I learned as a kid the best way—the best way for me, anyhow—to have a friend was just to pick someone and hang around and hope they assume they are your friend. I mean, you try and force them, which is what it comes to, to do the things friends do and hope that means you're friends.

If you can stand it, I'd like to pursue this a bit. During the summer after my freshman year in high school (quite undistinguished school, only a few students reached the level of mediocrity, such excitement as prevailed was centered on the football team and the choir, directed by a very colorful pedophile, whose detection and ejection sucked away the only creative energy which had been there)—during that summer, I say, I found myself without the easy means of doing with others things friends did. There were no classrooms, no gym changing rooms, no lockers, no enforced lunch periods. I lived a few miles away from those I wanted in my little friendship play. They didn't come to me or call me. I had no way to get to them (no car, city bus line a bit embarrassing, landing me on a wide street and forcing me to go house to house like a salesman, which I was, but without a product anybody wanted). So I would call them, one after another, and say, "Hey, let's go to a movie!" Movies were all I could think of to do. (Then and now.) Every so often, somebody would go and I would be very happy. But the acceptance rate was lousy, and I should have seen what was building up. These reluctant movie attendees were comparing notes. That fall, when school finally started and I swooped into my old drama with something more than relief, I was met by my mates, who, together, made a great show of laughing together and telling me they were anxious to go to movies with me. I wasn't especially hurt. I just saw what had happened, not that I was able to avoid it after that. It was all I could think to do, and my need remained greater than my wit.

You'd think my obvious yearning for friendship, my open advertisement of myself as friend-in-waiting, the clarity with which I expressed my liking for others, would have attracted somebody. Maybe it did. After a while, I did manage to be alone less, though the summers were never less vacant.

Two years ago, at a class reunion, Lynette Archer, a quiet and pretty girl, told me she had had an aching crush on me through high school. "Why didn't you tell me?" "Oh, Barton, you were always so popular, and I was so shy." She smiled and touched my coat sleeve. It was the best moment of my life, not because I could now entangle myself with Lynette Archer—she was now, happily I hope, Lynette Russell—but because what I had wanted all along had happened. I had had friends. I hadn't known it, really, but other people had. So maybe they were right.

But it isn't often I think so.

And it was your letter that came along, like Lynette Archer, only better.

In any event, let's talk about you. I am sorry that you are leashed to Snell, who doesn't strike me (even me) as having enough holes in his bowling ball. Tell me how I can help.

As for the book, that will go on as if nothing had interrupted it. It's sure that somewhere the sun is shining! And so the right thing to do is make it smile for you. A heart full of joy and gladness will always banish sorrow and strife! So always look for the silver lining, and try to find the sunny side of life. You know that lovely tune? I know it can be ridiculed, but I have never had much talent for ridicule.

So, the book will go on. I'll work with K and E, who seem (I must say) very good at receiving material and not quite so good at doing anything with it. Still, they are writers and must proceed at their own pace, assuming that the word "pace" applies to them at all.

It's important that K and E, E and K, know nothing of this pebble in our path, this temporary shower of trouble, this slight blip on the screen. I will be back where I was in no time, certainly, and there's no need for them to be distracted.

Nor you.

Your friend, your grateful friend,
Barton

Interoffice Memo

March 7, 2003

Dear Percival,

Since you're often accusing me of jumping the gun, being pre-emptory, getting my oar in ahead of the rest of the crew, I can only say, "well"?

I have been waiting and waiting. For your response, you know. Where is it? We got that stimulating letter from Wilkes (dated February 27) several days ago. What's your view? I can tell you my view, but that's what you always object to, me telling you my view before you tell me yours.

I sometimes think you are giving too much time to other things in your life: the other books you wrote a while back and are still publicizing shamelessly, this fucking English Department, your students, your stock portfolio, your pets, your exercise regimen, your arty-crafty projects, your partying, and those chemicals you ingest. Oh, and your wife. I am not being judgmental about chemicals. As you often point out, chemicals are in everything we swallow, like broccoli. I take your point, as an uncle of mine, who never understood any point unless he sat on it, used to say. Still, there must be a difference between broccoli and those pills you buy from that rummy-looking guy over by the Coliseum.

In any event, here's what I think. I know you don't care, but I do. I know you don't want me doing anything ahead of you. But what happens when you aren't doing a thing? Am I supposed just to wait? Add it up, ace. Looks to me like doing things that way is no way. Nothing would ever get done.

Therefore.

What do you think of this rough outline for the book?

Part I: Political History
a. Strom on Slavery
b. Strom on the War
c. Strom on Reconstruction
d. Strom on the KKK
e. Strom on The Dixiecrats
f. Strom on Civil Rights
g. Strom on Washington generally—amusing musings on blacks in politics and non-blacks too
h. Strom on our contemporary world and the blacks in it

Part II: Cultural History
a. Strom on blacks and music—real music, not gangsta rap
b. Strom on blacks and the theater
c. Strom on blacks and the domestic arts (making quilts—shit like that)
d. Strom on blacks and painting (? Query: have there ever been any?)
e. Strom on blacks and the dance

f. Strom on blacks in film, television, radio, journalism
g. Strom on black fashion models
h. Strom on blacks and sports

Part III: The People
a. Strom on blacks and the family
b. Strom on blacks and the schools—here's a real strong suit
c. Strom on blacks and public transportation
d. Strom on blacks and food—what they eat and how
e. Strom on blacks and religion—maybe we should write this for him?
f. Strom on blacks and domestic décor
g. Strom on blacks and dirt farming
h. Strom on blacks and criminality

I have some misgivings about IIIh. Don't you?

Hey, but isn't this a masterful idea? Masterful. We've got 3 Parts, 8 sections each, 15 pages a section, with some illustrations, it's over with. I can write 15 pages in one day on any subject. All we need's some hints from Strom and we can finish this book by the end of the term—easy.

Don't thank me.

Blesings on you,
Jim

FROM THE DESK OF PERCIVAL EVERETT

March 8, 2003

Dear Jim,

I WILL thank you, buddy. This is a very good outline. And when did I ever criticize you for displaying initiative? Never, that's when. Never had occasion to. Initiative, you see, is very different from blind panic and aimless flailing, both of which you are prone to. But this outline is by-Jesus initiative, Jim, and don't let them tell you any different.

As for the outline, the general idea seems fine to me. I'm not quite sure we want to separate "Cultural History" from "The People," as if The People didn't figure in culture. And do we want Strom writing on black cuisine? That seems odd, doesn't it? I mean, many of the things in Part III seem better suited to almost any other author.

Also, don't we want "blacks and literature" under cultural history? That, after all, was what Barton suggested to us.

I have a few other suggestions, but we can work these out later and fit them in—or not. I do like your idea, Jim.

Strom on blacks in literature
Strom on blacks in the waste disposal profession
Strom on blacks and penis size
Strom on blacks and their fondness for rape
Strom on famous black scientists
Strom on diseases caused by blacks
Strom on ebonics

Again, no matter what you say, I DO thank you.

Best,
P

March 9, 2003

Dear Juniper,

So nice talking to you, dearie. To hear that your job is so much better makes me glow, though I wonder if you're not shifting it into the sunlight to keep me from worrying. Anyhow, the pay is good; and as for the St. Patrick's Day party, well, you've had experience fending off Martin before. I worry about you, but here's some advice: just keep your body sideways to his. That way he can't do any real damage. Do you know Mother once told me exactly that? I was about 13, and I swear I didn't know what she was talking about. I still don't. I wonder if she knew.

I wanted to ask you a terrible favor, Juney. You remember my friend Septic? The one who has had such a hard time of it, such a time as you and I will probably never even have to glimpse. But that's just the point: our unwillingness to take a look, much less a sympathetic look, at the world of Septic is an evasion that, however understandable, is also too easy for us. By looking away, we allow this horrible world to roll along, grinding up bodies and lives, especially the bodies and lives of the weak and innocent.

Septic, as you know, took on her name—it is her only name—as a form of protest, an ironic reversal, she calls it. I think myself, without her authorization, that the name is used a bit as "Queer" or "Black" are—throwing it in our faces. But anyhow, Septic has somehow remained gentle-hearted through it all.

She's written a kind of novel/essay. I think you might call it a fictional polemic. It is very experimental in its form. I think it's important. Excuse me for taking so long to get to the subject of her work, which is a grind-your-nose-in-it look at the worlds of prostitutes and pimps. It's very provocative in its ideas on prostitution, sex in general, money, and class issues. The novel, appropriately (well, I hope so), is entitled CLASS ASS.

Yes, Septic has been both a pimp and a prostitute; has both sold and taken drugs; has acted in and directed porn (adult and child); has committed robbery, assault (several times), burglary, arson, and, though in a botched way (it makes the one comic part of the book), counterfeiting. That's just it: she fits none of the stereotypes. Maybe nobody does.

The book is a little long and wants editing. I can hear you screaming. But I think you might have something like Jack Abbott here. Septic seems to me absolutely authentic and dear.

How would you feel about (a) looking at it and (b) meeting her? You think I put in (b) knowing you would reject that and thus making it harder for you to say no twice. Why, Juniper! Would I do a thing like that?

Much love,
Sis

SIMON & SCHUSTER, INC.
1230 Avenue of the Americas
New York, NY 10020

March 10, 2003

Dear Barton,

The past is very cruel, humiliating. But you know, Barton, I sometimes wonder if it's the past that's at fault or our memory and the
way we tell ourselves stories about the past. You know what I mean?
For me, the past is really pretty malleable, and I can dredge up from
it stories for all occasions and moods. It's not, for me, a matter of
lying (though I'm sure I fill up my quota there) but of finding ways
to tell a tale or run a movie in my head that makes the past fit what
I want. I don't do this consciously; it just works out like that.

My own favorite literary character, Humbert Humbert, puts it
this way: "When I try to analyze my own cravings, motives, actions,
and so forth, I surrender to a sort of retrospective imagination
which feeds the analytical faculty with boundless alternatives and
which causes each visualized route to fork and re-fork without end
in the maddeningly complex prospect of my past." (I don't have this
memorized. I've been reading LOLITA as fall-asleep material.)

Anyhow, Barton, I wonder if your memories of your own past
and the desolation you see there doesn't say more about now than
about then? You unconsciously form the past to fit the present.
Don't you think so?

But look at it this way. First of all, you do have friends. I am your
friend, and Kincaid and Everett, I know, think very highly of you.
Senator Thurmond, this temporary rupture aside, is also your friend, I
am sure. And there are others too, of course. The thing is this, Barton:
you are in politics, surely the most unstable and wretchedly selfish
endeavor known to man. Friendships are probably impossible to form
there. Any person possessed of sensitivity and depth of thought
would find the whole environment harrowing, empty. It's the place,
Barton, not you. Anyone who fits there would never have acted to
save my job, could not have written that letter you then sent me.

You'll excuse me being so aggressively intrusive. Of course I
know little about Washington and the political life. Still, I'll bet I am
not wrong. Put yourself in any other area and you would not only
shine but gather around you many friends eager to share your

energy and luminosity.

Count on me to say nothing to K and E about the short-lived misunderstanding there. You're right: it would just throw them off the track. We'll go on just as we have been, and that way things will progress as fast as they can.

By the way, my impression is that K and E are really pretty enterprising fellows. I may be wrong, but my guess is—I'm a regular fortune-teller tonight—that they've been working hard and will probably spring something on you when you least expect it.

I've got to run. I have this neighbor, a very sweet old woman, who has taken it into her head that I love to watch a certain television program. I am ashamed to say I was about to skip the name, just so I wouldn't look like a dumb-ass. But it's one of those reality programs, teenagers in a house nagging and niggling. I would have thought they'd be doing drugs and wallowing in the bliss of all that young flesh; but no. They complain about who uses the phone too long, who cleans up, who is defensive, who alludes unkindly to the fat girl's fatness, as if those things were life. What a waste. And it's on MTV. My neighbor must be 80, which is what trapped me. You see, I thought it was really commendable that she would find something of interest on MTV, so I talked with her about it. I had never seen the show and am sure I said nothing either way about it, but she mis-read my blab as addiction to these dreadful teens. Now I must go over every week and watch with her. She fixes elaborate toastie things—toast rounds with various toppings that testify to her highly reckless ingenuity. I'm becoming addicted to the toasties, to Margaret, and (what a thing to admit) the show and the kids on it.

For the truth is I enjoy it all at least as much as she. Two weeks ago I took wine, which we (she) finished before the show was half over, so last week I took two bottles. Who knows? This may be love!

Your friend,
Juniper

From the Desk of Percival Everett

March 11, 2003

Jim—

I didn't mean to be critical or sarcastic. I was sincere in my expressions of admiration for your outline and the idea of writing a kind of suggestive, very wide-ranging history rather than a political or social history that would try to cover with some semblance of responsibility some specified ground. This way we can dip and glide and say what we want on a variety of wholly disconnected topics. I can see the top of the bestseller list crooking its finger at us---or giving us the finger.

But we're one on this. Could you tighten up the outline a little, incorporating the very few serious suggestions I gave you and ignoring the ones offered as jokes, poor jokes.

Don't be huffy now. You're always saying we should move forward, and you've moved us forward. You've stuck your thumb right up our collective ass and given us a timely goose.

P

March 15, 2003

Dear Reba,

Ides of March, and would that I had been stabbed.

Oh dearie sister, Martin's party turned out to include—as you warned—but one guest, who had to serve as dinner companion, game player, dance partner, and more. At one point, he decided we should go for a swim, so we set out to find an indoor pool at 2 a.m. I was surprised, as you would be too, that there were none that met our roving eyes. Martin decided the fountains outside the New York Hilton would do just fine.

I can say this: though I did not resist everything, I resisted some things. In the first category, the worst was that I put on a gown to dance with him. I have no explanation, beyond mentioning that this was the very first activity he had on his list, and it did seem churlish to start the evening with a refusal. Dinner wasn't bad either, really, though Martin, who has an immense dining table, sat about six inches from me. I kept thinking how sad it was that he had this big dining table and nobody to share it with.

I did resist (a) any games that involved undressing (the donning of the gown was done in discreet privacy), (b) weeping along with him as he told stories of his youth (though I did get a little misty once), (c) submitting to a massage, (d) letting him "do a lick job" on my toes, (e) playing a game he called "back seat at the drive-in," (f) joining him in the Hilton fountains. (In plain truth, I did give in on (c) and the first minute or two of (e).)

As for Septic, I take your word that she's something special. Have you read her stuff? I gather you have, since you say it needs editing. Well, here's what I'm going to do, though it's better as yet to say nothing to Septic about it. Her kind of material is not Snell's department, though he'd love to think he knew her world better than she. (The truth is he's a lonely man who has had no life and can find nowhere to steer his boat.) It is Vendetti's. I don't think I told you that I parted on good terms with him, though he is what he is, whatever that may be. Anyhow, I'll slip him the word on it without Martin knowing. If you can mail me Septic's manuscript overnight mail. Please <u>you</u> do it, Reba. The very idea of Septic scares the shit out of me.

You're the tops.

Love,
Juniper

SIMON & SCHUSTER, INC.
1230 Avenue of the Americas
New York, NY 10020

March 18, 2003

Dear Barton, Percival, and Jim,

As you are all my mutual friends—maybe we should start a barbershop quartet?—I thought I owed you some description of Martin Snell's early St. Patrick's Day party and other outstanding events going on here. First, Reba put me on to a friend of hers, one Septic (that's right—her real and only name) who is writing a book called CLASS ASS on the ins and outs of prostituting and pimping, a Marxist analysis too, I think. I decided to slip it to Vendetti, as Snell would do horrible things with it. Second, the party didn't have green beer or anything at all Irish. I don't think he remembered what the occasion for the party was.

That's the extent of the good news.

The pathetic old bastard, he ended the evening drunk and floundering in the New York Hilton fountain. What nice people there! They helped me get him out and in the car, said it happened a couple of times a month. Maybe it's Snell that does it a couple of times a month. I should have asked.

I wrote Reba a full account—of me donning a gown in order to dance with him, of several other disgraceful things, comic too, if it all weren't so sad. But throw somebody like Snell a life preserver and he'll pull you under, as a character in LUCKY JIM says.

I guess that's true. I'd like to help him, but not at the price he asks anyone to pay. And he doesn't mean to be so outrageous either. What he wants is a friend or two, but he's been without them for so long, it's driven him to a land of loons where he has lost his compass. He is not really dangerous: the moment I give out with any signs of reluctance, his merriment collapses and he begins weeping, or apologizing, or, most commonly, both.

My virtue is intact, in case you were wondering. I'd do a lot to try and help him, but somehow I think fucking him (or whatever would pass for that in his mind) might be a big mistake—for him, probably not for me.

Ah Snell, Ah humanity!

Love,
Juniper

p.s. Vendetti loves the project. I guess that's good.

James R. Kincaid
University of Southern California
University Park Campus
Los Angeles, CA 90089

March 20, 2003

Dear Barton,

Hope you're well and not letting the venerable Senator feed off your life's blood. That's a joke, naturally, but you know, Barton, I think there's some truth to the suspicion that the old often feed off the young. I mean, look at the old guys who are coaches or, I suppose, teachers. They drain the young. I mean, why do we chain all the young people in our land to desks hour after hour, until they're half-wild with boredom and bottled up vim? Partly to discipline them to our needs, I guess, keep them from doing anything disruptive or creative. But also, don't you think, so we can lap up that energy we allow no other outlet? Where can it go but to the old crumbling bodies before them? So watch out.

But I'm writing about another thing—and hope you are getting along fine with Strom, who must have much in the way of canny conniving to pass along.

What I have here is an outline, reflecting the enthusiasm Percival and I both feel for your idea about making this a cultural and social as well as a political history. What do you think of this? You'll see it's divided into 3 parts (but doesn't have to be).

Part I: Political History
a. Strom on Slavery
b. Strom on the War Between the States
c. Strom on Reconstruction
d. Strom on the KKK

e. Strom on The Dixiecrats

f. Strom on Civil Rights

g. Strom on Washington generally—amusing anecdotes on blacks in politics and non-blacks too

h. Strom on our contemporary world and the blacks in it

Part II: Cultural History

i. Strom on blacks and music—real music, not gangsta rap

j. Strom on blacks and the theater

k. Strom on blacks and the domestic arts (making quilts—shit like that)

l. Strom on blacks and painting

m. Strom on blacks and the dance

n. Strom on blacks in film, television, radio, journalism

o. Strom on black fashion models

p. Strom on blacks and sports

q. Strom on blacks and literature

Part III: Social History

r. Strom on blacks and the family

s. Strom on blacks and the schools—here's a real strong suit

t. Strom on blacks and public transportation

u. Strom on blacks and food—what they eat and how they cook it

v. Strom on blacks and religion—maybe we should write this for him?

w. Strom on blacks and domestic décor

x. Strom on blacks and dirt farming

y. Strom on blacks and criminality

None of these are, as our miserable fucking Dean says, "carved in stone." Percival thinks IIIu may not fit the Senator's agenda. But I say, "Let Barton and the Senator decide."

Anyhow, you see what we have in mind, following your lead. This will be a broader-ranging and less conventional "history," allowing the Senator to suggest topics for short essays, filled with

HISTORY OF THE AFRICAN-AMERICAN PEOPLE ...

personal experiences and good stories, on items that interest him. After all, what interests him will interest others.

Barton, does it ever occur to you that life passes us by—or that we wade through our lives looking down at the puddles and our galoshes without noticing much else? When you get to my age, such depressing ideas strike you, and I do mean STRIKE. It's like getting hit with a big paving brick right between your ear and eye. I only had one life and why didn't I even remark on it as I went through it?

Oh well, philosophy's for the elite, as a British idiot said about me in a recent essay in the TLS. What she actually said is, "irony is an elitist tool." Referring to me. What an idiot. She thinks she's being ever so sympathetic to those who, by her lights, haven't gotten to a point where irony can be used safely. That is, she's telling young people they'd better not be ironic. Thus, under the guise of liberal sympathy, she's the worst kind of conservative, robbing the young of yet another tool. Oh, it makes my semen boil!

I'd love to go on, but I have a class to teach. It's one of the great pleasures left me—eating the energy of the young.

Devotedly,
Jim

March 24, 2003

Dear Martin,

I wonder if you wouldn't like to get closer acquainted? We're not so far apart, and I think by now we have learned to climb those little lumpy hills that can separate those who ought not to be separated.

I haven't anything sexual in mind, just to ease your palpitating heart. Just social things and dancing. Moonlight movies. Rides in the country. Picnics. Rollerblading.

You'll be glad to hear that all goes very well with the project, very well indeed. K and E are now really rolling on a new plan for a cultural/social/political history. Much more lively and Strom-like. Won't be a chronicle of events, you know, but more a set of funny stories and telling anecdotes (or at least anecdotes).

I know you're busy but I just hoped you'd be interested in my little proposition.

Juniper, I gather, is really working so hard these days, he must be exhausted. Now, that's one reason I step into the breech, though my motives are really not that unselfish. Mostly I want to be with you. But Juniper is working now also on that CLASS ASS project (the accounts from the gritty, liquidy world of pimps and prostitutes by one SEPTIC, whose no-holds-barred account will tell it like it's never been told before.) I know this is Vendetti's project, coarse as it is, but it must rip Juniper in two directions at once.

I, on the other hand, am whole.

Badda-Bing,
Barton

March 24, 2003

Dear Juniper,

I just hit on a scheme for putting up a shield between you and Martin. I hope.

I wrote to him offering my very self for waltzing under the stars and fornicating in fountains. Of course I trust it won't come to that. I am an old hand at avoiding anything intimate, whether I mean to or not.

Also, I let him know how busy you are, what with that project on whores you're doing with Vendetti.

Are there stars out tonight? I don't know if it's cloudy or bright. Cause I only have eyes for YOOOOOOUUUUUUU.

Cheers,
Barton

SIMON & SCHUSTER, INC.
1230 Avenue of the Americas
New York, NY 10020

March 27, 2003

Dear B----

Just a note to thank you for the shield. You cannot know how much I need one. Snell found out about CLASS ASS and seems to be fixated on Vendetti. It scares me. Could he be worried that Vendetti is stealing me from him? What a grotesque idea—which makes it all the more likely in old Marty's case.

Whoooee. Martin is possessed, that's for sure.

Thanks!!
Juniper

Vendetti, you puss-pricked Sicilian yellow bastard,

I have my eye on you, you swarthy pig fucker. I fucked your mama, you know, me and all the other 11th graders at P.S. 122. She kept saying, "Give me more, give me more!" "Oh Ralphie!" she'd sometimes say, the senile old cunt. Or "Oh Rover, give me your raw red cock."

I hope you die, you cocksucker. I wrote your name all over the Grand Central toilets: "For a good dick-slurper call A. Vendetti (A. is short for assfuck)."

You aren't worth a pile of cowshit as an editor, you know that? Anybody's a better editor than you. That's why they give you all those books aimed at fairies and stupid women. You have a lot in common with them, right? You can only fuck your old stinking cow of a mother and the boys in the toilets. That's why they give you those books. And the ones on pimps and whores.

I may just run you down with my car, I'd have to back over you thirty times to get all the glop out of your fat body, all blood and loose cartilage and fat and no brain matter on the street.

I know where you work, Sicilian shitface fuck. Just keep that in mind. I don't know where you live, but I can find out.

A. Frend

Memo: McCloud to Snell

March 28, 2003

Dear Martin,

I typed up that note to Vendetti, but do you think it's wise? Don't you think he'll suppose it's internal? Maybe you should follow your first instinct and send the pencilled note. It's well disguised.

Anyhow, I did use the font you suggested—that comic Chinesey font. Are you sure you haven't used it before? It's so odd that if you have used it before, it'd be like attaching a picture of yourself to the letter—not so anonymous as you're hoping, I'd say.

Also, and above all, would you leave out that allusion to the pimps and whores project? Vendetti's been fine with me, but he might think I wrote the note. I mean, who else knows about it, except Barton? Well, you. But don't make me sorry I told you.

Juniper

Memo: Snell to McCloud

March 28, 2003

Jun—Send it exactly as it is, exactly, every word. I resent

your phrase "anonymous as you're hoping." You think I'm afraid of that bloated Wop? Jesus, what a fuck you are sometimes (luckily, not always)! I'm keeping it anonymous just to preserve company dignity and also to vex him even more, that shit-eating Sicilian son of a diseased whore!

Mar

SIMON & SCHUSTER, INC.
1230 Avenue of the Americas
New York, NY 10020

March 28, 2003

Dear Barton,

Our contacts until now have been entirely epistolary. Nothing in the flesh, I mean. Only paper has connected us (along with electrons, I guess; I refer to our phone calls and however it is phone messages are transmitted, electrons I think, though I was never good in science. Were you? I have found I seldom get along well with those who were good in science. I use the past tense because I know no one whose acquaintance with science is not in the past. i.e., I know no scientists, unless you want to call physicians and pharmacists by that term, which I don't.) I have never much liked talking on the phone, which is something of a disadvantage in my line, where phone schmoozing means a lot to some. But if it means that much, I always say, why don't our books come out with receivers attached?

The reason I mention our not having met in the flesh is that your letters have often made me quite afraid of you. Just to ante up and stay in the game, cards on the table though not face up, I will say that I can't tell if you are colorful, uninhibited, witty, or sociopathic. Now, that issue may not matter to you, but it does to me.

Let me be plain. I will not pretend that I am so busy I have no time for anybody in my life. I'd love to get to know you if you won't hurt me. By "hurt me" I don't mean anything remote or obscure. I don't mean break my heart; I mean break my arm.

I am, Barton, very lonely, and I am aware that such loneliness makes me act in ways I sometimes, afterwards, wish I hadn't. But I am not so lonely that I want to be abused—physically. Emotionally, I can take.

I know very well that Juniper has never liked me at all. He's an extremely kind boy is all it is. That and being pretty indifferent to his lovely, lovely body. I have never fooled myself that he was eager to do anything sexually with me. What little went on he just allowed and was nice about it. I almost let him get away, I guess because I was so humiliated by what I was doing to him. And I am so afraid of losing him, though I don't really HAVE him either.

Why am I saying all this? Usually I am not so introspective, you may be glad to find out. To swing to the conclusion: I would love to do things with you—you mention dancing and rollerblading—so long as you don't beat me up. Say when you're free. I am free any time except work hours, and often then.

Badda-Boo,
Martin

Simon & Schuster, Inc.
1230 Avenue of the Americas
New York, NY 10020

March 30, 2003

Dear Percival and James,

I trust things are going very well. I gather they are. Barton Wilkes tells me they are, and I am inclined to believe him. He said you were shifting from a strict history to something more enjoyable and more within the Senator's compass and your own. That sounds good to us, provided (a) it gets done soon and (b) it still connects the two key terms in the project, Strom and blacks. Abandon either term and the project has lost its moorings, become some-. thing else, something very good it may be but not what it was, not what we signed on for.

You'll be sorry to hear—I know I was—that Juniper McCloud, whom you have befriended, and very kind of you to do so, as he deserves it, a very nice young man and also well-featured, is laid up in the hospital. His injuries are said to be not critical but extensive. What that means in this case is that another editor here, Ralph Vendetti, a capable but coarse-minded man, assaulted him, i.e., beat him up pretty much all over, but not too horribly in any one place.

Why did Vendetti do it? Word is that Juniper sent him

an abusive note, though I cannot believe Juniper would do that. However, he probably has provocation, as he is, though you do not know this, working part-time (against my better judgment, which he surely should rely on) for Vendetti. I do not take this as a betrayal, since the project is a low-market thing about whores and such. Juniper is helping a friend. Some friend!

In any case, Juniper is at the 37th Street hospital, not the world's best, I might add, but the very place our insurance here at S&S lands us. His face is OK, but his jaw isn't, if you take my meaning. But he can talk. I know because I visited him and vowed to take things into my own hands with Vendetti, which vow I will fulfill, once I determine how best to do it.

Martin

~

April 1, 2003

Dear Jim and Percival,

I am reclined here in Dante's 7th circle, enjoying myself greatly, thanks to philanthropic painkillers I wish I had learned to spend time with earlier. I'll tell you, my dear friends, that these things do a lot more than kill pain. Oh yes. They give you a sense of serenity that recovering alcoholics pray for. I can see why they do. It's as good as any drunk---a little morphine, some codeine, some pills of some sort. And it's not lassitude I feel, but exhilaration. I feel like I'm all mind, as if my body were laid to rest somewhere over in the next township and all energy has been deposited in my head. And a happy head it is, filled with plans and promises and resolve to do good.

I should have said I'm here in the company hospital---or some hospital the company allows us to go to. It's a splendid hospital, a beautiful and even charming place. The nurses are very funny and gifted people, and the food---well, you won't find many 5-star restaurants to top it. I'm here because Ralph Vendetti took it into his head to punish me for a scurrilous note sent to him by poor Martin. I'll tell you why poor Martin in a minute.

Anyhow, Martin, driven by forces beyond his control--and most forces are--wrote a note to Vendetti. I said that before, didn't I? Sorry. I'm just so happy. This letter is being transcribed by Reba, my Venus of a sister, Venus and-----[I am simply NOT going to send this part, promise or no promise---R.]. You see, I can make myself understood but not sit up, really, or hold a pen, really. That's fine. I'm far from complaining. You should try it. I'll try to sneak some of this stuff for you. Maybe in LA you can get all the codeine you want? Lucky you!

Reba told me I was drifting, which put me in mind of a song, called Drifting Down the River on a Sunny Afternoon, the Sky above, the moon you love, crooning out a tune, the old accordion playing a tune that is a tune, cruising down the river, on a sunny afternoon-noon-noon-noon. I just sang that. Wish you could have heard it. [I do too--R.]

So, Vendetti went after me. I won't give you details about his motives, as they are perfectly reasonable but I forget what they are. Anyhow, he did. And here I am and there you are and here is Reba in this palace writing down what I say. Only thing bothers me is that I told Vendetti it was Martin who sent it. That was low of me, you'll say, and I agree. But I was in great pain at the time, I think, though now that's hard to believe, and I think pain must be an illusion. Still, I was afraid he'd give me more pain and seemed to be honing in on my balls, in fact, so I told him.

I love you and Reba and Reba loves you and me.

Juniper

There's this very pretty candy-striper kid (girl) comes by and sings. I sing with her. She's good and doesn't mind that I don't know the words. She, Whitney is her name and she's about 12 I think, says she's going to write out the lyrics for me. GO, GIRL! I say. Doncha know, baby. Reba says she really loves Whitney too but she's not going to go on writing this [no, I'm not]. Did I say she really likes Whitney too? [yes] Reba refuses to sing [right].

April 3, 2003

Dear Percival and Jim,

Well, the worst has happened and I knew you'd want to hear all about it. Reba says you couldn't possibly be interested; she says I'm bothering you. But that's women for you. Apart from that, she's a good sort. Actually, I like women a lot, generally. Almost always. I'd much prefer to spend my time with them, no offense. Men are not so comfortable for me, not easy. You know what I mean? It's funny, though. I'm highly sexed. Reba just said not to tell you that, but why not? My guess is that you two are highly sexed too, though probably not in the same way I am. Here's how I am: there's lots of men and women I'd like to have sex with, children too, though that's for some reason a big no-no in our culture. Why is that? Anyhow, my dilemma is this. Well, my REAL dilemma is that I am so seldom able to arrange circumstances where it turns out that I am sleeping with anybody, never mind man or woman or child. Reba said to say "child" was just a joke. It isn't a joke, though it's illegal. I tell her there's a big difference, though I don't think most people recognize it.

They changed my medication a bit. It's even better, if you can believe it. This kind sort of wears off, which is a bummer, but then when they give me another shot oh jesus! I am not sure what it is. They won't tell me. They told Reba, I think. [Yes they did and I told Juniper but he has a hard time keeping anything straight, as you've noticed.]

My dilemma is that there are more men I want to sleep with than women, leaving children out of it. Maybe it's just the luck of the draw--I mean by that only that the men I have met happen to be more attractive, some of them, than the women I have met, some of them. I don't have any special proclivities, of that I'm pretty sure. But I prefer being around women. Maybe I just haven't lived long enough to get it ironed out. I was going to say "get it straight," but that's a laugh, isn't it. But, when you think of it, it isn't all that funny. Yes it is.

The worst that's happened, as I said, has happened. Martin is in here, though not in my semi-private room. There's four of us in here, which lands pretty heavy on the semi part of semi-private, if you ask me. The others sharing my particular privacy are all wonderful and gifted men. Why they are all men I don't know. If college dorms can be co-ed, why not hospital semi-private rooms? But these guys are magnificent. Two of us, counting me, can't get out of bed, which means the other two have to initiate the visiting, which they do a lot. One is a football player or maybe polo. But it's Snell I wanted to tell you about, thanks Reba.

So, probably because I told Mr. Vendetti as he was bashing me with his big fists and then picking me off the floor so he could bash me again--he didn't kick me, to the best of my recollection and I don't think he's the kind of person who would--anyhow I told him Snell had sent the note. Pure cowardice you're saying. True.

So Vendetti got to Snell, easy enough since their offices are close, not next door but close. Kicked the shit out of him. Not like me but worse, I think. I have tried to call Martin Snell on the phone here, which Reba helps me with. They could do with less stuff or more furniture and drawers is my opinion. The top of this unreasonably small bedside table (otherwise very nice) gets crowded, not that I am a neat freak. But spilling is messy, don't you think?

But he's not there, Snell, or, I guess he is; he's just not answering. Probably he can't yet. But they tell me he's going to be OK. I told the nurse to give him what I'm getting. You know what she said? She said, "We only give that juice to the patients we love, sweet cheeks." Reba doesn't believe she said that, no you don't, but she did.

Well, you're up to date now, as they say. If you know anybody who'd like to have sex with me, I'd be grateful if you'd tell me about them or them about me. It doesn't matter which way, as it'll amount to the same thing in the end, and that is not a pun. Man or woman. Child I was just kidding about. OK, Reba?

Love,
Juniper

April 5, 2003

Dear P & J,

I now have my own laptop here with me and can save Reba some trouble. You know that she slept in a lounger here for two nights? What a dearie.

I go home tomorrow, probably. I sure hope so. I actually felt better before today, when they suddenly and mercilessly replaced the wonder drugs I was taking with, get this, Tylenol. What a fraud Tylenol is. Does nothing. Reba says, though, that the other drugs made me effervescent to a degree that others might not understand. Actually, she said they made me nearly incoherent in my bliss. I'm sorry if I gave that impression. Near as I can remember, I've never felt so confident or impressed with my own thinking, and I suppose that's bad. Fun, though!

I will be brief. Mr. Vendetti has been here every day. He hasn't once said he's sorry, but he hangs around for 45 minutes or so, being gruff or silent. Reba talks with him a lot, though, and several times I thought I heard Mr. Vendetti laugh. The drugs, you know. With me, though, he mostly stares straight into my face, as if expecting me to tell jokes or make an important announcement. It would embarrass me to do that, just stare at somebody, but it doesn't embarrass him. I asked him, as politely as I could, if there was something he wanted to say. "If there were, I'd say it." But he sort of smiled. "Is there something you want me to say?" I probed. "No." What do you make of that? Sometimes I think he just comes here to see Reba. If so, I wish he'd stare at her rather than me, though I don't mean to complain. He's obviously a decent guy. Ugly as hell, though not as much as when I first saw him. There's a way in which his face has a lot of character, but still, however you cut it, kind of ugly.

The other news is about Septic. She came here yesterday with Reba in the morning and stayed practically the whole day. Actually, that was fine by me. She's not ugly like Vendetti and she didn't stare at me. Get this. She's shy. Turns out Reba had practically dragged her here to talk about her book, CLASS ASS (as you remember).

Well, I was feeling right at the top of my game (or, as Reba would say, prime idiotic) since they hadn't begun tormenting me with Tylenol yet. I was curious about Septic anyhow, as she hadn't seemed the sort my sister would befriend. Turns out I was judging Septic only on her name and the title of her book. She looks a little like Audrey Hepburn or somebody just as fragile. I was expecting a motorcycle mama, I guess, or maybe Joan Rivers. But here was a shrinking violet, with blond hair I could tell was natural (I didn't say she was a duplicate of Audrey Hepburn) and a modest dress that was actually pleated at the bottom with those poofy sleeves. Didn't know they were in fashion. Probably they are not, as I don't think Septic has a lot of money or, I'd also guess, interest in fashion.

After a while, I got her talking about her book. I was sure after twenty minutes that it was all fiction. No way this well-spoken girl had been a pimp and prostitute. Wrong. She insisted she had "worked summers" while in college, three summers to be exact, in the body trade. The first two summers she had done tricks; the last one she had moved up to "administration," which seems to correspond more to Madame than pimp, sort of like second-in-command to Heidi Fleiss.

I didn't go into any of her experiences, though, just asked her to tell me more about the book. She called it "a kind of ironic mockery of shock fiction," which shut my mouth, I can tell you. She mistook my silence for puzzlement, maybe disapproval. "I mean it tries to be an expose at the same time it makes fun of the conventions of expose writing and the way such sensational stuff is marketed and, well, sensationalized." She blushed as she said this. Had I not been a little immobile I'd have bounced up and kissed her right there.

To get to the point: at my urging, she read a few pages, the beginning. They were so good that I asked for more, then more, then we had lunch, then more. She ended up reading the whole thing. Took all day and the next (she came back). It would have been faster, had she not kept apologizing and offering to quit.

It sounds like a set-up comic situation, doesn't it: a guy stuck in a hospital bed being forced to endure 19 hours of CLASS ASS, read by the author, one Septic. But it seemed to me the best day of my life. Sure, I was on some sweet chemicals, which may have made the best day of my life even better, but that's what it was.

Love,
Juniper

⌐꒰ᔭ꒱

April 5, 2003

Dear Ralph,

I want to thank you for your kindness to Jupiter and to me. I can tell that you hate to be thanked, and I will keep by my promise to hide from Jupiter that there were charges not covered by insurance, and that somebody covered them.

Far beyond that, your kindness in visiting so regularly and in listening so calmly to Juniper's wild ravings—certainly no other human is so susceptible to chemical pleasures—has been so important to both of us.

I know it is excruciating for you to read that, so let me move to what is excruciating to me. Two days ago, you began what seemed to me like a suggestion that we go to dinner or a museum together. If I am wrong, I am willing to be embarrassed. Life is too short to hide behind the fear of being embarrassed. If that's what you meant, I would love to do it (movie or museum or anything else short of extreme sports). If that's not what you meant, just ignore this.

But don't ignore our gratitude, however much you may cringe to have it directed so bluntly at you.

Your friend,
Reba McCloud
Reba McCloud

OFFICE OF SENATOR STROM THURMOND
217 RUSSELL SENATE BUILDING
WASHINGTON, D.C. 20515

April 5, 2003

Dear Juniper,

I am so sorry to hear about your hospitalization---and the pain you must be feeling. Funny how events like these seem to make the world over, place all of us---those hurt and those who care---in another drama, with new parts to play. I don't mean to sound insensitive to your agony, as if it were only a pretend thing. I know it's not a pretend thing, and I am not pretending when I say I wish I could help.

You've been very good to me, Juniper, and tolerant beyond any reason to be. I have a suspicion that I can help best by staying away, and you don't need to pain yourself by confirming that. Do stretch one more time to be kind to me and tell me what I can do to help. Do you need money, magazines, girls, liquor (the best!), a clown act? Anything at all.

Love,
Barton

... As Told to Everett & Kincaid

OFFICE OF SENATOR STROM THURMOND
217 RUSSELL SENATE BUILDING
WASHINGTON, D.C. 20515

April 5, 2003

Dear Martin,

I think I now have this all straight, thanks to Reba on the phone. If Reba in person is anything like Reba on the phone, she must be a stunner and a saint to boot. Far beyond me, that's for sure.

I am very sorry, Martin, that you are in pain. I can also understand acting on an impulse to free yourself from whatever emotions are grinding into your skull---or trying to get out. Others will tell you that the letter I gather you sent to Vendetti was unwise, but I am one who can sympathize and understand that wise or unwise does not enter in: the letter was necessary. It shot out of its own gun.

It is a shame that Juniper got mowed down in fire that was, when you consider it, friendly. The longer I live, the more I think there is never anybody to blame. Not even Vendetti. I hope you agree with me---even now, even where you are.

I am staying away for now, unless BOTH you and Juniper need me. But I am moving neither my body nor my heart from either of you.

Always,
Barton

April 7, 2003

Dear Barton,

Hey Barton, you're so fine! You're so fine you blow my mind. Hey Barton!

You know that song? It's a little young for you and me, but a sweet-spirited song. They play it at the end of a movie called "Bring It On." You'd love it. I did. Reba did. I think Martin didn't see it. He looked alarmed when I recommended it. True, it's about highschool cheerleaders, which arouses some people's resistance. If you don't let that part stall you, you'll be treated to a terrific ride.

Anyway, your letter was sunshine to me. But I shouldn't allow you to feel sorry for me. Better living through chemistry, you know. Whee!

But that's behind me now. It was like a holiday. I'm home now. It's poor Martin who is bunged up.

I keep forgetting to ask or mention or assume out loud: you're back with Strom now, right? All fences mended? All hugs and boo-hoo and kissy?

More shortly and thankee!

Fondly,
Juniper

OFFICE OF SENATOR STROM THURMOND
217 RUSSELL SENATE BUILDING
WASHINGTON, D.C. 20515

April 10, 2003

Juniper McCloud:

I have no idea what you are talking about.

This will be your only warning to desist. Otherwise, I will be forced to take action simply to protect myself. Nobody can blame me for trying to protect myself. Even if they do, I am resolved to keep myself as safe as I can.

You think it's funny. You think I'm funny.

Well, the ha-ha will be on you.

Barton Wilkes
B. Wilkes, Esq.

SIMON & SCHUSTER, INC.
1230 Avenue of the Americas
New York, NY 10020

April 10, 2003

Dear Ms. McCloud,

Thank you.

I've always been suspicious of people who flinch at

expressions of gratitude. Anyhow, please believe me, Ms. McCloud, that I'd be happy to accept your thanks, were I at all deserving of them.

I put your brother in the hospital in the first place, you know. As it turns out, it's not even that I had a reason. Give me a suspicion and a body that's handy and I'll start punching it. That's hardly admirable or deserving of gratitude.

Still, I'm glad I did it, since it gave me a chance to meet you. You seem very nice and I will pick you up Friday at 7 for a movie. Tell me where you live.

Sincerely,
Ralph Vendetti
Ralph Vendetti

OFFICE OF SENATOR STROM THURMOND
217 RUSSELL SENATE BUILDING
WASHINGTON, D.C. 20515

April 11, 2003

Mr. Vendetti
Simon & Schuster
1230 Avenue of the Americas
New York, NY 10020

Dear Mr. Vendetti,

I have an ear for these things, even if seeing is believing. Why should you care? There's no apparent reason, no reason apparent to most. But to me, there is. I just know it. You care. I do not know if you are generally a caring person, and I don't care. Does that surprise you? No it doesn't, and I am the one who knows.

Some people know one thing, some another. I don't dispute that, and I think we would all get on better if we took that for granted. Lyndon Johnson did.

As you know, I am writing to offer myself to you. In every sense of that word (but one). Promiscuity is not my thing, and that's not what I mean anyhow. I am a pro. And in that capacity I am making this offer.

It seems you have managed to disable, in every sense of the word, those who might have helped you. Doubtless some instinct drove you to it. I know that. Those two people, best left nameless as who wants to give them the pleasure? Not me and you. Those two people wouldn't have been the thing anyhow. Not the thing. Not the thing at all. I, on the other hand, am the thing.

Hire me for CLASS ASS. Hire me, work me, use me. I am used to it. I am not used goods. I know use when I see it. I am still of course attached here to the Senator, loosely but unmistakably. (That's all been worked out, our misunderstandings, I mean, if they can even be called that.) The point is that I can easily handle (well) two jobs—or more.

You could come to love me. Even if not, I can make allowances. Should I show up for work in 4 days? Make it 5.

Dutifully,
Barton

OFFICE OF SENATOR STROM THURMOND
217 RUSSELL SENATE BUILDING
WASHINGTON, D.C. 20515

April 12, 2003

Dear Percy and Jimbo,

I have heard nothing from you recently. Oh yes, you have written, but that goes for nothing. I wish I could say that I am not accustomed to such treatment, but I am. You suppose that means there is no end to it, but there is an end. That end is nigh. Even worms turn.

Still, as my uncle used to say, there's no moon like a new moon and no one like you! That's a song, I believe. Do you know it—I mean the lyrics, all of them? The lyric that applies most now is from, you guessed it, Snow White and the lovely song sung by her little friends as they go, in their words, "off to work." The most memorable part comes in Verse 2:

When there's too much to do,
Don't let it bother you!
Forget your troubles;
Try to be
Just like the cheerful chickadee!

You say you like the idea of a history that is primarily sociocultural, with an emphasis on music, dance, and the domestic arts. And literature. Well, I should think you would like the idea. I don't expect credit for it. I should receive credit, but that's another matter. What one deserves and what one gets seldom mesh like butts and toilet seats.

Here are more materials you should include.

Some white writers, just to give a full context. Also white singers and dancers.

Melville. Comment on the use of point of view in Moby Dick and how it compares/contrasts with point of view in Chestnutt and Morrison.

Show that Joel Chandler Harris was really black. It's not necessary to present this as a DISCOVERY. His blackness is less important IN ITSELF than the implications of that BLACKNESS for literary and cultural history and for the views Strom has about such matters.

Show that Strom himself is an important writer—I include some letters and memos he has sent me, along with 37 speeches, texts of. Show that he is, properly understood, a black writer. Strom has always understood "negro-hood" as a matter of spirit and capacity, at least as much as it is of blood. He thus encompasses but is not limited by his black writer capacities.

It will take all your skill to present this last point persuasively and to control by your prose (and illustrations) how this perfectly just claim is to be understood. It won't do to have it misunderstood. It could be easily caricatured. We know that. Strom knows that. All the same he and I feel you can do it.

Perhaps you should write up these pages right away and forward them.

I think you should be very careful what you say to you-know-who at S&S. Don't say I said anything. If you do, you'll find yourself having to deal with somebody a good deal more able to take care of himself than little junebug. Strom is doing well.

For a period of about 6 weeks when I was in high school, I would meet, every school day, this girl Dawn Ann Blaine in the woods between our houses. There was this small woods between our houses. We'd meet at exactly 6:45 so we could do this thing and still catch the school bus at 6:55. The woods were small and close to the bus stop. It was an urban sort of woods. What thing we'd do was exchange underpants, easier for her than for me, in terms of time, but I was good at it. Never missed the bus. Dawn Ann wasn't what you'd call pretty but she was nice.

Looking back now, I think it's the only innocent thing I ever did in my life.

Help me.

Yours,
B. Wilkes

SIMON & SCHUSTER, INC.
1230 Avenue of the Americas
New York, NY 10020

April 15, 2003

Mr. Barton Wilkes
Washington, D.C.

Dear Mr. Wilkes,
No.

Sincerely,
Ralph Vendetti
Ralph Vendetti

Interoffice Memo

April 15, 2003

Dear Percival,

You know what? I don't know what I'm doing on this project. I thought I did. You thought we did. I just finished up to page 73---I know you've done the bulk of it so far, but pp. 68-73 that I did are real good. Anyhow, I was just steaming along and then this comes from Wilkes.

You get it? Strom as a black writer? But that's not the half of it. Should we be frightened?

Jim

FROM THE DESK OF PERCIVAL EVERETT

April 16, 2003

Dear Jim,

Here's what we do. We write Wilkes a polite and very calm letter, explaining that we love what he says and just need a little time. Then we leave tomorrow for Washington to see Strom. I'll pick you up at 5:30 (in the a.m.—sorry but we want to do this in a day) and we'll get this straightened out.

Don't be scared. And yes, you can have the aisle seat. I know about you and your bladder.

Percival

Here's a copy of the letter to Barton:

Hi Barton,

Many thanks for the suggestions. They fit wonderfully with what we've been doing, and Jim and I were both delighted to get them. We can see now how they fit, though we would never have arrived at anything like this on our own. Yes, you are right about the skill needed to get the major claim established clearly and yet unapologetically. We'll need your help there.

And don't worry about either of us breaking any confidences. We are all professionals here, and you can count on us, professionally and personally.

Your friends,
P & J

[Jim—I know that "professionally and PERSONALLY" is a bit risky, but I figure it's better having him liking us and being a pain in the ass that way than shooting us and being a pain everywhere.]

OFFICE OF SENATOR STROM THURMOND
217 RUSSELL SENATE BUILDING
WASHINGTON, D.C. 20515

April 17, 2003

Dear Jim,

I can interpret your silence only one way. Don't tell me how to interpret it. You think you know, but you don't. How could I have been fooled so badly. You pretend to be one thing but you're another. Now I see.

And pretty soon YOU'LL see.

Barton

OFFICE OF SENATOR STROM THURMOND
217 RUSSELL SENATE BUILDING
WASHINGTON, D.C. 20515

April 17, 2003

Everett:

I thought you were the one I could trust.

I thought our mutual blackness would bond us. I am not black, thank God, but all the same things like that should count for something. It is not all your fault. It is deconstruction and moral relativism. But it really is nobody's fault but yours.

I do what I must do now painfully.

Yo da man.

Barton

OFFICE OF SENATOR STROM THURMOND
217 RUSSELL SENATE BUILDING
WASHINGTON, D.C. 20515

April 17, 2003

Martin,

Why would you lure me in and then throw me back, like a fish hooked out of season?

I know you're in bed, but so what? Hospitals never were fortresses in any time. Don't pretend they are now. What was true for Henry V is true for me. But not for you, apparently.

My family has long memories. Long. This is not a threat, but if you continue in your present conduct it could become one. You think you have it bad now? You in pain now, Martin? Real bad pain? Think of your pain, Martin.

I paid my taxes, honestly. My father always did too. He said one should always favor the government when in doubt. That says it all. Next to my father, Martin, few can stand. Even fewer deserve to live.

Barton

OFFICE OF SENATOR STROM THURMOND
217 RUSSELL SENATE BUILDING
WASHINGTON, D.C. 20515

April 17, 2003

Dear Juniper,

You are worst of all. I know you can be kind. It seems almost whimsical of you to mark me off as the one person to whom you choose not to be kind. I cannot understand that. Is it really something about me, or do you simply get pleasure from the cruelty? Do you masturbate there at your desk, picturing me in agony?

I keep thinking things could have been different. But they won't be because you are who you are. Maybe you can't help yourself.

But you deserve to be punished.

I could change, you know. You don't believe it, don't want to believe it. I can see very clearly when I've got off on the wrong foot and am very adaptable to what other people think. I have always been able to change and make people love me. Even at the age of 2, I could charm anyone, even when at first they didn't like me.

Please don't talk about me when I'm gone.

Barton

OFFICE OF SENATOR STROM THURMOND
217 RUSSELL SENATE BUILDING
WASHINGTON, D.C. 20515

April 17, 2003

Dear Reba,

Of all people to lash out at me and join in the thoughtless persecution of the innocent! I think it's almost enough to make me give up, to find you in this crowd. Others I can stand against. I can fight. I am no coward. But when I see you there, I falter. I can see you so plainly.

You really have the kindest face. You'll think I haven't seen it, but I have. Your brother once showed me a picture. He was very kind then too. I don't know what happened. I mean, what changed things? I try to remember, but I can't. That ever happen to you? All of a sudden everything is different and you can't trace why? I don't suppose it matters. We have to live with what is. Play it as it lays.

Honey you been dealt a winning hand. That's what Maria says in Play it As it Lays. I like that book. She also says, "Maybe I was holding all the aces, but what was the game?" I didn't use to understand that.

I'd like to get back to where I was, I guess. That occurs to me a lot. Maria would say there wasn't any "back there" and there sure isn't any now. That's so. Sometimes I remember it, though. I know I'm fooling myself. After Dawn Ann that I told you about, nothing has been very steady. Maybe Dawn Ann I'm making up. Did I tell you about her and me? Nothing to tell, really. At least that's good.

I can only see one way to go with this, Reba, and that is to clear my path. Clear it. Once it's clear, I can go.

Sincerely,
Barton

KINCAID AND EVERETT VISIT THURMOND AT HIS OFFICE

Jim and I took the Metro from National Airport (now sadly called Reagan Airport). We'd decided that another visit to the Senator was in order, needed, important. This then will be a description, if not a transcript, of that encounter. Jim, as you may have gathered from our correspondence, is an open and friendly person, possessed of a mean streak, but fun and loveable nonetheless. On the Metro he smiled at people and even once said to an Asian woman, who possibly didn't speak English given the way she stared at us, "We're on our way to see Strom Thurmond. Working on a book. There's a crazy man involved and we're somewhat afraid for our lives. Are you from Washington?"

"Jim," I said, pulling him by the tie he'd insisted on wearing, "leave her alone."

He straightened his tie and I looked at my own. He'd insisted I wear one as well. I can't recall his argument, but it seemed compelling at the time. Now, I was just uncomfortable. We'd called ahead of time and Thurmond was expecting us, so our names were on the list to get into the building. Still, Thurmond was not in his office. The place was buzzing with activity, aides and interns, secretaries and a detachment of South Carolina State Highway Patrolmen. As well, the space was being shared by the staff of Tom Daschle, his office still unfit for occupation.

"Are you seeing this?" Jim asked.

I didn't say anything. That was my affirmative response. Tom Daschle's people were mid-twenties to early thirties, mostly male, mostly homely, furrow-browed and pasty. Thurmond's crew was early twenties, cute in the South Carolina young beach Christian sort of way and white, white, white. Except for one black woman who was simply white, white. Her name was Dora and she had one of the best accents I ever heard.

"Are y'all the writers?" she asked.

"Yes, we are," Jim said.

Dora looked at me. "You're the one who started all that flag business, aren't you?" she said.

"I guess."

To Jim, "The Senator isn't in the office."

"We were told he'd be here," I said.

"He's here," she said, with what might be called a "tone," and added, "He just isn't in the office."

Two other aides stepped over. Dora introduced the blond bookends as Mary Lyn and Melinda Sharinda. "These here are the writers who are helping Daddy Strom with his book," Dora said.

"Daddy Strom?" Jim and I said together.

The aides giggled, covering their mouths like shy geishas.

"Where can we find the good Daddy?" Jim asked.

"He's downstairs in the gym. He's playing racquetball," Dora said.

"Racquetball?" I asked.

"Yes," said Mary Lyn. "He plays every Thursday with Senator Kennedy. Just take the elevator to the basement, the guards will direct you."

We rode down to the basement, walked past a couple of frozen-faced Marines, and found ourselves standing in front of a glass wall, peering in at a marvel of nature. Two of them. Thurmond, though slow, was moving about the court, whacking the blue ball, his spindly legs poking out of orange Clemson trunks. Ted Kennedy was leaning against the left wall, hands on his knees, stretching the fabric of his pantaloon-like sweat pants. Kennedy was not paying attention to the ball at all, but seemed to be concentrating on each and every panted breath.

"Nine zip, Teddy, old boy," Thurmond said.

The Senators came off the court. Kennedy stumbled wordlessly past us to the locker room. Thurmond stepped spryly and tossed himself into a wheelchair. We were somewhat startled by the sudden appearance of the thing, pushed of course by Hollis.

"A pleasure to see you boys," Thurmond said. "Of course, at my age, it's a pleasure to see anyone."

"Senator," I said. "Mr. Hollis."

"Follow me," Thurmond said.

We followed him to the door marked "Lockers of the Male Senators of the United States." Thurmond stopped and turned to me. "This is as far as you go," he said.

"Excuse me," I said.

"Kincaid can come in, but you can't."

Jim and I exchanged the proper glances.

"Gotcha," Thurmond said. Then he and Hollis laughed.

"That's a good one, Senator," Jim said.

"Take a steam with me, boys," Thurmond said. "Hollis will show you the guest lockers."

Jim, though a little shy about his body, undressed in front of me and I in front of him. We wrapped ourselves in the thick towels (nothing like the napkins passed out at my gym) and found our way to the steam. Hollis was stationed, in tie and jacket, at the door.

"You're not coming in?" Jim asked.

"No, sir," Hollis said. Then he let go a slight smile.

"Over here," Thurmond said as we entered. "Come over here and sit by me."

We found him and sat on either side of him on the tile bench. A few men sat scattered throughout the room. A man in a suit sat some ten feet from us.

"Who's that?" I asked.

"That's Tillman," Thurmond said. "He's a SLED man. State Law Enforcement Department, South Carolina. He's around all the time. Sometimes you see him, sometimes you don't, but he's always around."

"Was he at your house when we visited?" Jim asked.

"You betcha he was."

"Where was he?" I asked.

Thurmond shrugged.

We sat for a minute and sucked in the steam.

"What do you think of these towels?" Thurmond asked.

"Very nice," I said.

"Nothing but the best up here on the Hill." Thurmond stroked the towel covering his middle. "Egyptian cotton. Can you believe that? Goddamn cottom from a bunch of ragheads. We grow the best cotton in the world in South Carolina and Alabama and I'm sitting here with Egyptian cotton covering my ding-dong. What do you think of that?"

"What do you think, Jim?" I asked.

"I think it's a damn shame," Jim said.

"You're goddamn right, Kincaid."

Thurmond hummed a tune for a long minute.

I was about to speak when Thurmond started.

"I've got one for you. What do you say to a redneck in a suit?"

"What?" Jim asked.

"Will the defendant please rise." Thurmond giggled a bit, then added, "I used to tell that with 'N' word. But I grew older. I grew up. Hell, I keep growing up. Nobody appreciates it, but I'm a different man from the man who was governor of South Carolina." He leaned forward and put his elbows on his knees. "I think these steams might be the secret to my longevity. Steams and exercise. I used to be a high school coach. I'm as fit as I was then. I suppose Kennedy could say the same thing, but he'd mean something different."

Jim cleared his throat. "We're here because we're still experiencing a series of intellectual hurdles in figuring out just what you and the publisher have signed us on to facilitate or accomplish."

After a silent beat, I said, "We don't know what the hell we're doing."

"Oh, well, sons, that's simple. You've been hired to eradicate an image, regardless of its apparent or actual truth. You've been hired to make me a national hero to all Americans, to make it clear that I have been misunderstood my whole career, to put my face on a stamp, on the nickel or a fifty-cent piece."

Jim and I were stunned at the clarity of Thurmond's statement; we shared a glance.

Then Thurmond said, "What the hell am I saying? I've watched the colored people of this country rise from sharecroppers to good, decent, hard-working members of society. The good ones anyway. The good ones are just like any white person. They just happen to be brown or some shade thereof. I knew some Negroes back in South Carolina who were as white as you, Kincaid, with blue eyes and blond hair."

"How'd you know they were black?" Jim asked.

"Because they are," Thurmond said. "If you saw an all-white eagle fly down you'd say, 'Look at that white eagle.' Same thing. Don't you think, Everett?"

Jim appealed to me with his eyes, trying to calm me. But perhaps he was telling me to let the old sonofabitch have it. Anyway, I said, "Senator, we're here to ask you if you simply want us to write what you believe to be the history of African-Americans or if you'd like us to paint a pretty picture of the misery, destruction and lies you've contributed to black life."

"I don't think I like the sound of that," Thurmond said. "Say it again."

"Do you want us to tell the truth or lie?" I asked.

"Why, son, I expect you to lie. All truth needs some lies to keep it honest."

"You don't believe that," Jim said.

"Of course I do," Thurmond said. "And I'm right. I'm a thousand years old. I think I know a little more than you whippersnappers." Thurmond coughed up some phlegm and spat it onto the floor we couldn't see. "Let me tell you a story. When I was a boy my daddy forbade me to go to the town square where a bunch of Klansmen were going to lynch this poor colored man. But I went anyway. I sneaked out the kitchen, past my mother. She didn't cook often, but when she did, it was good. She was cooking up some candied yams that day and I remember the smell was just marvelous. Do you like the smell of cooking candied yams, Everett? I don't bother asking Kincaid because I know he's from North Dakota."

"Ohio," Jim said.

"Same thing. So, I sneaked past her. I couldn't have been more than ten. Have I told you this story? It doesn't matter. I never tell it the same way twice. That's what I mean about truth. I sneaked into the town square trying to see through the sea of bodies. Then I saw them string that poor boy up. His legs jerked and his feet wiggled. His eyes were open the whole time and I remembered that I had seen the boy before, on the street when my daddy and I were on our way home from Sunday school. He had beautiful hands. I remember that vividly. Long, thin fingers. I'll bet you anything he played the piano or maybe the organ in church. Anyway, Daddy caught me sneaking back into the house and he knew sure as a frog's got no hair where I'd been. 'Get a good look?' he asked. I told him I had. Then he asked me if it was ugly and I told him it was. I told him about the man's hands and he said it was all a waste. He said he knew that man to be a good colored and it was a shame to lose him."

"Okay, okay," I said. I felt my blood pressure rising and I made a mental note to see my doctor when I got home. "Are we allowed to editorialize or interpret what you pass on to us?"

"By all means, but my people get to approve your interpretation. I think that's only fair."

"That sucks," Jim said. "We're not free to write anything then."

"This is my book," Thurmond said. He adjusted the towel over his lap. "Hollis!"

Hollis came, suit and all. "Senator?"

"Have my chair brought in here. I don't feel like walking. And I feel like spending the night over at Walter Reed."

While the Marine struggled with Thurmond and the chair, Jim and I watched without speaking.

"Egyptian cotton," Thurmond spat.

April 20, 2003

Dear Barton,

Of course I know what you mean. You mustn't think that you are alone in finding the world suddenly changing, waking up to find yourself in a new land. One minute you're doing fine and can count on the people around you and can count on yourself. The next minute you can't.

Barton, I know you are frightened, but there's nothing that some relaxing chat won't cure. Most of all, I can see that you are blaming yourself, imagining that somehow you've failed everybody. I know you are lashing out at others, but you don't mean to do it. It's your way of handling a confusing problem. But Barton Wilkes would never hurt another creature. Your way is to help and heal. I can tell.

Why don't you come down and see me---or we could meet

where you say. Don't be frightened. I won't propose marriage or try to initiate you into a cult. I think we could have a nice afternoon talking. I think you would like it too.

Juniper and my friend Septic will probably drop by too, but not until you and I have had a chance to swap stories about what an uncertain world this is and how uncertain our own minds are to us. You're not alone in this, Barton, nor am I. We're not alone, you and I.

Fondly,
Reba

April 20, 2003

Dear Percival Everett and James Kincaid,

Did I ever tell you of what happened to Johnson Trotter? No? Well, I will. Johnson Trotter was the only son of the Trotters, who owned the jewelry store. It was a family with lots of money, most of which didn't come from the jewelry store, if you know what I mean. Johnson was one of those rich kids who try to be just like everybody else. He didn't dress any different, wore his hair like the rest of us, didn't have manicures (I did), and didn't even have his own car. He was kind of quiet and he hung around me a lot. I wrote stories then and Johnson Trotter said he liked them. Don't get me wrong. Johnson Trotter and I weren't handling one another behind the barn. I was very modest and he pretended to be. I never even saw Johnson Trotter's underpants, that's how clean and good our friendship was. The summer we were 16, I remember we were 16, his parents told him he had to go to Europe with them to see the sights. He said he wanted to invite me to go along. They said sure. I knew they were doing it to embarrass me, though, so I said no. Johnson Trotter told his parents that if I didn't go, he was going to stay behind. He asked me if he could stay with me and I said no. I didn't think he was trying to embarrass me, even then, but I was embarrassed. Really I was ashamed. So he said he would stay at the hotel. But I told him to go, that I didn't want him around. He went and got killed there, that summer. He died, I mean. Something got stuck in him and they did surgery and he died. And I never saw him again. It's all I ever wanted was to see him again.

I know the lives you two lead. I will admit I am surprised. Yesterday, Everett spent the whole day, though it was a school day, feeding a lot of animals, building a trellis or something for grapes I guess, digging a hole that has no purpose I can see, and gabbing with a woman I suppose is his wife. He did peck around at his computer a bit and read some papers. He went into a building with no windows, and I don't know why. I did catch a glimpse. Looks like a hideout to me. The day before, Kincaid got up real early with another woman (not the same woman at Everett's) and made some kind of health breakfast. I should say that both these women are good looking, which is the last way you'd describe E and K. Anyhow, after the woman left, K did some hopeless treadmilling at a speed appropriate for the crawling bug he is. Then he ate some candy and pecked away for hours at his computer—when he wasn't accessing sports sites to read about various professional teams from Pittsburgh. He also dug around a little in the dirt, but did not produce a hole. He seems less fit than E.

What does this tell you? Let's just say that I don't miss much. Perhaps you will take steps. That's what you're thinking. But I have already taken those steps. Any steps you take will lead you to where I already am. I'd think twice about going there if I were you.

Barton Wilkes

Interoffice Memo

April 22, 2003

Percival---

For once, you're listening to me. I have this student who works for school security. He knows that world of security and body-guards and general tough guys. He says he can get us a good rate on round-the-clock protection. I figure the school will cover it. I gave him a tentative go-ahead, wanting to confirm this with you. Confirmed?

Jim

From the Desk of Percival Everett

Jim---

Yeah, so he's looking in our windows. So what? If he wanted to hurt us, he'd do that. Probably he just wants to be invited inside. Whichever one of us sees him first ought to give him a beer (in your case, a diet Shasta, you cheap fuck) and ask him how his life is, after Strom. He must actually NOT be with Strom. But who knows? Wish we at least knew that. Maybe we can help him.

What on earth were you doing digging? Digging what? Watch yourself, Chubbo; you get all enthused with those uppers you take and imagine you're 62 again.

P

April 23, 2002

Mr. Martin Snell
Editor
Simon & Schuster

Dear Mr. Snell,

I am sorry to have missed your phone calls, but I do very much appreciate your interest in my book. I guess you are senior editor there?

Anyhow, Mr. Snell, I am a bit confused. I had been led to believe by Mr. McCloud that I was working with another editor, Ralph Vendetti. Is that not so? Please do not suppose I am trying any end-runs here or that I am trying to cause confusion. I'd just like to be less confused myself.

It may be a labor of Hercules to make me unconfused, but I would appreciate it so much if you could try.

Cordially,

Septic

p.s. I do not mean to ignore your questions about my past life or your inquiries about "contacts." It's just that I am in a position now where all of that, all that happened to me and all that I was, really is past—or so I hope. I wrote the novel to get control of that and give it form, to probe and question it but also close it off. You'll understand that, having done that, I am reluctant to revisit it in any other context. Also, despite the novel, I do not wish to exploit those experiences. I wrote the novel to help myself and to help others too. That probably sounds naïve, but it is so.

April 23, 2003

Dear Ralph,

I know I will irritate you horribly by appealing to your <u>kindness</u> and calling your kindness by its right name. You'll sputter and snort and be rude to the next three or four people who cross your path. That's just too bad. I want you to do a kind thing. It makes no business sense at all, this thing I want you to do, and it will settle smack into your round lap the most troublesome and wiggly of gifted and unstable babies to take care of. He'll make demands on your time, your consideration, and your passion. He'll force you to listen to what you do not want to hear and extend your interests to where they do not want to go. He is, as you would put it, a needy son of a bitch, and the person he needs is YOU.

Barton Wilkes, you've heard of him, former aide of some sort to Senator Thurmond and plague for some time of Martin Snell. That fact alone ought to make your heart leap out to enfold him, were your heart a ready leaper.

You would add stars to your crown by employing him, specifically to edit and consult on CLASS ASS. Given steady and focussed work, in a professional environment that would be stable and unquestioning, he'll be a real asset to you. He is smart. All you need to do is let him work, listen to him, and (hardest of all) don't confuse him by being (a) rude, (b) ironic, or (c) inconsistent.

Add to that a few hugs now and then, some inquiries after the state of his feelings, and the occasional tear, and you'll have the employee of your dreams. Well, not YOUR dreams, but anybody else's.

Do it for me?

Fondly,
Reba

You wonder why I am asking. Well, Barton is a curiosity, but he also went out of his way to help my brother Juniper, forcing Mr. Snell to re-employ him. Add that to your suspicion that I am a meddling do-gooder and you got it!

April 23, 2003

Dear Percival and Jim,

I have some inkling of what Barton is like when he's on the rampage, and I hope he hasn't been bothering you too much. I expect he's been bothering you some. Barton's perfectly harmless, you know, and I wouldn't say that were I not sure. Barton on the rampage is a little like Winnie the Pooh out for blood.

The thing to do is find him some focus. He doesn't really need sympathy; he needs work. I'm convinced he's a real pro, smart and efficient, if he's given something to do and a way to spare himself the always-waiting chores of hating himself and imagining that others must too.

C'mon, there must be something there at old USC for him. It's a private school, right, with lots of slush and slop in the way of administrative offices busy doing not much of anything? Barton could write wonderful reports, go on or organize retreats, institute task forces, manage Centers, coordinate initiatives.

I've written to Ralph Vendetti, trying to hook Barton in with him on CLASS ASS, which is going to be a big hit, you just wait. But Ralph has cultivated fangs, which bare themselves at the approach of anybody who might dent his protective shell. Barton is a practiced denter, so I don't know if that'll work out.

Hope you two are flourishing. Must be almost the end of term there, right? I don't suppose you guys teach much, publishing talents that you are. That's a shame, since I can tell how fine you'd be with the kids.

Juniper sends his love, and me too—

Reba

SIMON & SCHUSTER, INC.
1230 Avenue of the Americas
New York, NY 10020

April 25, 2003

Dear Reba,
 My Dad told me he used to go with a bunch of friends to church basketball games in the West Virginia little town he grew up in. They formed an unappointed and unwanted cheering section. He told me one cheer was:

> Methodist Once!
> Methodist Twice!
> Holy Jumpin Jesus Christ!

As for your proposal—Holy Jumpin Jesus Christ! I'll think about it.

Sincerely,
Ralph

James R. Kincaid
University of Southern California
University Park Campus
Los Angeles, CA 90089

April 26, 2003

Dear Barton, Martin, and Reba,

You know, if you take a step back and look at how this picture is forming itself, what you do is what satellites allow us to do with weather patterns and seats high in stadiums allow us to do with football plays or halftime shows. You get to see large movements and convergences that are hidden from you if you are close up. It was Napoleon, I believe, who first started viewing battles from atop hills not too close. That way, he could observe with perfect clarity what the cannon smoke and screaming and things in the way (he was short) would have hidden from him. It's called The Big Picture. It's what God has of us, for instance. Not that I'm God or even Napoleon (though I have had seats very high up in football stadiums, let me tell you), but I think I share that capacity with them. People at our department meetings are always saying to me, "Jim, you never get bogged down in facts."

Anyway, here's what's shaping up. It's shaping up on its own, but if we recognize what's happening we can save time and dollars by doing it faster and better. Martin, you should hire Barton to work on Strom, as he IS the project. Hire Reba too, as she knows Barton's mind and is, I can tell, an excellent illustration and copy-editing person. This team will do the job. And it's the team that destiny is forming in any case.

We're working on redoing the opening section, Percival and I. With that plus the outline you'll see where we are exactly. Have it to you in ten days, and that's not exaggerating.

Barton, I hope you have stopped looking in my windows. It's quite un-nerving, even though neither my wife nor I are especially modest or have anything to hide. It's just that we—make that I— am not easy with having my day logged. I'm sure I waste time, eat too much, dawdle, and, to be frank, do things on the Internet I shouldn't. OK. You got me. But in the scale of human activity, even in the scale of human criminal activity, does what I do weigh heavily?

Let me know when the Barton-Reba-Martin team is set. I'll send tee-shirts.

Best,
Jim

Interoffice Memo

April 26, 2003

Dear Percival,

Why don't you use the customary "Dear" in your salutations to me? By not doing so, you draw attention to your self-conscious avoidance. Avoidance of what? You can, after all, call me "Dear" without suggesting you'd like to fuck. It doesn't mean you're in love with me, pledging to me eternal devotion and a willingness to lend me money. Are you homophobic? Is that it? I wouldn't have thought so, but what else am I to conclude?

But set that aside. I bother you now to tell you that I thought I'd make things easier for us by writing the enclosed, which I sent to

Martin, Barton, and Reba. What I didn't tell them was that we thereby arrange Vendetti, Juniper, and Septic on that whore project and keep them away from us. I think it's an excellent way to distribute and distance our problems and make it appear that it was all a matter of kismet.

You've got to admit I can be cagey when I want!

XOOXOOXOOX,
Jim

FROM THE DESK OF PERCIVAL EVERETT

April 27, 2003

Dear Jim,

If you insist. I don't think I'm homophobic. I admit, though, that the idea of having sex with you doesn't present itself to me, even in nightmares. I avoid the "Dear" to save time and to do what I can to preserve nice words for nice times.

Did you realize you were sending the same xeroxed letter to all 3? That is, you made that plea to Barton about his peeking and the confession about your illegal Internet porn activities to all of them. Did you mean to do that? You think Barton's going to be happy with that? You think Martin is not going to use your confession against you? You think Reba isn't going to think you're trying to get Juniper fired again? You're going to have all three of them swooping down on you, angry and armed.

Just fooling you. Of course you are not in danger—probably.

But your idea of dividing all these people into teams is bad and the particular division you make outlandish. I bet when it was your turn to be captain and pick a team for recess softball you ended up with all second basemen.

Juniper is with Snell, and they'll do the Strom book. We don't want Barton within a million miles of that. We'll handle his continued meddling, but we don't want to give him official status. You want him empowered to force revisions on us?

Anyhow, the big picture you managed to miss, God, is this: Vendetti and Reba are an item, so he'll hire her. Septic, as author, is already there. Reba will cajole Vendetti into hiring Wilkes as well. Lots of cooks, but I imagine Septic's book is already about where it should be, so they'll do no harm.

Next time, lover, find a spot on a hill that's not right behind a tree.

P

April 28, 2003

P---

Horseshit and fuck you!

J

Memo: Septic, Reba McCloud, Barton Wilkes
From: Ralph Vendetti
Date: April 30, 2003

Just to confirm our conversations, some in person and some by phone.

Reba McCloud, hired for this project only, and Barton Wilkes, permanent special field and subject editor working for me, are assigned to do preproduction, marketing, copyediting, permissions, illustrations, and miscellaneous editing for the book known as CLASS ASS by Septic. Septic will be consulted on all details and have the right to appeal any disagreements to me. I trust there will be none. If not, I needn't be involved at all.

Mr. Wilkes, we are especially glad to have you with us and regard ourselves as lucky to have roped you in.

May 1, 2003

Martin:

Barton Wilkes is working for me on the CLASS ASS project. If you had any sense, you'd recognize this as a real break for you. But you don't and you won't. You'll be tempted to ask me questions. Better not.

Also, Reba McCloud has been signed on with a work-for-hire contract, this project only, at least for now. If you bother her in any way, I will eat your eyeballs.

Ralph

May 5, 2003

Dear all,

I remember in some group therapy session I was in—I've participated in so many, I can't keep any of the sessions or the disorders they were designed to keep under control straight—the leader made the observation that truly disgraceful behavior, so long as it is truly excessive, is usually rewarded. She said there were personality types who sensed this and lived their lives on that principle.

I hope I am not one. I'd rather think that I have fallen in among people so gracious that they forgive. I don't think any of you are neurotics who need and thus encourage neurotic (with me, psychotic) behavior for your own ends. I think you are good people who want to help.

It's a corny thing to say, but I feel redeemed. Of course, I've felt redeemed before, in some years several times. Still, I feel that this is different, that I have somehow fallen asleep in a sty and awakened in a new land.

To all of you, you who brought me here, I give you my thanks and the promise for many parties to come. That seems to me much more in your line than apologies. Strangely, parties now seem more in my line too.

Love,
Barton

May 5, 2003

Dear Reba,

Just a short addition to you. What you have done for me is so kind and so uncaused, you make me think of Cordelia. Were I of the stature of Lear, I'd propose that we two go off to prison too, singing old songs and telling old tales. As it is, I'll just say thanks.

Your friend,
Barton

Percival Everett
University of Southern California
University Park Campus
Los Angeles, CA 90089

May 6, 2003

Dear Martin and Juniper,

As promised, here is a draft of the opening pages of A HIS-TORY . . . . This may give you an idea of the tone Jim and I have settled on, of the pace we think fits the Senator's style, and the context we hope to establish. True, it doesn't get down to issues or details, but we think the most interesting thing about this history will be the absence of such things. This will be history without what is usually regarded as an "historical record." In a sense, this will be a far more vivid, even authentic history, in that it not only takes into account a particular perspective on the past, but IS that perspective. We do not make any pretense of empirical justification, of giving a world outside Strom. There is, for Strom and for the reader, no world outside Strom. He never was able to see one or make one. We might call that a tragedy, were it not for the fact that, in this, we are all Strom.

My daddy filled his life and mine with stories, stories that often had a point. It wasn't always very clear what that point was. I meant to say that it wasn't clear to me what the point was; but, come to think of it, I don't think the point was very clear to Daddy either. Maybe it was clear to him and not to me, but possibly it was the other way around, often as not. Maybe he had one point in mind and I garnered another. But what I'm talking about and not getting to is something else entirely. Maybe there weren't any points, just the stories. See what I mean? I am not trying to be fancy, but we Southerners put a lot of stock in stories, not just to entertain ourselves but to tell us and others about the world we live in and how we should live in it.

But maybe the stories were only stories, telling us not one damned thing. Maybe the stories manage to get in between us and a whole lot of nothing. Think maybe? All those stories and all that time spent telling them and listening to them. I wonder now why. It has always made me feel good to tell stories. Early on in politics, I realized that the best answer to a question is a story. People like to hear stories, maybe so they can go tell them to somebody else. But why is that? I always thought it was because stories gave us all something to chew on, set us straight, you know, on issues and the like. But maybe stories did just the opposite: gave us the satisfaction of thinking we were chewing, but there was no meat.

Don't get me wrong. I don't mean to say that stories were lies or that I developed the knack of telling them just to slither my butt out of tight spots. A few of the men I learned county politics from told me that, told me that "old fuck-yer-dog tales" would do more for you with folks around here than any sort of political position. But it wasn't just fuck-yer-dog stories and it wasn't just tight spots. I saw that they used stories all the time and, right away, so did I. Not just fuck-yer-dog stories but bless-your-mother and fling-the-sorghum stories too. Politics is just one story after another, stories inside stories. But I don't know what isn't.

Anyhow, when you look back on your life or, in my case, on the life I have shared with African-American people and their struggles, you realize that all you have are a bunch of stories, stories that may or may not pack a wallop but that certainly don't seem to me to pack anything else—like revelation. Maybe it's just me. That's possible. I've always been a man who knew the lay of the land for twenty yards on every side. Knew every detail. If you train your eyes that way, by frilly damn, you are harder than hell to beat in an election. You become the best politician you can be. Maybe I am the best politician of the twentieth century. I don't know who has won more elections and lost fewer. I also don't know whether that's a good thing to be, whether I haven't paid a high price.

What kind of a history can I write when I never looked past twenty yards? But then I wonder if anybody really does have much more range than that to plow in. What the hell do you say past that point? I mean, who knows what the big issues are anyhow?

My daddy loved to tell a story of Big Ed McClellan, the worst coon hunter in the county. Big Ed had the best dogs anybody could want and he even, it is said, bought a book on coon hunting. He'd lived here all his life, wasn't any youngster, and seems as if he'd done nothing but coon hunt. It wasn't that he was dumb exactly or handicapped, the way some are, with poor eyesight or real strong body smells that make hunting tough. Big Ed was greedy and he was a thinker. It was the last that got him in trouble. No sooner was Big Ed out with his dogs than he started to think. If the dogs headed one way, got a scent, Big Ed would think where other scents might be coming from. If they got a coon treed, he'd think where all the untreed coons was. Also, he'd remember coon hunts before and try to make 'em match up with the one he was on, so he could either copy the success or avoid the failure of the past. The result was he thought so much the coons was as safe with Big Ed hunting them as if they were in a zoo.

You get the moral of that, you kind readers out there? My daddy said the moral was, "When you got a coon treed, keep your eye on that there coon and none other." I was never too sure what that meant and am not too sure to this day. Maybe my daddy thought the idea was to keep a short, unwandering focus. I always thought the moral was to keep to the present, not to imagine that the past had any bearing on it or that the present would have any impact on the future. I guess that view came to be known as a kind of existentialism. That's what an aide of mine said, when I explained my view of that story. But if my view deserved a fancy name it was sure by accident. Anyways, I wonder now if Daddy didn't steer me wrong. Maybe he should have said that Big Ed was simply thinking at the wrong time and that there was a better thing for a thinker to do than go coon hunting.

Worst of all, my daddy taught me to believe that stories had secrets in them and that we could find them or reveal them. You would think such a belief would be good training for a historian, which is what I'm trying to be here. After all, history is just a big story with a lot of little stories inside it. But what if the stories ain't worth a damn? What if there's nothing at all inside them?

But I didn't mean to get off on that. I really meant to be talking about what it means to be a politician and to think always of what you can do right now under these circumstances. The politics I know always involved working as best you could to play a game whose rules were already there when you started. See what I mean? You always have to deal with what's there, whatever it is. Usually what's there is a tangle, some of which makes sense and some of which don't. In the case of the African-American people, lots of what was there might have seemed unfair and cruel to anyone not trying to make things better inside the conditions we had.

Let me try again. Until I started to write all this, I never thought of some things. That's not quite right. I never thought of things outside a certain way, outside the confines of that twenty-yard circle I was telling you about. I never had time, I guess, or the occasion. I wonder now about all that. I wonder if I could have thought different, not different things but in a different way.

Here's an example, just to jump right into the subject. Take schooling for Negroes. Now, when I was growing up, we were surrounded by people, lots of them just no good, who would exercise their lungs hollering against African-American people, "niggers" they called them (a word I never used to denigrate another human being). Long after slavery, long long after, they still didn't want black people to have any education. None at all. "They aren't fit for it!" they'd say. "Makes 'em uppity. Takes money away from decent white folks. Makes 'em think they can take our jobs. Makes 'em think they can take our women!" I don't think people today know how loud these people were or how many there were of them. "Poor white trash" is a phrase that doesn't cover them. Most poor Southern people, like most poor people everywhere, are very good people. I'm talking about scoundrels, and there were lots of them.

Now, my daddy and his friends hated these scoundrels and knew how much damage they did to South Carolina. My daddy and his friends did not hate the Negro. If you won't grant me that, please don't read any more. It's the honest truth. And it's true for me too. Here's how we saw the picture, the twenty yards we saw. It was a white problem, a problem of white scoundrels, not a black problem. I tell you and please believe me: most black people we knew were very hard-working, respectful, Christian people trying to get along in the world without causing trouble. Try not to pin a label on what I just said. I'm not apologizing, just trying to describe the game I grew up inside. I didn't make the rules. I guess I didn't know there were rules. I just saw what was . . . twenty yards around me.

When I got a job as school teacher, then various county posts, then as judge, I saw my work as a game where the players were these: the decent white people, the scoundrel white people, the decent black people. Of course there were black people who were trouble, but not enough to make it into the game. The problems were those of violence and the justification of violence, of the Klan and lynchings and horrible housing and education. At least, that was the world I saw and went to work in. I didn't make that world. I just saw it and lived in it. But I did try to make it better. I worked hard for better black schools, higher pay for the teachers, training in read-ing and writing for black people, even what we now call day care centers, also for black people.

Now people say I was the King of Segregation, that I never saw the answer to all these problems that came to be written: blacks and whites in the same school. That idea wasn't part of the world I was in. It just wasn't. Equality, for me, meant one thing and it meant another to people I couldn't understand.

I'll say this and get it out of my system: They couldn't understand me any better than I could understand them. They had their own twenty yards of compass and I had mine. To make what they saw morally superior to what I saw and to make me seem conniving and evil all along seems to me sim-ply a failure to see that none of us saw very far. I had a debate once with Senator Jake Javitz, a fine man and a dear friend. Javitz was going on about conditions in the segregated South, saying how we were systematically mistreating, deliberately and wantonly, every black citizen. What he was really saying was, "Hey, folks, New York is superior to South Carolina and I, Jake Javitz, am sure as hell superior to Strom Thurmond."

But what was the condition of black men, women, and children in New York? Were their schools better? Their housing? Their jobs? Were they safer, less likely to end up in prison? To his eternal discredit, I must say, Jake really couldn't see the point I was making.

To my eternal discredit, I could never see his. I wish I had been more like Big Ed, looking past the coon up the tree to try and see what the forest looked like.

You get the idea.

Best,
Percival and Jim

Jim

May 9, 2003

Dear Juniper and Reba,

Please rescue me. I was sinking deep in sin, far from the happy shore. Very deeply stained within, sinking to rise no more. But the master of the seas heard my despairing cry: from the waters lifted me, now safe am I.

Be the masters of my seas.

Barton Wilkes I thought was in L.A. but I have too much reason to believe he's not. I swear I saw him outside my apartment. I thought I would die from the shock. You know that scene in "Rear Window" when Jimmy Stewart locks eyes with Raymond Burr through the telescope Stewart has been using? Burr's a killer and now knows Stewart knows and heads right over to silence Stewart. We know all that in a flash as soon as their eyes lock.

Well, I was looking out my apartment window, just like Jimmy Stewart, except of course I was looking at the skies, not in somebody's window, which we all know is against the law. There are several young people in the apartment opposite mine, very nice looking young people, WHICH IS PRECISELY THE REASON I WOULD NOT PEEP AT THEM.

I looked down from the skies, and there on the street corner, sort of as in "The Third Man," stood a man in an overcoat, leaning on a lamppost, smoking a cigarette, and casting a long shadow. Don't tell me I'm hallucinating. I couldn't see his face, but that makes me even more certain it was Barton Wilkes stalking me. Who else would be out there on a foggy night at 3 a.m. or a little after?

Here's my plan. I know you two have moved in together and thus have room for me. I won't take up much space. I'll pay 40% of the rent. Now, that's more than fair. Cooking and cleaning can be divided in thirds. We each get privacy if we want it. No stringing wet underwear over the bathtub, I promise.

Through all kinds of weather! What if the sky should fall? Just as long as we're together, it doesn't matter at all. Though they've all had their quarrels and parted, we'll be the same as we started: Just travelling along, singing a song, side by side.

Love,
Martin

May 11, 2003

Dear Martin,

Reba and I both like your songs. That's a nice touch.
You can bring Pearl; she's a darn nice girl, but don't bring Lulu.

Lulu is the smarty who breaks up every party. Shamalan goo-goo! Don't bring Lulu! I'll bring her myself!

Reba thinks "Shamalan goo-goo" is wrong, but I just listened to the record and I know.

You can tell we're having a nice time here. I am afraid, Martin, that there's no room at all for another. I'm sure you understand. It's not just me and Reba but also our separate guests, who are sometimes or even often here. It's a two bedroom place, and they aren't kidding when they say two bedrooms. There aren't any hidden solariums, offices, studies, guest areas, or even closets.

More importantly, there is nothing to fear from Barton Wilkes. I am surprised you were not included in the conciliatory and kind message he sent out. I understand that he has been employed to work on the CLASS ASS project, which seems to me a splendid idea. (Also, the Strom project will probably go on just fine, allowing Kincaid and Everett to work on what they have so far and what they can worm directly from the Senator.)

Do be reassured, Martin. You sound so very distraught. Maybe you could come over to dinner. I could even invite Barton, just so you'd see. Next Friday?

Till then---

All best,
Juniper

p.s. It's "peaceful shore," Martin, not "happy."

SIMON & SCHUSTER, INC.
1230 Avenue of the Americas
New York, NY 10020

May 13, 2003

Percival Everett
James R. Kincaid
Department of English
University of Southern California
Los Angeles, CA 90089-0354

Dear Professors Everett and Kincaid:

This is to acknowledge receipt of your outline and few beginning pages, forwarded to me as Senior Editor from Martin Snell,
who is serving a probationary period as an assistant editor.

We will be in touch with you in due course.

Sincerely,
Arthur Sullivan
Arthur Sullivan
Senior Editor

May 13, 2003

Reba—
I guess I could bring this up while we're at work, but
that's not what I do. How about going out to the Met---La

Perichole---with me and dinner too on Friday. If you're busy, that's OK.

Ralph

May 15, 2003

Dear Septic,

I know it hasn't been very long, our acquaintance, or very extended, our dating. I know that what you have seen of my past history, even last month's, can't have been very encouraging. Still, I cannot justly or fairly speak for your heart but only my own.

I have felt bewitched since I have been with you, transported. I am aware that these feelings sound very much like being in love, temporary chemically-induced mush and very banal. Worse, very unstable.

So, the fact that I am in love with you is meaningless. You might be in love with me too, but that would also be meaningless. What counts is that I find you beautiful, reliable, kind, and with the sort of generosity that doesn't come from feeling insecure about yourself. I don't think you've outgrown your past or gotten over it or absorbed it. I think your past has nothing to do with you. You have made yourself new. You have made me new. You are also so potently erotic that I don't really care how long it is before we have sex.

Will you marry me?

Love,
Barton

May 17, 2003

Dear Percival and Jim,

I know I am off the case, and I think that's the best thing for the case---not to mention you two, Strom, the book, and me. Still, I wanted to pass along the few tips I had remaining. You two dearies will know what to do with them.

First, I think Strom's ability to connect his public or private life into any kind of coherent or linear story is so limited that you should just give up. He existed always, and exists now, inside the forces he feels, pretty acutely, are pressing on him at that moment. Don't sell him short. He's managed to survive so long by judging these complex, overlapping, layered pressures so astutely that a number of his constituents love him so thoroughly they'd die for him. Even some Senators, and you wouldn't suspect this, like him a lot and respect him, even seek him out.

Second, a man so trained and constituted has the weaknesses of his strengths. There are many. Strom is so sensitive to local and immediate pressures because he has no way of feeling any larger ones. In a way, he never judges or analyzes at all, beyond playing one pressure off against another. He has never considered either the root or the large pattern he operates in and often sets in motion. He works inside an ideology but has no idea what that ideology is. He has no idea that ideology exists.

Second, I'd focus on just a couple of areas, ignoring others.

Ignore anything that happened before Strom was born. His views on slavery, on the War, on 19th-century legislation and court decisions, on Reconstruction are, all of them, not worth hearing.

I'd focus on two areas. One, his childhood and early life in local politics. He is colorful and shrewd on the world he grew up in and on how he acted before he got very important. In those days, he was as much of a free agent as he ever could be. He made some decisions. Later on, he became such a fine politician that he never had to make any decisions. Even the Dixiecrat business was never a decision of his: it was just the result of certain force lines vectoring.

Two, the Civil Rights Bill he signed and the ones he opposed. He is fully aware that he changed with the times and that these Acts pushed him in ways he didn't think he wanted to go, but went anyhow. Strom might come close to telling you that he was never anything more than a sensitive recorder, a kind of conscienceless seismograph. Anyhow, he's troubled about all that and has given the whole period a lot of thought, or what passes with him for thought.

Finally, don't pay any attention to what he says about women. That's just my own view. Actually, I guess it's a request. Strom will talk endlessly and blindly about his success with women and his current performances in various bedrooms and cars. As anyone in Washington will tell you, his office is the main visiting spot for all the male interns working on the Hill, simply because Strom indecently showcases his own harem of young interns, all of them pretty close to parodies of Southern Belles, Little Miss Cotton Blossoms every one. I suppose they are of legal age, but they seem to be about 14. Strom will go through the office, goosing and fondling and pawing. I saw him at a reception this spring posing for a picture with two interns working for another Senator. They heard about Strom and wanted their picture taken with him. Right there, in full view of most of the Senate, with wives and guests, Strom joked loudly with the girls, putting his left hand square on the bosom of one and his right hand up the skirt and onto the ass of the other. I hope you will omit all of this.

Strangely, it's the part of his life that he is proudest of and the one that is least like the political and administrative Strom. Whatever else one might (and should) think about him, he is neither ruthless nor vindictive. He likes almost everyone and tries to shield others from hurt, at least on a local level. But with young women, very young women, he is brutish and cheap.

I'd love to see you if you get to New York. You have been awfully good to me, and I won't embarrass you with more thanks.

Knock 'em dead with STROM.

Your loyal friend,
Barton

⌐ℐ⌐

May 18, 2003

Dear Juniper and Reba,

Pity you're so cramped. I won't reference all I've done for you, since it would amount to nothing more than pouring water on a couple of ducks.

Dinner with Wilkes? What a charming idea—not!

I will manage alone or I will be slaughtered. I simply did not realize I had enemies of so many different stripes.

Our working relation, I trust, will go on as usual.

I may need your help with suggestions on office redecorating. A memo came through that we (editors) will each be allowed $25,000 for redecorating. Not a lot, but I have some friends in the trade and maybe you do too? We'll jolly well spruce up the place. Reba too.

Very cordially yours,
Martin

May 19, 2003

Dear Barton,

I have given much thought to your very sweet letter. I must say that it is probably the most intelligent and demanding proposal letter written recently. I say that only to note what an exceptional man you are, willing to be so trustful and respectful. All of that warms me, Barton, and makes me feel the compliment deeply.

I don't want to keep you waiting for an answer, but yet I don't know what to answer.

As I read your letter, I felt, deep in my heart, the truth of all you were saying. You did not tell me how to feel in return, but there was nothing you said that did not awaken an answering echo in me. I know that's a Victorian phrase, but there's something very Victorian about both of us; and I see nothing wrong with proceeding as if we were in a George Eliot novel.

That may be an unlucky reference, since marriages in Eliot novels so seldom provide happiness for anyone. But I don't foresee any unhappiness for us, any letdown, any disillusionment as we sag into the ruck of one day following another. If we can make one another new, we can work that same magic on time.

So why is my answer not clear? Maybe it is, but I simply cannot summon quite enough self-trust to say it straight out. We haven't known each other long. That doesn't matter at all, we both know, in terms of our sense of what is right and what is possible for the two of us.

I think it matters, though, in terms of the equilibrium I need to gain.

OK?

Love,
Septic

May 24, 2003

Dear Juniper,

I'm once again asking for help in the way of advice. I won't further burden you with apologies, since I know you'll brush them aside anyhow.

You may know that I've asked Septic to marry me. If not, please don't think the advice I'm asking concerns whether I should have done that.

Here's the question. She replied that she was inclined in that direction but needed more time. I didn't answer her letter—I've had it about 6 days—since I thought I might be rushing her.

Should I rush her or wait?

Love,
Barton

May 27, 2003

Dearest Barton,
   Wait.
   When life delivers such great news and brings together two peo-
ple in such perfect symbiosis-----like sharks and those little sucker
fish that attach themselves to them or oaks and lichen----you just
have to say, "Whoopee!" I can't help it, Barton. I'm just so happy.
   I guess I am happy for you, but it feels like I am happy for me.
   Can I be your best man?
   Don't wait more than two weeks, though.

Love,
Juniper

May 30, 2003

Dear Reba,
   Have I done the right thing? Barton proposed to me in such
a fine letter. I didn't say yes or no, but I didn't leave a lot of
room for no. I didn't want to.

Love,
Septic

June 2, 2003

Dear Septic,

Of course you haven't done the right thing. But what the hell.
You're doing what you're doing, and I will be head cheerleader
for you. (I'll need to get new tights, though, having split mine at
the big last game of the year against McKinley Heights, though
that's another story.)

Have I done the right thing?

I've been spending more time every day with Ralph. I thought it
was just habit, that he was easy and comfy. Well, he is easy and comfy,
in his uneasy and uncomfortable way, but he is so many other
things. Of course he never says a word about what's happening, but
it's almost like it's happening without either of us bothering to
mention what it is that's happening----whatever that might be.

Am I wrong?

Love,
Reba

June 5, 2003

Dearest friend,
   You're as wrong as wrong can be.
   We ought to set up as Advice Columnists.

Love,
Septic

SIMON & SCHUSTER, INC.
1230 Avenue of the Americas
New York, NY 10020

To: Juniper McCloud, Ralph Vendetti, Arthur Sullivan,
        Reba McCloud, James Kincaid, Percival Everett,
        Barton Wilkes, Septic, Miss Mary Jane Dawkins
From: Martin "Up a little, please" Snell
Date: June 10, 2003

I thought I had the date wrong, but I didn't. Next week
is Flag Day.
PARTY!!!!! MY PLACE!!!!! 5:30 P.M.
Costumes are required. Dress in—you guessed it—a flag.
Drape yourself. Let a flag be your umbrella on a rainy,
rainy day.
Flags only. No other drapery. Shoes OK and hats.
The smaller the country, the smaller the flag.
Hint—I'm coming as Monaco.
Theme of the Party—MAKE UP AND MAKE OUT.
The moon belongs to everyone—and there's worse things
in life than me.

June 10, 2003

Dear Reba,
 I would really like it if you would marry me. I can't imagine why you'd like it or why my liking it would be much of an inducement, but if you're willing, Barkis, then WOT LARX.

Love,
Ralph

June 10, 2003

Dear Professors Everett and Kincaid,
 It strikes my old pate that we should be getting this book done. You up for it?
 I should ask if you are up for dinner with me. My place. Next Tuesday? That not good for you, Monday is OK too.

Devotedly,
Strom

DINNER WITH STROM

Saturday, 6:00 PM, Washington, D.C., a rental car, some kind of mid-size Ford with ice-cold air-conditioning that can't be shut off or turned down. Everett is driving. Somewhere on Wisconsin Ave. approaching M Street:

KINCAID: God, it's cold in here. My nipples are hard.

EVERETT: That's a little more than I needed to know.

KINCAID: Do we really have to do this?

EVERETT: What are you griping about? You're not the one he insults.

KINCAID: Yes, and how insulting is that?

EVERETT: What?

KINCAID: It's like being found attractive by the ugliest girl at the party. Imagine how I feel not being insulted by the good Senator.

EVERETT: That's perverse, but I'm afraid I get it. You know, I think we should simply publish our correspondence on this thing and call it quits. Or go on with our fake Strom voice.

KINCAID: That's what I think. We'll never figure out what's in his head.

EVERETT: I have figured that much out.

KINCAID: Well, yeah.

EVERETT: A parking space right in front. That's a bad omen.

KINCAID: Omens. I don't believe in omens. I bet you could turn to religion in a really bad time.

EVERETT: Any minute now.

KINCAID: How do I look?

EVERETT: [nothing]

KINCAID: What is it?

EVERETT: I'm looking for a hint of irony in your question.

The door is opened by Hollis.

EVERETT: Hello, Mr. Hollis.

HOLLIS: Mr. Everett. Mr. Kincaid. The Senator is in the media room. If you'll follow me.

THURMOND: Hi, boys. You'll forgive me if I don't get up. I'm just watching the end of *Flubber*. God, I love this picture. This and *Gone With the Wind* are my favorite movies. Have you ever seen *Flubber*?

KINCAID: I think so. Long ago.

EVERETT: No.

THURMOND: You think they could really make up some stuff like that? This is the part I really love. Ha! That cracks me up.

HOLLIS: Sir, I'll get your coat.

THURMOND: Hollis, go get my coat. I can't keep these boys waiting. I'm sure they're hungry enough to eat a...a...a...

HOLLIS: Cow, sir?

THURMOND: Cow. Mr. Kincaid, have you ever milked a cow?

KINCAID: When I was a boy, I did once.

THURMOND: Good man. Ever see *Gone With the Wind?*

KINCAID: Senator?

THURMOND: *Gone With the Wind,* ever see it?

KINCAID: Long ago.

THURMOND: What about you, Mr. Everett?

EVERETT: No.

THURMOND: I don't blame you. If I was colored, I wouldn't see it either. You boys ready to go?

The BOYS: We're ready.

THURMOND: Head 'em up and move 'em out. Mr. Kincaid, you ever milk a cow?

KINCAID: No.

Restaurant in Georgetown—Estelle's Southern Cuisine

THURMOND: Is this table okay? It's my usual place. I like to be close to the toilet.

EVERETT: It's fine. We might find it convenient as well.

KINCAID: [pointing to a nearby table] Is that . . .

THURMOND: Tillman. You've met him, I'm sure. He's always around. He's here to keep some commie pinko bastard hippie lowlife from trying to cheat me out of the last couple years of my life.

EVERETT: Yes, these are your golden years.

THURMOND: You bet your sweet ass. The food is great here, just like my mammy used to make when I was a young whippersnapper. I especially like the fried okra and the lima beans. Their cornbread makes me feel like I'm home.

EVERETT: We've been considering abandoning the project.

THURMOND: Do you like grits?

EVERETT: There's a raging fire behind you.

THURMOND: There's nothing better than grits for supper.

EVERETT: [to Kincaid] He's gone.

KINCAID: Senator, we're not going to write *your* goddamn book.

THURMOND: Kincaid, why are you swearing?

EVERETT: [taps Thurmond] Senator?

THURMOND: I'm sorry, Mr. Everett, but I can't hear anything on my left side.

EVERETT: Jim, tell him we're leaving.

KINCAID: Percival wants me to tell you that we're leaving.

THURMOND: Why, boys? I thought we were just coming to some kind of understanding.

KINCAID: We can't figure out what you want this book to be.

THURMOND: It's supposed to be a book. The title is *A History of the Colored People by Senator Strom Thurmond, America's Oldest Living Lawmaker.* What's so hard about that?

EVERETT: Tell him he needs to find some other guys, some Bible college professors maybe, to write *his* book.

KINCAID: You might be better off hiring somebody closer to your own politics to write *your* book. We're going to write *ours*.

THURMOND: But I want Everett. He's from the South. He's colored. That's a good thing, for my book anyway. I don't know you, Kincaid, from Adam, but you're a Yankee and that's kinda like being colored, in some people's eyes anyway. Are you boys serious about leaving?

KINCAID: We're serious, very serious.

THURMOND: Well, I'm not listening. You boys think it over some more. We'll just eat tonight. You can ask me questions and I'll answer them and then you decide. Where're you going, Mr. Everett?

EVERETT: I'm just moving over here next to Jim so you can hear me better. How's this? Can you hear me?

THURMOND: Yes.

EVERETT: We're doing *our* book, not yours.

THURMOND: Let's talk about this.

Clarence Thomas stops by the table.

THOMAS: Senator Thurmond.

Tillman stands.

THOMAS: Senator, it's me, Justice Thomas.

THURMOND: It's okay, Tillman. It's Justice Tom. Tom, how are you?

THOMAS: I'm fine. How about you?

THURMOND: If I were any finer, I'd be sick. Justice Tom, I'd like you to meet Professors Kincaid and Everett. Gentlemen, I'd like you to meet Justice Charles Thomas.

THOMAS: Pleased to meet you.

THURMOND: The professors here are helping me with my book. It's about your people.

THOMAS: Republicans? [Thomas and Thurmond laugh]

THURMOND: Remember that song we sang at your house the night of your confirmation?

THURMOND and THOMAS: [to the tune of the Fats Domino song] I found my thrill on Anita Hill. [they laugh]

THOMAS: Let me tell you a story about this man. One night I was standing on E Street, outside the Corcoran Museum, in the pouring rain. It was coming down in sheets and not a single taxi would stop for me. I waved at one after another and none stopped. The drivers would look at me and just drive by. Then the Senator came out and he put up one finger and three cabs pulled up. Of course he let me take one. That was some night.

THURMOND: Where are you sitting?

THOMAS: We're over by the kitchen. In fact, I'd better get back over there. I think my food's arriving. I really hate cold chitterlings.

THURMOND: See you later, sweet tater. He's a good boy, that Clevon. Dumb as a plucked chicken in a truck, but a good boy.

EVERETT: What do you mean by a "good boy"?

THURMOND: You know, does his job, doesn't try to upset the pineapple cart.

KINCAID: Kisses ass.

THURMOND: [laughs] He has beautiful hands. Did you notice them?

EVERETT: Do you think he belongs on the Supreme Court?

THURMOND: Why not?

EVERETT: You just said he was dumb.

THURMOND: Lots of people are dumb. So what? He's not so dumb that he's not useful. Hell, nobody's that dumb. Except maybe that Clinton. He just couldn't keep his puppy in the house. Well, nobody can really, but he let everybody know about it. It's good to let people play with your puppy, but hell, you can't put a big neon collar on it with your name and address and everything. You've got to be discreet. Tom wasn't too discreet with that Blueberry Hill woman, but we got him out of that mess. We need more like him.

KINCAID: Let me ask you this: Do you believe that black people have it better now than they did in 1950?

THURMOND: What do you mean by "better"?

KINCAID: Do you think black people are treated equally?

THURMOND: I believe they always have been treated equally. They had less, but, hell, that's just the way it was. If they had the money, they could have bought what I bought in 1950.

EVERETT: An education?

THURMOND: Of course.

EVERETT: Equal education?

THURMOND: Yes. Equal, however separate. But that's all changed now. Heck mercy, man, you teach with Kincaid here at that College of South California?

KINCAID: Lordy.

THURMOND: This happened in the war. I was a tank commander and I was at the Battle of the Bulge. We were well away from the front line, but I could hear the artillery all night and the real distant bangs of mortar fire. It was cold and wet and we were stuck in the holler waiting for orders. It was a mess. About four hundred men stuck in there and I remember a lot of them boys were from New Jersey for some reason. Where it wasn't muddy, the ground was frozen hard. So when those Negro soldiers showed up, we put them right to work digging us some latrines. Boy, they really saved the day for us. As I remember, they dug real nice latrines. They tickled me too, the way they wanted to go fight some Germans. Those diggers were a godsend.

KINCAID: That's some story.

THURMOND: You see, that's partly why I want to write this book. I want the diggers of the world to know that I appreciate them. I want them to know that we white people don't think of them simply as dirty diggers or lazy diggers or even agitating diggers.

EVERETT: You really are nuts, aren't you?

THURMOND: I don't mean to be offensive.

KINCAID: God just made you that way.

THURMOND: God. That's the other reason. I'm getting old. I don't know if you noticed. I know I'm not going to live forever. And when I die I'd like to have a seat at the big party, if you know what I mean. You probably don't. I'm talking about heaven, boys. I'm cramming for finals, trying to make amends, trying to have my parking ticket validated.

EVERETT: Even if the cows have already left the barn.

THURMOND: I realize I've done some underhanded things and that I've hurt a lot of colored people. But hell, I hope I've hurt as many liberals and Jews. But we're all Americans, aren't we? And that's what counts. The world has changed. You got that Colin Powell now and that Rice woman in the damn White House with a Republican president. Granted, he ain't the sharpest hoe in the shed, but he is a Republican, and peaches grow in trees and not on vines, you know what I'm saying? Times are different. Now we got Muslims and Arabs to hate. You know a lot of them are pretty dark. What's that tell you?

EVERETT: Okay, that's enough.

KINCAID: Let's go.

THURMOND: But we haven't eaten.

Everett and Kincaid walk to the door. Thurmond follows.

THURMOND: Wait up, fellas. Maybe we could just hang out.

KINCAID: Where did we park?

EVERETT: Hell if I know.

THURMOND: The air out here is nice, ain't it. Hey, watch this.

EVERETT: He's standing on his head again.

KINCAID: I think we parked up that way.

EVERETT: Jim?

KINCAID: Yeah?

EVERETT: He looks funny.

KINCAID: What do you mean?

EVERETT: Look at his face. And he's not talking.

KINCAID: Oh, shit.

EVERETT: Where's Tillman? Tillman!

TILLMAN: What is it?

EVERETT: He's not talking.

TILLMAN: Oh, shit.

KINCAID: What is it, Tillman?

TILLMAN: Fucking shit.

EVERETT: He's dead.

KINCAID: Dead?

EVERETT: You know, not alive.

TILLMAN: Shit, shit, shit. Hollis! Hollis! [pulls out his cellular phone] Hollis! Where are you? Well, get the car over here.

EVERETT: Shouldn't you get him down?

TILLMAN: I think you two should just get out of here.

KINCAID: I'm for that.

MAN IN RAGS AND A SHOPPING CART: Senator Thurmond?

TILLMAN: Stand clear, sir.

MAN IN RAGS: That's Senator Thurmond.

WOMAN IN A TIGHT RED DRESS: Look at that man on his head.

MAN IN RAGS: That's Senator Strom Thurmond.

TILLMAN: Everybody get back.

HOLLIS: Oh my good lord. Tillman, help me get him into the car.

EVERETT: Jim, let's get out of here.

HOLLIS: Watch his head.

TILLMAN: Why?

Simon & Schuster, Inc.
1230 Avenue of the Americas
New York, NY 10020

June 23, 2003

Professor Percival Everett
Professor James Kincaid
Department of English
University of Southern California
Los Angeles, CA 90089-0354

Dear Sirs:

    I regret to inform you that the materials you have sent us do not justify our going forward with this project. By actually reading the contract, you will see that we are simply exercising our rights, enumerated therein in any number of clauses.

We wish you all good fortune in finding another publisher. I am sure you will have no difficulty doing so.

Sincerely,
Arthur Sullivan
Arthur S. Sullivan
Senior Editor

Other selections in the AKASHIC URBAN SURREAL series

DON DIMAIO OF LA PLATA
by Robert Arellano
200 pages, a trade paperback original, $13.95, ISBN: 1-888451-51-3
"Fear and loathing with Don Quixote at your side! Herein another savage journey to the heart of the American dream—but with *sabor* and *saber latino.*"
—Ilan Stavans, author of *Spanglish: The Making of a New American Language*

BOY GENIUS by Yongsoo Park
232 pages, a trade paperback original, $14.95, ISBN: 1-888451-24-6
"*Boy Genius* is a modern-day *Candide* . . . Yongsoo Park's combination of popular culture, high ideals, comedy, and serious intent makes for a joyride of a read."
—*Education Digest*
"Superb writing!" —*Clamor Magazine*

MANHATTAN LOVERBOY by Arthur Nersesian
*From the author of the cult-classic bestseller *The Fuck-Up**
203 pages, a trade paperback original, $13.95, ISBN: 1-888451-09-2
"*Manhattan Loverboy* is paranoid fantasy and fantastic comedy in the service of social realism, using the methods of L. Frank Baum's *Wizard of Oz* or Kafka's *The Trial* to update the picaresque urban chronicles of Augie March, with a far darker edge . . ." —*Downtown Magazine*

Also available from Akashic Books

LIMBO by Sean Keith Henry
270 pages, trade paperback, $15.95, ISBN: 1-888451-55-6
"*Limbo* is a smart, honest novel about displacement and the meaning of home. It struggles in turn with the embracing of identity and the welcome comfort of escape."
—Percival Everett, author of *Erasure*
"*Limbo* is a strong, unsettling novel about race, dislocation, and the fragility of human connection."
—Nina Revoyr, author of *Southland*

ADIOS MUCHACHOS by Daniel Chavarría
Winner of a 2001 Edgar Award
245 pages, paperback, $13.95, ISBN: 1-888451-16-5
"Daniel Chavarría has long been recognized as one of Latin America's finest writers. Now he again proves why . . . [L]ed by Alicia, the loveliest bicycle whore in all Havana."
—Edgar Award-winning author William Heffernan

SUICIDE CASANOVA by Arthur Nersesian
370 pages, hardcover in videocassette case, $25.00, ISBN: 1-888451-30-0
"Sick, depraved, and heartbreaking—in other words, a great read, a great book. *Suicide Casanova* is erotic noir and Nersesian's hard-boiled prose comes at you like a jailhouse confession."
—Jonathan Ames, author of *The Extra Man*

These books are available at local bookstores.
They can also be purchased with a credit card online through www.akashicbooks.com.
To order by mail send a check or money order to:

AKASHIC BOOKS
PO Box 1456, New York, NY 10009
www.akashicbooks.com, Akashic7@aol.com

(Prices include shipping. Outside the U.S., add $8 to each book ordered.)

PERCIVAL EVERETT   **JAMES KINCAID**

PERCIVAL EVERETT is the author of fifteen works of fiction, among them *Glyph, Watershed,* and *Frenzy.* His most recent novel, *Erasure,* won the Hurston/Wright Legacy Award and did little to earn him friends. Everett lived in South Carolina from age five to sixteen. In 1989, he was invited to address the South Carolina State Legislature, but during his speech refused to continue speaking to them because of the presence of the Confederate flag, thus touching off a controversy that ended with the flag being removed from the Capitol building some years later.

JAMES KINCAID is an English professor at the University of Southern California and has written seven books in literary theory and cultural studies. These books and Kincaid himself have gradually lost their moorings in the academic world, so there was nothing left for him to do but to adopt the guise of fiction writer. Writing about madness comes easy to him.